UKULELE MURDER

UKULELE MURDER

LESLIE LANGTRY

W🌐RLDWIDE

TORONTO • NEW YORK • LONDON
AMSTERDAM • PARIS • SYDNEY • HAMBURG
STOCKHOLM • ATHENS • TOKYO • MILAN
MADRID • WARSAW • BUDAPEST • AUCKLAND

WORLDWIDE™

Recycling programs
for this product may
not exist in your area.

ISBN-13: 978-1-335-42505-8

Ukulele Murder

First published in 2016 by Gemma Halliday Publishing.
This edition published in 2024 with revised text.

Harlequin Enterprises ULC
22 Adelaide St. West, 41st Floor
Toronto, Ontario M5H 4E3, Canada
www.ReaderService.com

Printed in U.S.A.

This book is dedicated to Erin Mahr, who taught me how to play the ukulele when I took her class at West Music, to the Quad City Ukulele Club—an amazing group I follow and dream of joining someday—and to my ukulele heroes: Jake Shimabukuro, The Ukulele Orchestra of Great Britain, and the incredible Victoria Vox, who was the inspiration for Nani.

ONE

If anyone requests "Ukulele Lady," I'm out of here. I'm not going to do it. Not again. Not for the millionth time. Is that the only song tourists know? Yeesh. Please, tiki god of the Ukulele, don't let me kill a tourist today.

"'Ukulele Lady!'" a dumpy, middle-aged man in a *Frankie Goes to Hollywood* T-shirt screams. He gives me a knowing nod with his balding head to indicate he's the only one in the room who knows true Hawaiian culture.

I hate him. I imagine bludgeoning him with my koa wood uke.

But I don't. Do you know how hard it is to get blood out of koa wood? Well… I don't know either, but I'd guess it isn't easy.

Instead, I play the damn song—smiling as I imagine shoving his pineapple drink up his…

The crowd cheers as I perform. I know—it's not so bad having an adoring audience. But this isn't the audience I want. This is Judah Horowitz's bar mitzvah. One of the few gigs I could get in Aloha Lagoon.

My name is Hoalohanani Johnson. My mother, Harriet Jones Johnson, is a bit of a Hawaiian-obsessed nut. It's so bad that it's to the point where she believes she is the reincarnation of a Hawaiian princess and says that my name came from a dream from an ancestor god. In reality, it probably came from the bottom of a rum bottle.

To her endless annoyance, my redheaded, green-eyed mom comes from a long line of English ancestors and grew up in Kansas. Dad was a third-generation blond, brown-eyed German whose name was shortened to Johnson due to the inability to pronounce whatever the name really was. Neither of my parents had ever been to Hawaii until Mom and I moved here after Dad died.

I go by Nani. And I now live in Aloha Lagoon on the Hawaiian island of Kauai, with my mother, who now calls herself Haliaka and dyes her hair and eyebrows a ridiculous shade of black that does *not* look natural. I've never understood where my dark-brown hair comes from, but I look more native than she does. Always dressed in a muumuu, Mom wears hibiscus flowers in her hair and hangs out on my lanai, singing island songs all day and night, much to my neighbors' dismay. *Sigh*.

I finish my set, tell the crowd "aloha," and am cut off by the DJ who decides suddenly to play a gangsta rap song.

"Thank you!" Gladys Horowitz of Trenton, New Jersey, and Judah's mother, slips an envelope into my hands before running to the dance floor to shimmy disturbingly. Thirteen-year-old Judah hangs his head in shame.

I make my way through the crowd to the bar and order a decidedly un-Hawaiian vodka tonic.

"Here's the ten bucks I owe you." The bartender smiles, handing me money.

I gulp my drink, slapping an empty glass on the bar.

"I told you, someone requests it every time." I take his money and head to my car. My shift in hell is over.

I did not study music at Juilliard for this. And no, Juilliard doesn't have a ukulele program. I started with classical guitar, but once I discovered the ukulele, I developed an independent study program for the diminutive instrument.

And yet, here I am in paradise, playing gigs like this bar mitzvah and teaching fingerstyle ukulele to kids. My dream of being a ukulele virtuoso, hailed by critics and in demand as a performer, was rudely interrupted by reality.

Which means I'm a white outsider from Kansas in a state full of true, native Hawaiian musicians. They call me *malihini*—which means newcomer. Things are different from the mainland. Hawaii has many words to remind you that you don't really belong here.

I can't complain, because I get by. I have ten students—all from a local military base—play parties like today's or in a few bars on weekends, and am the regular musician at the Elvis-inspired Blue Hawaii Wedding Chapel. And my inheritance from Dad helps me keep Mom flush with hibiscus-flower leis and mai tais. But this is *not* the way I pictured my life.

My biggest problem is my competition. There are three native Hawaiian ukulele musicians on this island. *They* play the big luaus at the huge resort in this town. *They* teach and lecture at the local community college. And *they* play at all the holidays, official commemoration events, and in the two concert halls on Kauai.

They're good—real good. Alohalani Kealoha is a

50-year-old professor at Aloha Lagoon Community College. I probably know him better than I know the others—but even that qualifies as *barely*. As the only one of the Terrible Trio who's somewhat nice, he is actually fairly complimentary. His exact words? "Doesn't suck."

Then there's Kahelemeakua Lui, or Kua, as he's known locally. He's young—in his 20's, I think. A serious child prodigy, Kua travels all over the world performing when he's not surfing here at home. He's a lot more open in his hatred of me—I've heard murmurs that he's afraid I'm better than him—something I'm pretty sure he wouldn't want me to know. I don't know him very well, but I've heard he calls me "that mainland pretender." Nice.

Last but not least is Leilani O'Flanagan. Only half Hawaiian, or *hapa*, she's a cutthroat 30-year-old musician who has a killer instinct and brutal temperament. I avoid her socially. If she thinks you're competition, she'll do anything in her power to destroy you. In fact, I've never heard anything nice about her. Rumor is she was raised by rabid badgers. The only nice thing she ever said about me had three expletives and an exclamation point. I have no idea if Kua and Alohalani hang out with her. I wouldn't.

Don't get me wrong. I've seen all three perform, and they're all brilliant. It would be beneath me (and 100 percent true) to say I wish they'd move away or die peacefully in their sleep of natural causes. Okay, so maybe Leilani could get eaten by a shark. That would be okay.

It's late afternoon when I toss my ukulele on the front seat of my car and head to the Aloha Lagoon Resort for a concert on Polynesian music. The bar mitzvah made me a little late, but I'm hoping I'll be there in time to see most of it.

Leaving my instrument in the car, I race into the concert just in time to see Alohalani performing with a group of visiting dancers from Tahiti. I grab a bottle of beer from the bar and settle in to watch. He's good. Better than good—Alohalani is probably the best I've seen since I'd moved here. Even so, I wish it was me up there playing the ukulele.

"Hey, haole." Kua sidles up as Alohalani plays "Aloha O'e," my favorite piece—it was written by Hawaii's last queen. "Bet you wish that was *you* up there," he snickers. Great. The fun begins. I was kind of hoping to be off the radar here so I could relax and enjoy it. I guess that's not happening.

I turn to him. "And I'd be willing to bet you wish the same thing." I smile. "I wonder why they didn't ask *you* to play?"

Kua turns into a beet-red tower of volcanic rage. "I'm sure it's a 'respect for your elders' thing." He doesn't look like he meant that. Apparently, I've hit a nerve. "You mainlanders have no respect for our ways!"

To my dismay, Leilani joins us. She'd apparently seen Kua get pissed and decided to come rub it in.

"I miss all the fun." She grins meanly. "Both of you upset they went with Alohalani?" She sips from a huge daiquiri that looks like it has more umbrellas than alcohol. Not that I mind. But I have heard that Leilani is even worse when she drinks.

"Don't put me in the same league as *her*!" Kua thunders. This guy has a serious temper.

"Oh?" Leilani's eyebrows go up, as if she's surprised by his reaction. "And why's that?"

I know she just asked that question because once again she wants to hear how unqualified I am to be playing a traditional Hawaiian instrument. She lives for moments like that.

"Because she's not Hawaiian! Not even a local," Kua growls. "She can't understand the nuances of the music because she didn't grow up here!" He shoves an index finger in her face. "And you! You're half haole! And don't you forget it!" He gives us one last sneer before storming away.

Leaving me with the worst of the Terrible Trio. Great.

Leilani bridles, nostrils flaring. "That bastard. He's just jealous that a woman can play better than a man!"

"I agree," I say, even though I know she isn't taking a stand for female musicians everywhere. Leilani does *not* mean me. She means herself.

She gives me a sharp look. "Why don't you just go back home and quit stirring up trouble?" Leilani O'Flanagan curses under her breath. "Things were fine until you showed up!" She stalks off in the direction of the bar.

Yes, that's right, they all blame me for just about everything bad, even though I know that before I arrived, those two, Kua and Leilani, had duked it out many times over who should get what gig. I turn back to the stage to see the performers are taking a break.

"Nice job!" I say brightly to Alohalani as he sits at a table, nursing a glass of water. Why not be civil to one of them? Someday he might want to do a duet, and I would be the lesser of two evils. Maybe.

The older man looks up at me. Alohalani is still fairly attractive. He's stayed in shape through the years, with only a little gray at the temples.

"Mahalo." He motions for me to take a seat. I jump at the chance and obey immediately. "It is too bad you weren't born here," he says softly.

I flinch. Yes, I know I'm an outsider. These three fling it in my face every chance they can. Other natives and locals had been warm, welcoming, and wonderful when I'd moved here. Like my friend Binny. She comes from several generations of Hawaiians. She isn't like these three. Her family is practically my *'ohana*. Which, by the way, means family.

"Are we ever going to get past this?" I ask with a sigh.

Alohalani looks at Kua and Leilani, who are now engaged in an epic argument. I expect human-propelled glassware to fly through the air at any moment.

"Unfortunately, no. It's not completely your fault. You are a better player than Leilani and probably equal to Kua. But this is how our culture is."

"You think I'm equal to Kua's talent?" I ask. I know I am, if not better. But I could never say it out loud. The culture here shies away from bragging. Being humble is held up as an ideal. I wonder why Kua and Leilani don't know that. Or they do and don't care.

Alohalani ignores my question. "Musicians, like any artist, have fragile egos." He looks at me for a long time. "I'm sure *you* understand *that*."

I bite back a response. Arguing with him won't help me in the least. This guy is a legend around here. If I turn him into an enemy, I might as well move back to Kansas. At least there, I was the only ukulele player.

"Well," he says as he places his hands on his knees and hoists himself to his feet. "Back to work."

And that is as close as I'll ever get to a compliment, even though he made it clear I had no business touting myself as a ukulele virtuoso here. Well, you work with what you're given, I guess. Still, I have to admit, he had said I was better than Leilani. That in and of itself is a win. I'd go home tonight a little happier.

I stay in my seat up front. It seems rude not to keep it, especially since I was invited to sit there by the performer himself. The remainder of the concert is amazing. A couple of times, I hear Leilani shriek at someone at the back of the room, but I ignore it. When the performance ends, I join the rest of the crowd for a standing ovation. Unfortunately, Alohalani doesn't come back and sit with me. Oh well. It's time to go home anyway. It's almost dinnertime, and Mom will be expecting me to throw something together.

As I pass through the parking lot, I spot Kua standing about 50 feet away, staring at the beach. After a second or two, he starts walking toward it. I toy with calling out and saying something brilliant, but I really need to see what mischief Mom is up to.

"Mom! I'm home," I call out as I enter our modest bungalow, happy that the Horowitz bar mitzvah and the concert are over. The cottage was a fixer-upper when I bought it three years ago. Now it's just an upper. But it has a lovely view of the jungle, and if you stand just right in the bathtub and lean to the left, you can see a sliver of the ocean.

There's no reply, because Mom is taking a nap on the lanai. She'd fallen asleep on her chaise lounge chair, with an empty wineglass in her hand. It's shady where she is, so I leave her there to go change. Inside, I swap my muumuu for a T-shirt and shorts. While I like the traditional dress of Hawaii, I feel like a fraud wearing it day to day. Kind of like how I feel like a fraud every time I play ukulele on this island.

I might be giving you a false impression. This state is full of very loving and friendly people. You won't find anyone like them anywhere in the world. They are the best hosts and treat you like an honored guest. But that's the problem. You're just a guest. Anyone who is not native or local is an outsider. The basic attitude is, *It's so nice of you to visit—but you have to go back to your home now.* Of course, there are exceptions. Like my friend Binny. She's awesome.

Why don't I leave? Because I truly love it here. The beauty of the landscape, the mild weather, seeing the ocean every day, and the rich culture has held me in its thrall since the day I arrived. I can't imagine living anywhere else.

So here I stay—the visitor from the mainland who never leaves. I wonder if there's a Hawaiian name for that.

The doorbell rings with the voice of Don Ho—an old recording of one of his songs. I don't know why I agreed to having that installed. Mom can be stubborn, and some fights aren't worth it.

"I'll get it!" I shout, knowing full well she's asleep.

The shadow of a man fills the opaque door window. I'm not expecting anyone, except maybe the crème of Hawaiian society insisting I join them in all their future musical events.

"Miss Johnson?" The man flashes a badge. He's wearing an aloha shirt and khaki slacks. He looks like a native.

"Yes?" I wonder what this guy is doing here. With my luck, he's the ukulele police here to arrest me for playing crap songs at bar mitzvahs.

"Detective Ray Kahoalani. Do you have a few minutes?"

I stand aside. "Of course. Come in."

I lead the detective to the kitchen because I have no idea how Mom left the living room. One time she draped ten state flags from the ceiling. Another time, she filled the room with 53 pineapples. It was safer to go the kitchen.

Why was a policeman here? I pray Mom will stay asleep outside. I can't imagine her coming in right now and doing something…inappropriate. The neighbors have submitted dozens of complaints to the police over the past year—mainly for her very loud singing but also because they've found her rum bottles in their yards.

"I was just pouring some iced tea. Would you like some?" Detective or not, I never forget my manners.

"Thank you," he says as he wipes the sweat from his forehead. "I'd appreciate it."

I pour the tea over ice, trying to get a sideways glance in. What is this all about?

"I'm afraid I have some bad news," he starts as he reaches for the glass.

My eyes go automatically to the backyard. Did Mom die while I was changing clothes? And if so, how did the police find out so quickly? Or maybe the neighbors really have called the police to complain. I sit down at the breakfast bar and prepare for the worst.

"I'm sorry," the man says sheepishly. "I should've phrased that better. It's not your mother." Now I know things are bad with Mom—when the first thing a detective tells me is she's not the reason he's here.

I breathe a sigh of relief. "What is it, then, Detective Kahoalani?"

"Please, call me Ray. Everyone does." He pauses. "One of your colleagues, a Mr. Kahelemeakua Lui, or Kua, was murdered at the music festival."

"Kua was murdered?" I gasp. "I just saw him! Like, half an hour ago!"

The detective writes something in a notebook. "So it's true that you were the last person to see him alive?"

Uh-oh. "I don't think I was the last person to see him alive. I just passed him in the parking lot." A little shiver went through me. Was I really the last person to see Kua before he was murdered?

"Wait," I say. "What do you mean 'it's true'? Did someone tell you that?"

The detective looks at his notes. "A Miss Leilani O'Flanagan said you'd fought with him and followed him out the door when he left."

I shake my head. "That's wrong. I was leaving and just spotted him in the parking lot. I went straight to my car."

Leilani—what a stark-raving loon! I know she is

mean, but to imply that I might've killed Kua? That is a serious reach. Besides, Kua was a big dude. And the last time I'd seen him, he'd been a huge, angry dude. Who could've murdered him? And why didn't the killer murder Leilani instead?

Ray Kahoalani writes something in his notebook. "No one else at the concert remembers seeing him leave."

I think back. I was the only one heading to my car. I'd assumed the rest of the folks were socializing. Kua and I were the only ones in the parking lot before he walked out onto the beach.

"How was he murdered?" I shiver again. It's horrible to think that someone I just saw was now dead.

Detective Ray says nothing. His eyes are on mine, sizing me up. "We found him on the beach. He was alone. Bludgeoned."

I stifle a gasp. "I barely knew him. And I certainly didn't kill him."

"We were led to believe that you were colleagues." He looks through a notebook. "Miss O'Flanagan said so. In fact, she said you two were close friends. She also said you had a nasty argument at the concert."

Of course that psycho would pin this on me. It's ridiculous, really. I shake my head, trying not to laugh. Kua would hate hearing that we were close.

"That's not true at all. I'd seen him perform a few times. I only spoke to him once or twice. I don't know anything about him."

Except that earlier I wished he was dead—but I decide that it's in my best interest not to mention that.

"Can you describe what happened when you left?" he asks.

"Seriously? I'm a suspect?" My concern starts to turn to anger.

"Just answer the question, please." Detective Ray takes another drink of tea but keeps his eyes trained on my face.

I sigh. "I just walked out to my car, got in, and drove here."

"So no one can confirm what time you got home?" He frowns.

"No, I guess not." My stomach drops to my ankles. I have no alibi. But then, I hardly have any motive. I mean, wishing your competition was dead isn't a thing. Is it?

The detective finishes his tea and sets it on the table. "Thank you for your time and for the tea." He hands me a card. "Please call me if you have any thoughts. You aren't planning on leaving the area anytime soon, are you?"

Well, I am now...

"No," is all I say as I follow him to the door.

"I'll be in touch then, Miss Johnson." Detective Ray gives me a nod and leaves.

I close the door behind him and slump against it. I didn't kill anyone.

TWO

"WHO WAS THAT, NANI?" Mom comes up from behind and startles me.

"Um, no one," I tell her quickly. To be perfectly honest, I'm still trying to wrap my head around Kua's murder and being told I might be a suspect in that murder.

"All right," Mom says as she waves me off, indicating she has no further interest in our conversation. "Don't forget we have company coming for dinner tonight at eight."

My mouth drops open. "What? I didn't know anything about a dinner! Who's coming?"

"A new friend of mine," Mom says, ignoring the fact that I'm caught by surprise. "Perseverance Woodfield and her son, Nick. Try to dress up a little. You look like you're going to work in the garden."

"It's almost seven thirty now, Mom." I start to panic. "Did you make dinner already?"

I know the answer to that before she answers. The answer is no. It's always no. I do all the cooking. And it's a good thing too. But a little guilt trip never hurts.

She shakes her head, oblivious to my attempt. "Don't be ridiculous, Nani! I told Perseverance that you were an excellent cook."

Uh-oh. This woman is coming over with her son. And Mom told her I'm great in the kitchen. This is a setup.

I throw my hands up in exasperation. "There's no food in the house! I was going to go shopping tomorrow!"

Mom pats me on the shoulder. "You're a smart girl. You'll figure it out." She starts humming and wanders back into the yard.

I'm on my own. Guests are coming over in an hour. I'm underdressed, and even if I had all the ingredients, I still couldn't pull off dinner in that short amount of time. My mind races as I run into the bedroom and throw on a slightly nicer black T-shirt and white capris. It takes me a few minutes to find my black ballet flats and comb my long, straight hair into a ponytail. This will have to do.

Now I have very little time until the guests arrive. I grab my cell and dial up the Loco Moco Café at the resort and order dinner for four. As I race over there to pick up my order, I debate whether to admit I ordered dinner or pretend I made it myself. Somewhere along the line, I decide to be honest about the whole thing. After the bar mitzvah and visit by the police, I just don't have it in me to lie right now.

It's not worth getting angry at Mom. She's done this to me so often that I realized a long time ago she doesn't listen. The only thing to do is just get through it. None of the boys or men Mom has ever set me up with have turned into anything worth bragging about. With the exception of my father, she has terrible taste in men.

Woodfield. I've heard that name before. But where? My brain reaches for the information, but it's eluding me. I guess I'll figure it out when I meet Perseverance and her son…what was his name? Scott? Nick? Nick. That's it, right?

Somehow, in spite of all these hurdles my mother has thrown at me, I manage to get the table set and the food plated just before the doorbell rings.

"I'll get it!" Mom sails through the room and out into the hallway.

Fine by me. I'm in no hurry to see what kind of idiot my mother is fixing me up with. I try not to flinch as I throw the restaurant's packaging in the garbage. The last time she tried matchmaking, the guy was the nephew of one of her mahjong friends, Mabel Percy.

Ned Percy had turned out to be a scrawny little jerk who thought he was God's gift to women. An insurance salesman, Ned not only bragged about himself incessantly (which is fine unless your only claim to fame is collecting *Star Wars* memorabilia), but he also tried to sell us life insurance policies. And he asked me why I played a toy for an instrument. The man barely made it out of the house alive.

"She's in here!" I hear Mom say.

So it really is a setup. I guess I'd hoped against hope on that one. Oh well. There's nothing to be done but get through the evening as quickly as possible with as little humiliation as I can manage.

"Nani!" Mom says as she leads two people into the kitchen. "This is my new friend, Perseverance Wood-field, and her son, Nick."

I wipe my hands on a dishtowel and reach for the woman's hand. "Nice to meet you both. Welcome to our home."

"She's charming!" Perseverance exclaims. Definitely a setup.

The woman is in her 60s with dark-brown hair peppered with silver. Tall and proud, she smiles warmly as she shakes my hand. I like her already. The man with her is, to my shock, very attractive. Brown hair and eyes with a trim beard and mustache, Nick Woodfield isn't bad at all. At least the view during dinner will be pleasant.

"Nani made dinner for you," Mom says, and my heart sinks. "I told you she was a wonderful cook."

I guess I won't be confessing that this came from the Loco Moco Café.

Perseverance smiles and elbows her son. "It's always good to marry a great cook, Nick."

Ugh. I feel sorry for Nick Woodfield. At least there we have something in common.

"It smells great," Nick says with a smile as he shakes my hand. He winks. And it's utterly adorable. Okay, so he's cute and charming. That's not so bad.

"Thanks," I say, hating to take the credit for the Loco Moco. "What can I get everyone to drink?"

"And a wonderful hostess too!" Perseverance nods to Mom.

Everyone wants wine, so I pull a bottle of chardonnay from the fridge. Nick offers to open it, and I let him. As I grab the glasses, I try to give him a surreptitious once-over. Definitely gorgeous. If Mom doesn't blow it, maybe I could squeeze at least one decent date out of her exhausting habit of fixing me up.

As we sit down to dinner and begin passing the food around, I think things might be looking up a little for me. When Nick winks at me again, I know it is. Why is it so charming when men wink? I don't know, but it has always worked on me. I wonder if Mom told him that.

"So I said…" Mom has been talking, and I didn't realize it. "How is it your family has been here for so many generations but your name is Perseverance instead of a Hawaiian name?"

"Please call me Vera," Nick's mother insists. "I can't stand my name. It comes from my ancestor who came over here in the 1800s. I guess the Puritans gave their children names like this in hopes they'd develop the same qualities."

"I like Vera," I say with a smile as something tugs on the edge of my memory. Woodfield. How do I know that name? "That's why I go by Nani. Shorter names are easier."

Vera nods as she takes a second helping of yummy pork. "So much easier." She holds out her glass, and I fill it with more wine. "Haliaka tells me you're a musician. And you went to Juilliard. That's impressive, right, Nick?"

"Please!" Mom begs dramatically. "Call me Hali. Everyone does." I can tell, though, that she's thrilled Vera used her fake Hawaiian name.

Um…no one does. I've never heard her use that nickname before. In fact, I cringe whenever someone is deceived into using my mother's so-called Hawaiian name. But there's nothing I can do but play along.

"That is impressive," Nick says as his eyes linger on mine. "What do you play?"

"She's a ukulele virtuoso!" Mom jumps in before I can speak. "Just like Jake Shimbakoko."

"It's Shimabukuro, Mom," I correct gently.

"My Nicky has a PhD in Botany!" Vera boasts. "He works at the resort. Head of landscaping." She shakes her head. "He should be helping plant crops for starving people in Africa, but no...he wanted to come home."

Nick rolls his eyes, and I stifle a giggle. It's nice to know someone else has mother problems. He sees me and winks again. I'm in danger of really liking this guy.

"I love it here, Mom," Nick says. "I wouldn't live anywhere else."

Vera points her fork at him. "He had offers from the Department of Natural Resources and the University of Hawaii, but he turned them down to work here." I couldn't tell if she was disappointed or proud. "At least you could work for Limahuli Garden or Allerton Garden instead of the resort."

Definitely disappointed.

Then Mom starts in (I've heard it so often, I could lip sync what she's about to say). "Nani is the same way, Vera! She should be doing concerts and the big luaus and festivals instead of bar mitzvahs and weddings at the Blue Hawaii Wedding Chapel!"

Like I have any choice in the matter. I decide not to argue in front of our guests. Mom wouldn't hear it anyway.

"That's enough, Mother," Nick says with a smile. "I like working at the resort. I'm in charge there. I wouldn't be at one of the botanical gardens. And I'd have to kowtow to their standards. The resort lets me do whatever I want."

I like him even more. He's stuck in the same situation I am with a crazy mom.

"This dinner is excellent, really, Nani." Vera grins, forgetting the dispute completely.

She's a good match for my mother. Maybe they were separated at birth. I'd better not tell her that. She'd probably make Vera submit to a DNA test in hopes that they really were.

I start to confess, but Mom cuts me off. "She gets her cooking skills from me."

This time I roll my eyes. Harriet Jones Johnson can't even boil water. I had to teach her how when I was 12. If she had her way, we'd live on takeout. My father did most of the cooking. And I am very good in the kitchen. He taught me everything he knew.

For the most part, the rest of dinner goes smoothly, considering the chaos that preceded it. Nick even helps me carry the dishes to the kitchen. He opens the dishwasher and begins loading. Wow. This guy may actually be out of my league.

I watch as Mom leads Vera out to the garden. The hibiscus bushes are in full bloom as the slowly dimming sky casts the bright-pink blossoms in a lavender wash. This is my favorite time of day, and the garden is my favorite place to be. I'm a little nervous that Nick won't like it. I didn't really follow any plan—just used what was already there and threw in what I liked. For all I know, I could've committed a botanical crime or something.

These thoughts surprise me. I genuinely liked Nick. That has never happened before with someone Mom's set me up with. Either she got this one bizarrely right or Nick's putting on an act and is secretly an evil villain or worse…a collector of *Star Wars* memorabilia and personal friend of Ned Percy.

"Sorry about my mom." Nick's voice brings me back to cleaning up. "I'm sure you noticed that this was a fix-up."

I nod. "Sorry about my mother too. She means well, but I do have a confession to make."

Nick's right eyebrow shoots up, and it makes him even more attractive. "Oh? Let me guess—you found out we were coming just before we arrived?"

I laugh. "How did you know? Are you some kind of psychic botanist? Because that would be very cool."

He smiles. "That's when I found out. The moment I got off work, Mom handed me a towel and told me to take a shower because we were going to dinner."

"Me too…except for the shower part." I blush, imagining him in nothing but a towel. "But my confession is different. I didn't make this dinner."

"Loco Moco Café," Nick says as he nods. "I knew it had to be their laulau pork. It's the best on the island."

"I really can cook," I insist. "I had no time. I'd just walked in the door from the Horowitz bar mitzvah and then the music festival at the resort, and she said dinner would be in an hour. I hope you don't mind."

Nick shakes his head. "It's my favorite thing they make." He shoves the last dish into the rack and, after pouring a liberal amount of soap, closes the door and turns the dishwasher on. It's a very, very sexy thing for a man to do. If he takes out the trash, I'll have to propose.

"Then it worked out," I say.

"Did you say Horowitz Bar Mitzvah?" Nick asks. "From Trenton, New Jersey, right?"

I stare at him. "You really are a psychic botanist!"

"No." He laughs. "They're staying at the resort. Mrs. Horowitz has been picking flowers for her hair all week, even though I asked her not to. The hotel provides leis and blossoms for the guests, but she said she wanted the freshest ones."

"I can totally see her doing that. That's awful."

"Oh, it is awful. You'd be surprised how many people think that's okay." Nick wipes his hands on the dishtowel. "The worst is the mainlanders who pick rare orchids."

I flinch at the word "mainlanders." I hate being reminded that I'm an outsider. It's not his fault. It's not anyone's fault but the three other uke players. They're the only ones who make me feel this way.

Nick sees my response. "I don't mean that in a negative way," he apologizes. "Really, I don't have any prejudices about malihini."

I sigh. "Well, that's good to know. I get enough of that from the Terrible Trio."

He looks questioningly at me, and I tell him about Alohalani, Kua, and Leilani. And then I remember that Kua was murdered, and I'm a person of interest.

Nick frowns as he studies my face. "What is it?" He really looks concerned. About me. A woman he just met. It seems like a good sign.

I think for a moment before explaining. The news will be in the paper anyway. Besides, I don't have any special information, and that detective didn't tell me to keep quiet. I fill him in on the whole Kua mess. And like an idiot, I mention that I am a suspect.

"Wow. I've never been attracted to a potential murderer before." He grins.

Attracted? Now that's interesting...

"I know that detective," Nick continues. "He's all right but a little slow. I doubt he'll find any evidence implicating you. Especially since I know you didn't do it."

I laugh, feeling a sense of relief. This cute guy doesn't mind that I didn't cook dinner, and he doesn't think I murdered anyone. Nick Woodfield is definitely a person of interest in my book.

"How do you know I didn't do it?" I tease. "You just met me."

He looks very seriously into my eyes. "Because *I* killed the ukulele player."

My heart stops for a split second before he starts laughing. Of course he didn't do it. What was I thinking?

"I'm so sorry," Nick apologizes. "That was a very bad joke. I barely know those people you described. In fact, you're the first ukulele player I've ever really talked to."

I take the dish towel from him and whip him with it. "Not many botanist musicians, eh?"

Nick shakes his head. "Nope. You're the first performer I've ever hung out with."

And from the way things are going, I kind of hope I'll be his last.

We join our mothers on the lanai. I inhale the hibiscus fragrance and look up at the stars. Unlike the mainland or even Honolulu, there aren't many city lights out here. As a result, the evening sky and its brilliant stars are in sharp focus.

Nick starts walking around the perimeter of the garden, and I join him. He inspects every plant in the yard, taking his time as he goes. I try not to stare at his body. It's a good body. A very good body.

"Did you do all this?" he asks. "Because this is one of the best private gardens I've ever seen. And that's saying something for the Garden Island."

I shake my head. "No, I can't claim credit for that either. A lot of it was already here when we moved. I added the things I like, but that's it. This is my favorite place."

He nods. "You've done a great job. No weeds. Everything is healthy and lush. Maybe I should hire you as my assistant."

"I don't really know much about plants," I confess. "I love them, but I could never do more than maintenance."

"I guess I'll have to come over in the daytime and give you some helpful hints." Nick smiles.

Is he asking me out? Okay, so it is to my own yard, but still…that counts, right?

"It's a deal," I say. "I could use some expert input."

Nick smiles again. Even in the darkness I can see the sincerity and warmth there. "No, it's not a deal." He laughs at my expression of confusion. "It's a date."

THREE

NOT BAD, I think as I unload the dishwasher. We sent the Woodfields home with leftovers, and Mom has long since gone to bed, so I'm alone with my thoughts. I went from alleged murderer to potential girlfriend in just a couple of hours. Life is getting interesting. Stuff like this never happened to me back in Kansas.

My cell rings, and I answer it. It's my friend, Binny Finau. Probably my only friend here, except for the handsome Nick Woodfield, who I hope will be a friend—at the very least—or more.

Binny is a local. Half Hawaiian like Leilani, her grandmother on her mother's side was from Alaska—which seems to be about as far from local as you can get. Her father, on the other hand, can trace his ancestry back to King Kamehameha. She was the first friend I made when I moved here, and she and her family treat me like one of their own. Her mother is great—not even a *little* crazy.

"I just heard!" Binny says breathlessly. I can picture her eyes wide, teeth biting her lip.

How did news get out so fast?

"It's just a fix-up," I say. "But it went well, I think. We actually have a date planned."

There's silence on the other end for a few moments.

"What are you talking about? You have a date?" Binny asks.

"What were you talking about?" I'm a little confused. What could Binny be referring to?

"Kua's murder!" Binny squeals. "It's all over the island! And my cousin's best friend works at the police department. He mentioned you were being interviewed."

I deflate. "Oh that. I'm not sure really. A detective came by and asked me questions, but that's all I know." I'd rather she asked about Nick.

"Are you a suspect?" my friend asks. "Wow."

"I didn't do it, Binny," I say with a bit of annoyance. "He just asked a couple of questions." And asked me not to leave the island—so, yes, I guess that really does make me a suspect.

"I know you didn't. It's kind of fascinating that they think you did."

I could hear her smiling on the other end. Binny is the happiest person I know. It takes a lot to depress her. In fact, I've never seen her upset. Never.

"Any buzz on who really killed him?"

This is a small island. Only about 65,000-plus people. Rumors have to be swirling around by now. If Binny has any ideas, soon everyone will. She isn't a gossip, but she is plugged in. When you live in a small town, bad news is something to chew on. Makes the place a little less dull.

"I'll be right over," my friend says before hanging up.

Great. I was just about to go to bed. Oh well. Binny won't rest until she milks me for all the information I know—which honestly, isn't much. The doorbell rings immediately. The woman only lives a block away. She probably ran here.

"Tell me everything," she insists breathlessly as I open the door. Definitely ran here. And yet there isn't even a hint of perspiration on her face. How does she do that?

I fill her in on what the detective told me. There's not much. Just that I was the last known person to see Kua before he was bludgeoned (by someone who is not me, of course) somewhere on the beach. There's been no mention of the murder weapon, I realize. That's weird. Either the detective is hoping I'll confess or he just doesn't know.

"I think Leilani did it," Binny says as she stuffs some of the leftover laulau into her mouth. Too bad she was eating the last of it. The pork was perfect—it fell apart nicely and melted in my mouth. Oh well. I know where I can get more. I pour us both a glass of wine and we move out to the lanai to avoid being overheard. I don't need Mom waking up and getting involved.

"That's possible." I nod. "They did have a huge fight at the concert. It would be just like that crazy woman to try to eliminate her competition."

"So she might come after you next!" Binny cries, "How exciting!"

I hadn't thought of that. That is all I need. I just find what might be the right guy and then get killed by a psycho ukulele player. How poetic.

"There have to be other suspects," I think out loud.

My friend shrugs. "He was a competitive surfer too. It's possible he was killed because he took someone else's wave."

That idea gives me a little hope. *Please be a surfer*, I pray silently.

"There's no way to know until we hear more, I guess."

Truth be told—I don't really like the thought that it might be one of the other musicians on the island. If Leilani is coming for me, I want to be ready. I'd have to give that some thought. There are no weapons in my cottage. I wouldn't know how to use one if I did have something. I am athletic, however. So maybe I could outrun a killer. That's something to consider.

"So who's the dude?" Binny grins. There's no way she's going to leave until she gets all the juicy details.

I tell her everything, getting a little more excited as I babble. The idea of Nick Woodfield as a boyfriend has a lot of potential. He seems like the total package—smart, funny, talented, and hot to boot. And like me, he has a crazy mother. We might as well get married right now.

Binny hangs on every word. She's a very pretty girl with a silky black bob and the largest brown eyes I've ever seen. Seriously, they could make one of those Blythe dolls weep with shame. Add a killer bod, and she could be a model. But that's not her style. Binny is the nicest, kindest person I've ever met. Modest as the day is long, the girl would never consider herself gorgeous. And I've never felt threatened being with her. She can put anyone at ease and make them feel like the most important person she's ever met. Every time I see my friend, I consider it lucky that we met.

"I can't believe it! You, going out with a Woodfield!" Binny actually giggles.

I stare at her. "What? What's so funny?"

Binny sets her wineglass down gently. "They are one of the wealthiest families on Kauai! They've been here since the first missionaries set foot on the island in the 1800s. Didn't you know that?"

Ah. That's what I was missing. I knew I'd heard that name before. The Woodfields live in a huge house about ten miles from Aloha Lagoon. I've driven past that property hundreds of times. They keep to themselves mostly and own a lot of land here on the island. It's controversial because the Hawaiian sovereignty movement has tried repeatedly to get them to release their property to the natives of Kauai. You're surprised I know that? I'm kind of a history geek.

"He's not like that," I protest. "His mom's a little flaky, but she's very nice."

How on earth did my mom meet this woman? I doubt that Perseverance Woodfield slummed it with the mah jong crowd at the community center. And we certainly didn't move in the same social circles. We didn't move in any social circles here.

"If you say so." Binny gets up from her chair. "I'm looking forward to meeting him if it works out. And I hope it does. He's hot."

I throw a dish towel at someone for the second time today and make a face. "I'll let you know."

Binny hugs me and leaves. I slump against the front door, feeling defeated. There's no way it will work out with someone like Nick Woodfield. Once again, I find myself out of my league here in this beautiful place. I turn out the lights and go to bed.

"Hoalohanani!" Mom is standing over my bed. Uh-oh. She used my full name. That's usually bad.

I sit up, rubbing my face. "What is it?"

Mom is wearing her best muumuu. The white one with pineapples on it. That's not good. Something's up.

"There's a man here to see you." She frowns. "He's too old for you. Why would you be interested in anyone other than Nick?"

I get out of bed and stagger into my bathroom, shouting, "Nick and I aren't a couple." *Yet.* "I'll brush my teeth and be right out."

Mom leaves, and I throw on some shorts and a T-shirt. As I walk into the living room, I'm surprised to see Detective Ray sitting on the sofa, notebook out, looking around at the dozens of coconuts with googly eyes my mother has now arranged around the room. She even has grass skirts on some of them.

"Mom," I say. "Please get the detective some iced tea."

My mother's face pales a little, but she nods. I should've told her last night. However, if it makes her worry that the neighbors have complained about her singing loudly in the yard again, maybe it will be the wake-up call she needs.

I sit in a chair next to the sofa. "Detective Ray, what a pleasant surprise."

The policeman frowns, as if he'd hoped his appearance would make me shake in my shoes. But this is Hawaii. We don't wear shoes inside.

"A few things have come up, and I need to ask you some more questions." He says it slowly, as if choosing each word for the first time.

I nod. "Okay, shoot."

He looks at me, startled. Poor choice of words when being investigated for murder.

"Please," I say. "Go ahead."

"Miss Johnson," the detective says slowly. "Some new facts have come to light in my investigation of the murder of Kahelemeakua Lui. Could we go into your garden, please?"

I'm not sure what to make of this. Maybe he just likes being outside? Maybe the googly-eyed, grass-skirted coconuts are making him nervous. I can understand that because I'm starting to feel creeped out too.

"Of course." I stand and indicate that he follow me. "This way."

We cross through the kitchen, where Mom hands off the iced tea to the detective, and soon find ourselves in my backyard. I sit on the lanai, but to my surprise, the policeman starts to wander.

"Are you looking for something in particular?" I ask as I catch up.

Detective Ray stops and looks at me. "The coroner found splinters of kauwila wood in the victim's scalp. She says Kua was struck by something heavy. Something made out of kauwila."

I freeze to the spot. I have something made out of kauwila. It's the hardest wood in Hawaii and native to Kauai. So hard and dense that the ancient indigenous people used it in place of metal. It's one of the few woods that sinks in water. How do I know this? Because I once asked a local woodworker to make me a ukulele out of it. He told me he'd never heard of an instrument being made from that particular tree. And then he made me one.

"Do you have anything made of kauwila?" the detective asks.

I nod and begin to babble. "I do. One of my ukuleles is made of that wood. But that can't be the weapon. It's stored in my room. I haven't taken it out to play it in months." In fact, I rarely ever take it out. The wood, it turns out, is too heavy to hold for very long.

"Could you get it for me?" he asks, taking a long sip of iced tea.

"What's this all about?" Mom makes an appearance, startling both of us. Great.

I can hear Detective Ray explain to my mother as I go inside to fetch the ukulele. My ears are buzzing, and I start to sweat. It couldn't be my instrument. I didn't kill Kua. I wasn't even there. Panic rises in my throat, causing me to gag.

Calm down, I tell myself. This is ridiculous. Just get the ukulele so you can prove to the detective once and for all that you are innocent. This is all just a mistake. Mistakes happen all the time. At least, they do on TV.

I store my instruments inside their cases, on shelves in my room. There are six soprano ukuleles that I use in performance, two baritones I have just for my personal use, and one travel ukulele. Each uke has its own case. The kauwila ukulele is one of the sopranos and sits on the bottom shelf because it's so heavy.

I count, one…two…three…four…five…six (including the travel uke) and two baritones. Wait! That's not right! There should be seven here! With shaking hands, I open each case and set each instrument on my bed. The other ukuleles are there. But the kauwila uke is not.

Opening the two baritone cases, I find only baritones. My eyes grow wide, and I sweep the room, pulling everything out of the closet. I still can't find it. Running out to my car does no good either—the ukulele isn't there.

Oh no! Where's the kauwila uke?

I have no choice but to rejoin my mother and the detective in the yard. What am I going to do? Go on the lam? Where exactly can you go on the lam on an island? Wait—I didn't do anything wrong. I sure as hell didn't kill anyone. There had to be some mistake.

"I… I can't find it…" I stammer, feeling my cheeks reddening. "It's gone…maybe stolen." I look to my mother for help. "You didn't take one of my instruments, did you, Mom?"

Please let the answer be *yes*. Even though I'd be furious, I hope she did take it.

"Why on earth would I do that?" Mom asks, her face twisted with disgust. "I wouldn't touch your instruments after the fit you threw last time."

She's right. I caught her once out on the lanai, strumming my $2,000 concert soprano ukulele and let her have it. Mom wouldn't have touched my instruments after that.

"Maybe you took it out to be cleaned?" Mom asked hopefully.

I grimace. She knows so little about my job it's pathetic. "You don't take a ukulele anywhere to be cleaned."

"Repaired then? Maybe you broke a string?" Mom is trying to help, and I get that.

Shaking my head I insist, "I do all my own stringing and repairs."

"So," Detective Ray says slowly. "You have an instrument made of kauwila wood, but it is missing?"

Nothing gets past this guy.

"I'll find it. It has to be misplaced, or maybe it was stolen," I say. "Are you sure it was a ukulele that killed Kua? Maybe he was beaned by a branch from a kauwila tree? They're all over Kauai."

The detective looks at me. "You mean like this tree?" He points to a tree in my yard.

Mom and I follow the path of his finger. Sure enough, in my backyard, there stands a kauwila tree.

"I can't help it that I have a kauwila tree in my backyard. A lot of people do. Right, Mom?"

She shrugs and shakes her head. "I don't do yard work." Mom turns to the detective and smiles. "I do, however, do all my own decorating. What did you think of the coconuts in the living room?"

I can't hear his reply because my heart is hammering as if it wants to burst out through my rib cage. How could this happen? How could I not notice that the ukulele was missing? It doesn't look good.

"So," the detective says. "The murder weapon could have come from your house."

I close my eyes, waiting for the other shoe to drop. He is going to accuse me now in the murder of Kahelemeakua Lui. This is bad. I'm going to jail. Have I been framed?

"Huh," I hear Detective Ray say. "I'll have to look into that." He hands my mother the empty glass, and I wait for him to cuff me.

"I'll be back. Do not leave the island, please," he says

as he walks to the house. "I'll let myself out. The tea was good. Mahalo."

Mom and I watch as the man leaves us standing there, jaws on the ground. We turn to each other.

"He didn't arrest you," Mom says. "I wonder why? It seems like he should have."

"Seriously?" I ask. "You think he should arrest me?"

She shakes her head. "No. It's just that the evidence against you looks pretty bad. He told me that you were the last one to see that poor man alive and that you'd been seen having a big argument with him earlier."

I want to yell at her. Shout that she's not being very supportive. But she's right. It does look bad. In fact, if I were the detective, *I* would've arrested me.

"He liked the coconuts." Mom puffs up with pride. "Is he single?"

This is the first time my mother has shown an interest in another man. I'm guessing it's because Detective Ray is Hawaiian. That would be a feather in her cultural stalking cap.

My cell rings. I don't recognize the number. "Hello?" I ask, wondering if once he got to his car, the detective changed his mind and is calling me to turn myself in.

"Nani?" It sounds like Nick Woodfield. "It's Nick. I was wondering if I could come over this afternoon—take you up on your offer of a date in your yard? I'd love to see the foliage in the daylight."

Nick. Nick's a botanist. He might just be what I need. "Nick! I'm so glad you called! Yes! That would be great! How soon can you get here?'

He laughs. "Boy, are you eager or what?"

I blush, grateful he can't see me. "Sorry, I mean, yes, drop by. Now's great."

We hang up, and I see my mother grinning at me.

"I knew you two would hit it off!" She nods. "I knew it. But try not to appear so desperate, Nani! Really! You practically threw yourself at him!"

I watch as my mother trots toward the house. "I'll go over to Vera's and leave you two alone," she shouts over her shoulder.

So now she hangs out with Vera at the Woodfield mansion? When did that start happening?

A few seconds later, I hear the door slam and my mother's little car backing down the drive. Racing inside, I freshen up before Nick arrives. He probably won't want to see me ever again after discovering the damning evidence against me. But I should still look nice. Just in case.

The doorbell rings, and I answer it. Nick stands there looking like the best Christmas present ever. He's carrying two takeout containers from the Loco Moco Café.

"I brought a couple of Hale's Hawaiian Hamburger Platters for a picnic. Hope you don't mind."

I pull him into the house and slam the door behind him. "That's awesome. But before we eat, I really think we should do something."

He cocks his head adorably. "Um, okay…"

I realize what I just said and shake my head vigorously. "No! I mean, it's something else. I have a strange question, and I think you're the only person who can help me."

Nick smiles, but am I imagining it, or does he look disappointed?

"I'd be happy to help,"

"Oh good. Because what you think might determine whether or not I'm a murderer." A request rarely heard on first dates, I imagine.

FOUR

I EXPLAIN AS Nick follows me out to the yard and over to the kauwila tree. He sets the bags of food on the ground and steps up to the tree, carefully checking it out. Too bad he isn't checking me out.

"It's an old tree. Maybe a couple of centuries old. Unfortunately, there's some problem with the growth. It might have a disease." He looks sad. I guess it would be like me finding a uke lying in a puddle.

"What does this tree have to do with the murder?" Nick asks.

"It's not the tree exactly. I was wondering if this is a normal thing to have in your backyard here on Kauai."

Nick shrugs. "It's fairly common. Was Kua killed by a tree?"

I tell him about the splinters of kauwila wood found in Kua's hair. Then I tell him about the ukulele and how this makes me seem more likely a suspect. My heart sinks with every word. It's like I'm driving him away on purpose.

"Well, kauwila wood is common here, and I guess a branch or wood sculpture could've been the murder weapon, so it could still be anyone. That's weird about your ukulele going missing. I'd be willing to bet it was stolen."

"You…you believe me?" I ask.

Nick nods. "I'm a pretty good judge of character. I don't think you did it. Besides, striking someone that much taller than you, armed with a heavy instrument, doesn't make a lot of sense. Your mother is tall, but I don't think she could swing something that heavy with enough force to kill someone."

For a brief moment I'm amused at the thought of Mom using my ukulele to kill off the competition so I could have better gigs.

"Oh good," I say. "At least you believe me. I don't suppose you'd testify in court on my behalf?"

He smiles. It's a great smile. A warm smile. I feel like I might be okay with a smile like that.

"The detective didn't arrest you. He doesn't have a bloody ukulele covered with Kua's hair. There's no case. Yet."

"Yet?" I ask. His first words were better. Yet?

Nick picks up the bags and leads me into the kitchen, where we plate the food before coming back out to the lanai. There are several chairs, but he chooses to sit next to me on the wicker love seat. My heart begins pounding again, just for a better reason this time.

"I have an idea that might help," Nick says in between bites of mango. "But it's kind of unorthodox."

I shrug, swallowing a bite of burger. "I'll do anything." Then I blush. Ugh. I probably should've chosen my words a little better.

Nick winks, and I melt. "The detective could find something and come back to arrest you. I think we should investigate this ourselves."

I stare at him. "Are you serious? I don't know anything about investigating a murder!" Well, other than the fact that I think Leilani did it and framed me, but how does one get proof of that?

He shrugs. "I don't either. But I've read every Sherlock Holmes and Agatha Christie book ever written. Some twice. How hard can it be?"

"You read mysteries?" I didn't see that coming. I'd be worried, but since he didn't mention sci-fi souvenirs, I figure he's okay.

"And it certainly couldn't hurt," he continues, ignoring me. "I mean, what's the worst that could happen? We don't find anything, and I get to spend a lot of time with you."

He wants to spend time with me? That's the best news I've had in a year.

I sigh. "Well, at least we will have gone on a date or two before I'm incarcerated for life."

"It's not going to come to that. We can do this," Nick insists.

I wonder. I mean sure, the amateur-sleuth thing works in books, TV, and movies...but in real life? And what does he get out of it? The man barely knows me. Why risk anything for a girl he's never met before last night? It doesn't really add up. Huh. I guess that's the kind of thing you say when you're investigating.

On the other hand, Detective Ray doesn't seem too bright. What if he screws up the investigation and I end up in prison because of his incompetence? That would suck. I'm really not cut out for prison. Not that I know anything about it, but I'm just pretty sure it wouldn't exactly work for me.

"What would we have to do?" I ask weakly. I guess I've just agreed.

"Well…" Nick thinks for a moment. "Tell me everything you know about the Terrible Trio. That might be a good start."

I take a deep breath. "Okay. You're right. It can't hurt. Let's see…" I bite my lip as I think.

"Kua is… I mean, was, in his twenties. Tall, physically fit, talented…"

Nick frowns. "I'm a little glad he's dead."

I roll my eyes. "You cut me off too soon. He was also incredibly arrogant. He hated me. My very existence seemed to piss him off."

"Did he get along with the other two?" he asks.

"He always fought with Leilani. I don't think they ever got along. But I don't think he was that way with the professor. At least, I never saw them fight. I never saw them talk to each other either. I think Kua grudgingly respected him, but I can't say they were friends."

"What else do you know about him?" Nick asks.

"He was a surfer. I've heard people say he's pretty good. He participated in competitions on occasion. I have no idea who he hung out with." I shrug. "Surfing isn't really my thing." A thought pops into my head. *Binny surfs. That might be useful.*

Nick asks. "What about Alohalani? What do you know about him?"

"He's older, teaches at the community college. Alohalani gets the lion's share of gigs around here. He's pretty amazing talent-wise." I tell Nick about my conversation with the musician a few days back.

"So he likes you?"

I nod my head. "I'd like to think so. And he kind of hinted that he thought I had some talent—it's just my ancestry that gets in the way as far as he's concerned."

Nick cocks his head to one side. "Do you think he could've killed Kua?"

"I don't think so," I say, testing the words on my tongue. "He doesn't seem like the type, really. And Kua wasn't any strong competition to Alohalani."

I think about that for a moment, turning the thoughts around in my mind. I'd never seen Kua and the older musician together. But that didn't mean we could rule him out either. For all I know, the two could've been best friends at some point—at least teacher and student.

Nick sighs. "He doesn't jump to the top of my list. Even though in mysteries, it's always the person you least expect."

"Leilani's definitely more likely," I agree. "She's a real nasty piece of work." I fill Nick in on her lineage.

"So she's half native, half non-native?" Nick asks. "That doesn't make her a suspect."

Oh right… Nick is the same way.

"I'm telling you this," I say a little too quickly, "because it seemed to really matter to Kua and Alohalani."

I think about how Alohalani had told me he wished I'd been born here.

"Leilani makes everyone crazy," I continue. "She probably doesn't have one friend in Kauai."

"Which could mean a lot of enemies," Nick muses.

"You can count me in as one of those," I say. "She told the detective that Kua and I were close. My guess is she's framing me."

But did she do it? Was Leilani capable of murder?

"You think she did it," Nick says as he studies my face. "Well, she's definitely my first choice to investigate."

I nod. "She probably thought Alohalani was going to hand his gigs over to Kua when he retired. Rumor has it that might be soon. Like in a few years."

"Does anyone ever retire from playing an instrument?" Nick asks.

I shrug. "I wouldn't. I'll do it until my fingers are bent with arthritis. But if he's retiring from his job at the college, he might be retiring from everything."

"And Leilani would be next in line…now that Kua's out of the picture."

I nod. "At least she thinks so."

"What else can you tell me about her?" Nick asks.

"Not much," I answer. "She's not married, doesn't have a day job. Her grandmother died in Ireland recently and left Leilani some money. I have no idea what she did for money before that."

How did I know that? The evil redhead told me. Practically rubbed it in my face that she still gigged even though she didn't have to. She probably had no idea I'd find the information useful.

"Does she perform for the love of music?" Nick asks.

"Huh," I say. "I never thought of it before. I guess not, really. The other two do, but I've never felt it in her music. She's like some musicians I knew at Juilliard.

They had a lot of talent but not a lot of passion. Some studied because their parents wanted them to. Others simply had no idea what they wanted. I'd put Leilani in that boat."

"How do you mean?" he asks.

"Her technique is flawless. She's mastered the ukulele, but when she plays, it's kind of sterile. There's no heart. No emotion."

I'd never really thought about it before, but I was right. To an untrained ear, she sounded great. But if you looked for the nuances, they weren't there. I played because I adored the instrument. I let the music flow from my fingers, and if I closed my eyes, I saw the notes as living, breathing things telling a story. I'd bet Leilani never felt like that.

"So," Nick says, getting back to the investigation. "By killing Kua and framing you, she'd really stand to benefit by getting two competitors out of the way."

I nod. "So it would seem."

But did Leilani frame me? Did she steal the ukulele? I supposed she could've stolen the instrument. Mom sometimes drinks too much and passes out, leaving the door unlocked.

"I want to believe she did it," I say finally. "But I'm just not sure. Something seems a little off about the idea. I'm not sure what that is, but there's something bothering me about her as a suspect."

"She didn't feel that way when she told the detective you'd fought with the victim and was the last person to see him alive," Nick says. "Don't give her too much credit."

I nod. "That's true. This is so crazy. I still can't believe Kua is dead."

"If it wasn't Leilani," Nick thinks aloud, "it could be a surfer. Or someone else, for that matter. You said he had a temper."

"That narrows it down to the tens of thousands of people who live here." I throw my hands up in frustration.

"I disagree," Nick says. "Seems to me it had to be someone who knew him…someone who lives here. Someone who knows you have a kauwila ukulele."

I swallow hard. "I still can't believe it was my instrument that did it. It seems almost too obvious."

Nick nods. "Yes, it does. That's what makes it so devious. Whoever murdered Kua knows who you are. I think we can definitely narrow it down to someone in Aloha Lagoon or the surfing beaches on Kauai."

I shudder as if an icy shadow passed through me. "I hate to think that it's someone I know."

I don't really know that many people here. I'm ruling out my private lesson students first off. Those kids are under the age of 12, and I barely know their parents. There are a few bartenders and waitstaff at the various places I've played. And then there's the staff at the Blue Hawaii Wedding Chapel…

Oh no! I glance at my watch. Dammit.

"I've got to go!" I scramble to clean up and race for the kitchen, with Nick hot on my heels.

"What is it?" Nick asks.

"I totally spaced. I have to play a wedding in twenty minutes at the Blue Hawaii Wedding Chapel!" I shout this over my shoulder as I run into my bedroom and slam the door behind me.

"Can I go?" Nick asks through the door. "It might help. I can at least check out the staff there. See if there's anyone who hates you."

I pause for a moment. It couldn't be Pastor Dan. He's just a sweet old guy with an unfortunate Elvis obsession. Maybe Mary Lou—the wedding coordinator. She does double duty as the florist and photographer. She's never really liked me, so maybe that's something.

"Sure," I shout as I shimmy into my blue muumuu and step into my matching blue ballet flats. "Why not? But stay in the back, okay?"

After selecting my favorite soprano uke, I race out the door, with Nick trailing. I stop dead in my tracks in the driveway.

"You drive *that*?" I ask before I realize I'm being rude. Why should I care what my future husband drives?

A beat-up 1970s Cadillac in a disturbing shade of green sits in the driveway. We'll have to take it because my car is trapped inside the garage.

Nick points at the monstrosity. "It was my first car. Mom bought me a Jag, but I love this rattletrap."

"Fine." I climb into the passenger seat. "I hope it goes fast."

After all, I can't judge a future husband by his car... can I?

FIVE

WE ARRIVE JUST in time. The couple, a modestly obese twosome with bored expressions, stand waiting. The groom is middle aged and balding. He's wearing a brand-new aloha shirt and khakis—the equivalent of a suit here. The bride is youngish with long, badly bleached hair with black roots and a sundress that definitely does not show her body to her best advantage.

"Finally," Mary Lou barks as Nick takes a seat in the back. "I was about to call my cousin Myrna."

I take my place at the front with a quick "Sorry." Myrna has never had to replace me, and she never will. The woman can barely play even the most basic chords and can't carry a tune. Mary Lou knows this, and therefore I know it's an empty threat. Still, I feel bad for holding everyone up.

I start to play the "Hawaiian Wedding Song" as the couple gets into place in front of Pastor Dan. He's looking extra sparkly tonight in his '70s Elvis costume. *Nice call*, I think as I continue playing. This couple looks like they'd be more suited to a fat Elvis in his declining, drug-addled years than the fit, better looking '50s Elvis. Unfortunately, Pastor Dan's '50s Elvis outfit comes complete with super-short shorts. Just like the ones the King wore in *Blue Hawaii*—Dan's favorite movie and the namesake for this chapel.

Nick waves from the back, and I try to avoid smiling. Mary Lou scowls a few feet away as she snaps photos on a cheap digital camera. Once this is over, she'll slip into the office and print out the photos, slapping them in a tacky plastic frame.

I'm always amazed that people choose to get married here. There are so many striking, natural locations on the island, from the Fern Grotto to any one of the lovely beaches. Oh well, no accounting for taste. Besides, Pastor Dan pays me in cash, so I keep my mouth shut.

"Do you…" Dan drawls in his best Elvisy accent. It's something he does very well and makes it almost worth the cheap wig and polyester costume. "… Roberta Wilder take Robby Lugosi to be your lawful, wedded husband? Thank you very much!"

He adds a pose with his arm held high, his head bowed, and his legs in a lunge. Over the past year I've trained myself not to giggle when he does this. It wasn't easy. Quitting heroin would be a walk in the park compared to this.

Robby Lugosi? Wow. A man shouldn't be a *Robby*, *Ricky*, or *Bobby* after the age of ten. And Lugosi? I wonder if he's related to the actor Bela Lugosi. That would actually be kind of cool.

"I do." Roberta sounds bored and swats away a fly. She doesn't even make eye contact with Robby. I wonder what this is all about. These two don't seem to be into each other at all.

"And do you, Robby Lugosi, take Roberta Wilder to

be your lawful, wedded wife? Thank you very much!"
Pastor Dan swivels his hips lewdly.

They must've paid for the Blue Suede Shoes package—our most expensive. At Dan's age, he only attempts the gyrations if he is paid to. He's thrown out his hip more than once, and it's disturbing every single time.

"Yup," Robby says as he stifles a yawn.

Yeesh. What's wrong with these two? There's no chemistry at all. This is an awesome job for people watching. I've seen some really strange things. Once, a couple insisted they get married with their pets present. Oh sure, you say, that's normal. You've seen a wedding or two where they have their dogs in the church. But have you ever seen one where each person has a six-foot iguana on a leash? I have.

I spot Nick covering his mouth with both hands. He's about to lose it.

"By the power vested in me, the King"—Pastor Dan swings his arm around widely like he's power stroking a guitar—"I now declare you man and wife! You may kiss the bride."

Robby gives Roberta a weak peck on the cheek, and she frowns at him. I think my being late is the least of this couple's problems.

"I'll be right back with your photos!" Mary Lou fakes a smile that instead looks like she's on the verge of vomiting and disappears into the back.

I play the usual rousing recessional tune as Mr. and Mrs. Robby Lugosi walk limply back down the aisle. These events are usually a little more fun. Maybe this couple didn't really want to get married. They certainly don't seem like they just made the biggest commitment of their lives.

Mary Lou returns, waving a large envelope and an eight by ten of the couple's nuptials in a bright-blue frame with seashells glued to it. I suspect Mary Lou decorates the frames herself. We all wish the couple well as they exit the Blue Hawaii Wedding Chapel.

"Next time," Mary Lou barks as her face slides back into disgust, "be here when you are supposed to be here!" She turns on her heel and disappears into the office.

Pastor Dan wiggles his eyebrows. "Don't worry about her, Nani. She's just upset because I said 'no' to her demands of covering the whole room with blue suede fabric."

I laugh, because Mary Lou, in her endless attempts to redecorate, always comes up with some ridiculous idea. Last week she wanted to add 30 neon signs to give it more of an Elvis-in-Vegas feel. (Pastor Dan's excuse was we didn't have enough electrical outlets.) I'm surprised she didn't want to scatter pills and hypodermic needles artfully around the chapel.

To his credit, in spite of the tackiness of his costumes and act, Pastor Dan really has a lovely little place here. The pews and altar are made of teak, and he polishes them until they shine. Behind the altar are floor-to-ceiling views of the ocean. The floor is quarried stone. It's simple and pretty. Adding anything besides flowers would be garish overkill.

But I still wouldn't get married here. Even with a deep discount on the Blue Suede Shoes package. I'd like an outside wedding without an Elvis impersonator, thank you very much.

"Who's your gentleman friend?" Dan asks as Nick joins us. He extends his hand, and Nick shakes it.

"Nick Woodfield," I say. "Meet Pastor Dan Presley."

Nick cocks an eyebrow, and I know what he's thinking. He's wondering if Dan is related to Elvis. He isn't. He just legally changed his name the minute he turned 18, about 50 or so odd years ago. This man really, really, really loves the King.

"Nice to meet you." Dan frowns as if he's trying to remember something. "You're not Vera's boy, are you?"

Nick nods, and I recognize the look on his face. It's the same look I have when someone asks about my mom. We are wondering if it's good or bad to be associated with them. The best way to deal with this is to say nothing because what comes next could go either way.

"Ah," Dan says. "She's a nice lady. Even if she has tried to run me out every five years."

I look at Nick, and he blushes. This man couldn't get any cuter if he had a kitten dangling from his arm.

"Yes, well, sorry about that. Mom has this need for things to be a certain way," Nick apologizes. "I think she believes she owns this island."

Pastor Dan waves him off immediately. "Sorry, son. I didn't mean it like that. Your mom isn't a problem for me. I'll never sell this place. In my will it's going to Nani here."

I laugh—it's an old joke between us. Dan never had any children and, as far as I know, has never been married. Not that Mary Lou doesn't keep trying. That woman is a bit of a stalker.

"Don't forget we have another wedding tomorrow, Nani," Pastor Dan says. He turns to Nick. "Nice meeting you, Nick. I hope we'll see you again soon."

With that said, Dan disappears into the back, probably to get out of his costume. I can't really be sure, because I once saw him dressed in his 1950s Elvis costume in the parking lot of the grocery store. Wearing the short shorts. It was *not* a good look for him, and I was worried he'd be arrested for indecent exposure.

"He's fun," Nick says as he opens the door to his beater Cadillac for me. Nice.

I get in, and he joins me on the huge leather bench seat on the driver's side.

"Pastor Dan's great," I say as Nick starts the engine. In spite of its dilapidated appearance, the engine hums as if it is brand new. "He gave me my first job when I moved here."

Nick pulls out of the parking lot and onto the street. "Is he really leaving you the chapel?"

"No idea," I answer. "I just assume he's teasing me. Mary Lou hates it when he says that. She'd like to marry him and run the place herself after he's gone."

"The angry woman with the teased-out hair?" Nick frowns.

"I should let you know, I've never seen her in any other hairstyle. It's possible it's made of plastic," I say.

"How old is she? She looks a little young for Pastor Presley," he asks. Nick turns onto the road that doesn't lead to my house. Where are we going? Am I being kidnapped? Maybe I misjudged the man. It just now occurs to me that I barely know him. Oh wow. I barely know him. And he's helping me investigate Kua's murder. If he's a bad guy, then I walked right into this trap.

I think about this. No, I'm pretty sure I'm not being kidnapped. Nick seems to genuinely like me, for whatever reason. I've never heard anything bad about him. But then, I've never heard *anything* about him. Good guy or not, I should definitely get to know him better before we take this much further. Oh—how awful for me, right?

"Mary Lou is in her forties," I say. "But she's mad for Pastor Dan. He knows how she feels but doesn't have any interest in her."

Nick slants his eyes at me. "Does he have any interest in you?"

I laugh out loud. "No. You don't understand. The good pastor is gay. He's not interested in women period." I know this. Everyone in Aloha Lagoon knows this. But Mary Lou seems to think she can defy biology and change him.

We turn onto a country road about ten miles out of town. He's taking me to the Woodfield mansion. The man is actually taking me back to his house. Whoa—slow down, Casanova. I'm not ready for hitting his bachelor pad.

Nick hits the brakes, as if he's reading my mind. "Sorry! I'm just so used to driving home from town."

"It's okay. Mom's at your house anyway," I reply. I am kind of eager to see the inside of that mansion. If it's that gorgeous on the outside, I can only imagine what the interior looks like.

"Are you sure? I can take you home," Nick asks, searching my face to see if I'm just being nice.

"Yes," I insist. "I'd love to see your house. I've driven past it so many times. I'm curious about the inside."

He shakes his head. "You'll be disappointed."

"Oh? Why's that?" How could I be disappointed in a place like this? Okay, I would be disappointed if there are skeletons posed like they are eating in the kitchen. Or if he hoards cats and taxidermies them when they die. I guess it's better to find out now before things get too serious.

We pull up into a large, circular driveway. Mom's little blue hatchback is parked out front. I guess she hasn't scared Perseverance Woodfield off yet.

The manse rises up imperiously from the ground. It's modeled in the traditional Hawaiian style with a huge wraparound lanai on the first level and another porch on the second. Painted white to avoid absorbing the heat of the sun, the design is simple and elegant all at once.

"It's boring. Totally dull," Nick answers as he parks the car.

"You call this dull?" I ask in shock as we remove our shoes and cross the threshold.

The hardwood floors practically glow, and a giant koa-wood staircase parts the large foyer. Huge ceiling fans shaped like palm fronds circulate the air so you don't even feel the heat. The walls are covered with large ancestral portraits in beautiful, polished frames. The craftsman furniture is old yet inviting. A huge vase of freshly cut flowers takes up a small table in the middle of the room, and I see tables on the side wall, covered with potted orchids.

"It's lovely!" I breathe, afraid that if I speak too loudly, it'll all collapse around me.

Nick shrugs. "I don't know about that. It's okay."

I turn to him. "Okay? This is way beyond okay! This is amazing! You have an amazing house!"

Nick looks around himself, and I wonder if it's the first time he's really seen it.

"I grew up here. Everything just seems old to me."

"How could you not appreciate the beauty of this place?" I wonder as I walk over to the portraits. "I'd have loved growing up here."

The largest two pictures are dead center of the wall and clearly from the 19th century. A native Hawaiian woman smiles sweetly in such a way that you don't notice her English-style clothing. The portrait next to her is of a stern-looking Caucasian gentleman with a trim beard and huge eyes. His hair is parted in the middle, and his frown seems to be in response to the woman's grin. He probably thought that evened things out.

"My great-something grandparents," Nick says beside me. "She was the cousin of King Kamehameha, and he was Charles Endicott Woodfield—a Congregational Church missionary."

"She's so gorgeous," I muse as I step closer to the image. Dark hair cascades in waves over her shoulders, out of sync with her Christian clothes.

"She was," Nick says quietly. "According to family lore, she married shortly after Charles converted her to

Christianity." He points at the man. "And he was something of a jerk."

I can't help but laugh. "He looks like it. As if by glaring at us he's diminishing her happiness."

Nick looks at me. "That's it. I never could put my finger on why it bothered me so much that he's frowning."

The portraits that fan out in a circular radius around the couple feature men, women, and children in various time periods. These are Nick's ancestors.

"I think it's wonderful that you have this family history to look at every day," I say.

"You don't?" Nick asks, genuinely surprised that everyone else doesn't have family trees on their walls.

I shake my head. "Not really. We had pictures of my grandparents at home in Kansas, and I've seen photos of my great-grandparents on my mom's side, but that's it."

"Why is that?"

I shrug. "Maybe it's because my ancestors were pioneers to the Midwest. And photography was rare and pretty expensive. It was a big event to have your picture taken, and probably happened only once a year. And my parents aren't really into genealogy."

Dad's parents are probably too busy to think about it, and Mom most likely doesn't want anyone to know she isn't Hawaiian. I suppress a shudder. It's not right to glom on to another culture's history. I've actually told her that before. It didn't do any good.

"The Hawaiians are big into oral history and traditions." Nick is back to studying his grandmother. "Family stories are passed down from generation to generation in order for the dead to still be with us."

That is sheer poetry. My heartbeat skips a little. Nick really is adorable.

"I think that in the Midwest," I say slowly, "people envision that their children will do better than them. Have a better life. Hanging on to the past is just a reminder of those who came here with nothing."

"Huh." Nick turns his attention to me. "That's a pretty astute observation."

I smile. "Thanks! I just made it up."

We laugh, and Nick starts giving me a tour of his house. As we wander from room to room, I really look at him. Initially, I liked him because he was pretty cute and very funny. Now I'm starting to see that there's more to him than that. It's a good feeling.

By the time we reach the largest kitchen I've ever seen, we start to hear our mothers' voices trickling in from the backyard. Nick grabs a couple of beers from the fridge and hands me one. I drink it as we walk out onto the back patio, where Mom and Vera are laughing hysterically.

"Nani! Nick!" Vera waves us over to the set of wicker chairs they are sitting in. "I was going to suggest you two come over!"

Nick ushers me onto a large stone bench with huge cushions, and I sit. He sits next to me.

Mom acts as though she knew we were coming all along. "Nani had to work in that horrible little Elvis church today." She grimaces as if she had to endure it. I decide not to talk about today's wedding. It would only give her ammunition.

Vera nods. "That place is awful and takes up some

prime real estate on the beach, by the resort. I've made an offer to that pastor every year since they opened, but he won't sell. He's so stubborn."

"Mom." Nick glares at her. "Nani works there. Don't be rude."

My hero!

Vera apologizes. "I didn't mean anything by it, Nani. I'm sorry it came out that way."

"It's really quite pretty inside," I say in an attempt to smooth things over. "If Pastor Dan ever sells, it would make a nice quiet place to think or meditate or something."

Mom rolls her eyes. "Oh please. You're just protective of him because he gave you your first gig when we moved here."

A normal person would be embarrassed if their mother said something like that. I just ignore it. Mom has a knack for saying things without thinking. And deep down inside, I know she's proud of me and wants me to do well. At least... I hope she is.

"Whatever." I wave her off. "What have you two been up to? Nick just gave me a tour of your wonderful home, Vera. It's so beautiful! Did you do the décor yourself?" I think of the hula-skirted coconuts that currently reside in my living room.

Vera sits up straighter and blushes with pride.

"Oh, I can't take all the credit," she says. "It's pretty much the way my ancestors set it up, but I do maintain it and arrange the flowers. I think flowers really make the room, don't you?"

We launch into a relaxed conversation about flowers, and that's when I notice for the first time that the

Woodfields have an *unbelievable* garden. Of course Nick, being a botanist, would have set up a garden to die for. And this is that…on steroids…to the tenth power.

"Oh wow." My eyes grow to the size of cantaloupes as I look around. "I've never seen anything like this!"

Mom seems to notice the yard for the first time too and gets to her feet. "I was so busy talking I didn't notice what a gorgeous garden you have!"

There are flowers everywhere. One million colors envelop us in a happy, cozy den. The trees are perfectly landscaped and full of oranges, bananas, mangos, and coconuts. I've never seen grass so green. It's not even green. It's green-est-er.

"Is that a hedge maze?" I ask as I start to walk into the yard.

Nick joins me as I stop just short of it. "My great uncle designed and grew it. I just keep it up."

The hedge in front of me is at least eight feet tall. Full and lush foliage makes it impossible to see through. I can't imagine anything more awesome than this.

"I'll bet," I say, "you played in this a lot as a kid."

Nick winks at me. "I still play in it. Care to go inside?"

Yes. I do want to go and get lost in the maze with this incredible man. I look at my watch. But I can't. I have a lesson to give in half an hour. I get angry at my watch, as if it's to blame.

"I can't. I've got a lesson in a bit. Can you drive me home?" I ask, feeling awful as I say it.

Nick nods. "No problem. I'll take a rain check for the date in the maze."

We say our good-byes, and as we pull into my driveway, I see that my student Twila Grant is standing on the front porch, waiting.

"Sorry! Thanks for the ride—got to go!"

And then, without thinking, I kiss Nick on the lips before dashing out of the car. I blush furiously as I walk up to the door and unlock it. I don't even look back, but I have the sneaking suspicion that Nick Woodfield is smiling at me.

SIX

"MISS JOHNSON? Is that your boyfriend?" Twila asks. As children often do, she's not teasing me or making fun of me. She's just curious. I probably shouldn't have kissed Nick in front of her though. With little kids, kissing is as good as married. Nick and I weren't quite there…yet.

We are sitting in the living room, each holding a ukulele, each with a music stand in front of us. Twila is seven years old. Her father is in the military and very stern. He wants his daughter to take everything seriously, including her music lessons. If she doesn't go home with any progress to show him, she and I will both be in trouble.

"I don't know," I answer honestly. "Let's go over the music one more time, shall we?"

Twila nods and begins playing "Twinkle, Twinkle Little Star." She concentrates so hard her tongue sticks out of her mouth. The child struggles to manage the chord changes, but she gives it her best.

I'm only half paying attention. My mind is swirling from too much stimulation over the past couple of days. It all started with me being a suspect in a colleague's murder. And now it has ended with me kissing Nick— a man I barely know and just met. What could possibly happen next? And do I really want to know?

"That's very good, Twila!" I clap.

The little girl grins. She's missing her two front teeth. I can see why her tongue was sticking out. The doorbell rings, and I rush to answer it. Twila's mother, a very quiet woman with an uneasy smile, removes her shoes and enters.

"Is she ready?" Mrs. Grant asks tentatively. The woman always looks like she thinks she shouldn't be wherever she is.

I nod. "We're done. Perfect timing."

Mrs. Grant smiles a little more this time, and I manage to wrangle Twila, her music, and instrument to the door.

"Keep working on your music, and next week we will start another song," I say with what I hope is an encouraging grin.

The two nod and quietly walk out to their car. For some reason, I linger in the doorway until they drive off. I like working with kids. Mom says I should be a music teacher in the area schools, but I'm not sure I like kids that much. I'm still standing there when Binny arrives. She has excellent timing. I lead her into the living room, where I collapse.

"Sorry to barge in unannounced," she says, kindly not mentioning all the coconuts.

She's not sorry. Binny always shows up unannounced. I've gotten used to it and, as a matter of fact, look forward to it. This time is no exception, because I want to tell her what's going on.

Binny's jaw drops when I tell her about the missing uke. She giggles at the antics of Pastor Dan and Mary

Lou at the wedding and is awestruck by my description of the Woodfield home.

"You've actually been inside?" my friend gushes. "I don't know anyone who's ever been there before. You're the first!"

I shake my head. "Come on. It's a small town. They're the big kahunas. I'm sure someone you know has been to a party or fundraiser there."

"Nope." Binny shakes her head. "I really don't know anyone who has. What's it like?"

I tell her about the portraits and the hedge maze. She seems to hang on every detail. I'm shocked that this is the first time she's heard anything about the huge house just outside of town.

"The Woodfields are notoriously secretive," Binny says with a shrug when I ask. "That's probably why Nick drives a beater car. A jaguar would definitely stand out here."

"That's weird. Nick and Vera are the nicest people. Vera's practically adopted Mom."

How is it that the people who've lived here for generations haven't seen the inside of their house, but Mom, who's only been here a year, has? I turn this thought around in my head and inspect it from all angles. I come up with nothing.

"So," Binny says, "Nick is going to help you solve Kua's murder?"

I nod. "That's what he said. This relationship has moved a little quicker than I'm used to."

I tell her about the kiss.

"I can't believe you did that," she says.

I nod. "Me neither. I hope it didn't look too desperate." I change the subject. "So what do you think about us trying to find out who else disliked Kua?"

"Well, I'm in," Binny says. "I'm going to help too."

I hug my friend. It's probably a good idea to have her—until I decide if Nick is for real.

"You'll help a little or a lot?" I ask.

"I will do everything your boyfriend is doing," she says. "You have to give me everything he's got...except for the kiss."

We agree to meet up the next morning, and I call Nick. He's in, he says. I go to bed that night wondering where all this is going.

I wake up with no answers.

I sit on the lanai, eating a bowl of sugar-something cereal, staring out into the garden. My eyes alight on that stupid kauwila tree. It all comes rushing back to me. Kua's murder, the missing uke, Leilani indicating to Detective Ray that I'm connected—all spins around in my stomach like a bad case of acid reflux.

Since I have a moment alone, I should start piecing this together. What do I know that I haven't thought of? Well, there's that argument Leilani and Kua had the night he was murdered. She'd come over to get into a fight. And I'd seen them arguing later too.

But that wasn't anything out of the norm. The two of them bickered all the time. They certainly had an adversarial relationship. I think about Kua and me—did we have an adversarial relationship?

We basically had no contact. The few times we'd spoken, Kua had sought me out to pick a fight with me. I never started it. Oh wait. There was the first time we'd met. I guess I'd initiated that.

It was almost a year ago, shortly after I'd moved here. If you asked me to pin down the date—I couldn't. The weather is always the same here. It's impossible to gauge time by the weather. It's always sunny, and the temperature never varies that much. This is the only problem with living in paradise.

Anyway—there had been an open house at a new concert hall in Lihue, and I'd heard a lot of the island's musicians were going because the concert hall was going to have an open mic as a way to feel out future acts. Thinking this would be an excellent time for networking, I'd grabbed my ukulele and went.

My attitude back then was annoyingly optimistic. I'd just moved here, found a great little cottage, and the future was full of promise. Once at the concert hall, I sat in the audience and marveled at the acoustics. It wasn't a large auditorium. It held maybe 400 people. But whoever designed it had paid exquisite attention to the acoustics. The result was that no matter where you were sitting, you heard the same concert as someone in the front row.

I watched as the Terrible Trio performed—each separately, of course—and decided to jump up next. I wanted to be measured against these amazing talents. It was my chance to make my mark.

I'm a very good musician. I enjoy each and every note and chord and feel the music swelling in my bones as I play. My teachers at Juilliard were shocked when I switched from classical guitar to the tiny instrument.

But in the end, they encouraged me. At least they didn't kick me out.

After Leilani—the third of the Trio to play—finished performing, I took my chance and walked out onto the stage. After introducing myself, I played probably my best performance ever. I did a fingerstyle performance of a collage of old Appalachian folk songs. This was a tribute to one of my favorite composers, Aaron Copeland, and one of my favorite violinists, Mark O'Connor. And it went very, very well. I didn't miss a note.

When I finished, I took a bow, and amid what I thought had been very enthusiastic applause, I headed for the wings. Full of the high of an appreciative audience, I walked over to the Terrible Trio, who had been watching me from the backstage.

Alohalani spoke first. "Not bad, for a haole." He turned and left.

"Why would you play that redneck crap here?" Kua spat.

Leilani rolled her eyes. "I was way better than you."

"Oh." I fumbled, a little shocked by their bitterness. "Well, I thought you three were all great!" A little sugar can take the sting out of the angriest bee, my father always said.

He was wrong.

"I was great." Kua snorted. "Alohalani was good. Leilani sucked. And you—I don't even have words to describe whatever that was."

Okay…

"It was Aaron Copeland, you moron!" Leilani hissed at him. "Even if she didn't do it justice."

Kua glared at me. "Why are you here?"

I couldn't believe this was happening. "I just moved here…" I said. "I'm hoping to work here on Kauai."

"With that?" Leilani pointed a crimson-painted nail at my mahogany ukulele. "I don't think so."

"I'm not sure what you mean," I said.

"She means it's a haole ukulele played by a haole mainlander," Kua sniped.

I started to get angry. I'd been completely complimentary and respectful. But these two…

"That was an excellent performance." I pointed toward the stage behind me. "And the audience loved it."

Leilani narrowed her eyes. "That audience would applaud an epileptic basset hound playing the xylophone. They know nothing of our true art." She shook her head, as if I was an idiot. I tried to imagine said dog playing the xylo, so maybe I *was* an idiot.

The two of them left the backstage area, leaving me to wonder just what had happened. After that moment, I avoided the three musicians. I never initiated conversation with them. And I aimed a bit lower to get work. Which is how I ended up giving lessons and working bar mitzvahs.

Since then, I've had no relationship with any of them. Leilani implicated me as being closer to Kua than I was. She had to be involved somehow. But could I see her as a murderer? I wasn't sure. Granted, it would make things easier if she was, but could she actually kill him?

Did Leilani sneak into my home, steal my instrument, then bludgeon Kua in order to eliminate the competition? If she did, what is stopping her from taking Alohalani or me out too? (Weirdly, I'd be flattered to be included in this group.) Maybe the only thing keeping me alive is that Leilani knows it would be obvious if the professor and I were both murdered. Chills race down my spine as I realize Leilani might consider killing me. She never thought I was a real threat, but she certainly hates me. That would suck. I just got a boyfriend, and everything is looking up. Well, she's not going to get me. What's she going to do? Kill me with my own ukulele? Does she think that would implicate me as well? Who bludgeons herself to death with her own instrument?

I could just see the headlines: "Idiot and Untalented Haole Performer Kills Self with Own Uke." Mom would probably believe it. I pictured her giving an interview to the media, saying, *I always knew it was possible. She could not come to grips with her mixed Hawaiian heritage.*

No way am I going to allow myself to get killed so Mom can say something like that. I think about the detective and how he was slowly…very slowly…stringing together circumstantial evidence to condemn me. If I leave it in his hands, it could take months before he finally arrests me.

Nope. Not going to happen. I pick up my phone and call first Nick, then Binny. Both agree to meet me at the Loco Moco for lunch. I'm going to take them up on their offer. We are going to investigate this before I get arrested.

"Mom!" I shout as I grab my keys. "I'm heading out."

There is no reply. Should I check on her? After breakfast, she started watching TV in the sunroom.

"Okay, Nani," Mom shouts back. "I'm watching a *CSI* marathon so I can help you after you get arrested for murder."

I sigh.

For a moment I picture my mother in one of her muu-muus, looking through a magnifying glass at a test tube. It makes me shudder as I unlock the car and get in. As I back down the driveway and onto the street, I think that I'd better figure this out before Mom gets involved. There's no telling what that woman is capable of. She even thinks I'm going to get arrested.

The Loco Moco is packed, but Nick has scored a table. Binny arrives right after me and follows me.

"Nick Woodfield," I say, motioning toward her. "This is my friend Binny Finau. Binny, Nick."

We take our seats, and the harried waitress drops off menus as she rushes past our table. It's super busy here.

"You aren't Minnie Finau's daughter, are you?" Nick asks.

Binny's jaw drops. "How do you know my mom?" I'm sure she's surprised, since she said she's never met the Woodfields.

Nick grins. "My dad knew your mom. They worked together once."

I'm confused. "What did they work on?"

Nick hasn't mentioned his dad, and for some rea-son, I'd never asked. Binny's mom stayed home. Min-nie Finau never had a job that I knew of. How did they know each other?

"It was a long time ago. Before we were born." Nick

unfolds his napkin and places it on his lap. I love that he has nice manners.

"My dad," he continues, "used to be on the school board. They teamed up to get Hawaiian taught at the elementary school."

Binny's face lights up with recognition. "Oh, right. Mom told me that when I was a student. She told me I had her and your dad to thank for having to take two languages."

"You've never mentioned your dad, Nick," I say, trying to find a delicate way to ask if he is still alive.

The waitress joins us at that exact moment. A girl in her 20s, she looks like she hasn't had a break since 1992. Her face is flushed, and her hair is a mess. I wonder if she's new.

"What'llyahave?" Her words all run together in an effort to hurry us along.

We all order burger platters. She writes them down so fast I wonder if she'll remember it correctly. The girl disappears as quickly as she'd appeared.

"My dad died five years ago," Nick says simply, without much emotion. "My parents were divorced, and he'd been living on the Big Island for a while."

"I'm so sorry," I say as I take his hand. "My dad died a year and a half ago. It's why we moved here."

Nick puts a hand over mine and gives me a sweet look. Binny grins lopsidedly. Nick and I are getting a little too flirty for her. She's not big on public displays of affection.

"So…" My friend steers the conversation back to the

present. "How are we going to help Nani avoid a life in prison?"

Her choice of words startles us out of our little moment, and Nick starts to laugh self-consciously.

"Right. That's why we're here. We should talk about that." He blushes a little. Is there anything this man can do that isn't wonderful?

A cell rings, and Nick frowns at his phone. "I'm sorry—I really have to take this." He gets up and takes the phone outside.

"Must be a botanical emergency," I say.

Binny laughs. "I like him. He's perfect for you. It's just…"

"What?"

"It's probably nothing," she says as she stares thoughtfully at the ceiling. "I guess it's weird that I grew up here and never, ever bumped into him. After all those years, we finally meet, and it's like we are old friends or something."

I nod. "He does have a way of putting people at ease. I don't think that's a bad thing."

The waitress dumps our platters and drinks on the table in one fluid movement as she walks past. It's kind of like a drive-by—only with food instead of bullets.

"You're right." Binny tucks her napkin in her lap and squirts ketchup on her fries. "I'm being weird." She dips a fry in the red puddle and pops it into her mouth.

"Right or not, I'll take any help I can get right now." I follow her lead and begin devouring my lunch.

"You'll be fine. I doubt Detective Ray will arrest you.

He doesn't have any concrete proof." Binny looks at the door. Nick is still talking outside.

"How well do you know the detective?" I ask. I feel a little bad eating without Nick, but since it's just fries and not our burgers, that's okay, right?

Binny shakes her head and dips another fry. "Not well. I've seen him around town and all, but never did anything that would bring him to my house." She frowns, "In fact, I don't remember there ever being a murder in Aloha Lagoon before."

I sit up straighter. "Really? No murders?" That seems a little weird to me. The odds must be off the charts.

"Nope," she says. "I mean, there've been deaths before, obviously. And an accident a few years ago when some guy tried to jump off the cliffs outside of town."

"Are you sure it wasn't suicide?" I think about the cliffs she means. There's nothing but a rocky gorge below.

She shakes her head. "I'm sure. He wasn't the smartest guy. His friends who were with him said he figured he'd float down to the bottom. There was some talk about drugs being involved."

I stared at her. "You think?"

Nick joins us, sitting down and digging into his food. "Oh good. You started. I was going to tell you to do that. No point in waiting for me."

Something's a little off. He seems distracted somehow. I watch as he takes a bite of his sandwich and chews. It's as if he shoved food into his mouth so he wouldn't have to talk.

"What's wrong?" I ask. "Something happen at work?

Mrs. Horowitz mow down a whole garden of rare, endangered flowers?"

My joke only receives a weak grin.

"Who's Mrs. Horowitz?" Binny asks, and I fill her in.

"Ugh," Binny says. "I hope she's gone. I can't stand tourists like that. They act as if we should be so lucky to have them here."

Nick has stopped chewing. He looks like he's gotten some bad news.

"What's wrong?" I ask again.

The man sighs and shakes his head. "There was another murder—this time at the resort."

"What? Who?" I ask.

"It's Leilani." Nick looks directly at me. "Apparently she was pushed off a cliff and into the ocean while performing at a wedding at the Overlook in one of my gardens at the resort."

My eyes are bulging. I can actually feel them. "Leilani's dead?" And she was doing weddings? That's kind of *my* thing.

Binny looks from me to Nick. "How? What happened?"

Nick sets down his burger and gives us a look I can't decipher. "It happened this morning. Just the couple and a priest. All three say a woman with long brown hair ran out of the bamboo trees and shoved Leilani over the cliff. They're guessing the body hit the rocks before falling into the sea. They haven't found it yet."

Now he looks straight at me. "The person who pushed Leilani shouted something about Leilani stealing her gigs."

I'm unable to move. Unable to breathe.

Binny speaks the words I can't. "It sounds like you, Nani. They could be describing you."

SEVEN

When I finally am able to speak, I struggle with the words. "But…but it wasn't me! I didn't do it!"

Nick takes my hand this time, and Binny pats me on the back.

"Of course it wasn't you!" my friend says.

"I know it wasn't you," my future boyfriend says.

"It sure as hell sounds like me," I say dimly. The room is spinning, and I feel light headed.

"Why did they call you?" Binny asks Nick.

He nods. "Detective Ray is the one who called. He asked some questions about the copse of bamboo trees where the killer had been hiding. He wants me to look at the damage done, for some reason."

"That doesn't really make sense." Binny frowns. "Why call you? What does a botanist have to do with this?"

Nick shakes his head. "I have no idea. I think he's either some weird savant who sees things differently or he's just not very smart at all."

My mouth opens and closes like a fish out of water. "He's going to come find me next. He's going to think I did it…"

"You didn't do it," Binny insists. She looks at Nick.

"What time did it happen? And didn't you say they haven't found the body?"

Nick shrugs. "The detective didn't give me much information."

My friend puts her hand on my shoulder. I barely feel it. "I'm sure you have an alibi for this morning. Your mother had to see you. Right?"

I think about Mom sitting there watching *CSI* and taking notes for the arrest she was sure was coming. It's not like her to be right like this. I wonder how she knew.

Burying my face in my hands, I mumble, "Well, yes. Mom was home. That's true."

"See?" Binny smiles, but she looks worried. "It'll all be okay."

"Someone is definitely framing you," Nick adds gently. "By going after Kua and Leilani, they are trying to establish a pattern of you eliminating the competition."

"And wearing a disguise to look like you. It's ingenious really," Binny adds.

"I'm afraid I can't share your enthusiasm for the details of the plot." I pick at my food. I don't really have an appetite anymore. I shove the plate away from me.

"You shouldn't go home just yet," Nick says quietly. His eyes are darting around the restaurant. "Detective Kahoalani is probably headed there right now to arrest you."

I throw my hands up in the air. "Of course he's heading to my house. Someone's out to get me, and I have to admit—they're doing a great job."

Binny nods. "It does sound bad."

"Not helping…" I growl through gritted teeth.

"Sorry," she says. "What can we do now? How can we help?"

I shake my head. "This is out of control. Two murders, that I'm being framed for, have occurred in the last two days. Witnesses saw me at the scene of the most recent murder. I'm screwed."

Nick squeezes my hand. "No, you're not. You have us, and we aren't going to let them railroad you."

"Who is 'they'?" I ask. "We have no idea who killed Kua and Leilani. We don't even know how or where to begin!"

Nick stands up and throws several 20s on the table. It's more than enough to cover our bill and a tip. Binny reaches for her purse, but he holds up his hand to stop her.

"Come on," he says before leading us to the door. "Let's get out of here."

We walk out into the sunshine, but I don't see it. The beautiful day seems stained somehow—tarnished by murder. Nick urges us into his car and starts it up.

"Where are we going?" I probably should've asked before we got into the car. My brain hasn't caught up with reality yet.

Nick looks right and left before pulling out into traffic. "Somewhere they won't be looking for you. Somewhere we can think this thing through before you talk to the detective."

As if in response, my cell rings. It's the same number that Detective Ray called me from before. I let it go to voice mail.

"Are you sure this is a good idea?" Binny asks. "Won't it look like Nani's going on the lam?"

I'm impressed with her lingo. Maybe she's been watching *CSI* too.

"We can say we went to Na Pali or Waimea Canyon for fun," Nick says. "Cell service there is pretty spotty."

"What about the call you just took from Kahoalani? Won't he be suspicious that we disappeared right after you two talked?" Binny asks. "And there'll be witnesses who can put us in the Loco Moco at that time."

Everything looks like it's in black and white and moving in slow motion. My heart is pounding, and my mouth is dry. Words are spinning around me, and I can't quite grasp them. I picture myself running at Leilani and pushing her off the Overlook. I see the anger in her eyes turn to fear as she falls backward, arms flailing but finding nothing.

"He didn't tell me all that," Nick says as he turns onto a dirt road. Where are we going? I haven't been paying attention. "I made assumptions based on what he did say. He'll probably just think I'm a moron."

I start to sit up. "I should turn myself in. This is crazy…"

Nick and Binny look alarmed. They must think I've gone off the deep end. Maybe I have.

Slumping back against my seat, I close my eyes. This cannot be happening. It's all a bad dream. Somewhere out there, Kua and Leilani are hating me as much as they ever did. They're alive.

"Where are we going?" I ask again. I'm not sure about running away. Won't it make me seem more guilty?

Nick looks at me, which isn't good, because he's driving. "I thought you'd want to get away. Have some time to think."

I shake my head. "No, I'd rather go in and get this over with."

Binny agrees. "He can't arrest her, can he? He has no real proof."

"Except for a witness. And that's enough to arrest her," Nick adds, but he pulls over, as if considering going back.

"I need to know what I'm up against," I say finally. "I have no idea where to start, but having the details of Leilani's murder might help. And the only way we are going to get that is from the police."

Nick brightens. "Not necessarily…" He turns the car around. "I have an idea."

Which is how we end up at the Overlook. Nick called the chaplain who performed the service to meet us there.

"Don't you get it?" Nick asks as we stand on the breezy, bright-green cliff, waiting for the minister. "If he doesn't recognize you, that discredits the other witnesses!"

In the distance, a short, heavyset man wearing all black, except for a white collar, approaches. I don't know Reverend Blake. Pastor Dan knows him, but he's never said much about the Presbyterian minister. I have no idea what to expect from him.

"Thanks for coming, Reverend." Nick offers his hand, and the man frowns but takes it. Nick introduces us to the man, who glances at us with no sense of recognition in his eyes.

"What's this all about, Woodfield?" the man grumbles. "I don't have a lot of free time today. I missed two meetings with parishioners because of that murder this morning."

Well, he seems totally charming.

"I apologize," Nick says solemnly. "It's just that Detective Kahoalani is questioning me later today on the murder, and I wanted to know what happened before I meet him." He shrugs adorably.

It doesn't work.

"Look, son," Reverend Blake says. "If it wasn't for the large donation your mother made to my church recently, I wouldn't even be here."

Wow. I'm secretly happy I don't go to this church. I wouldn't be surprised if this guy makes his congregation feel awful with every sermon.

Nick nods. "And I'm very grateful for that. In fact, my mother was saying the other day that she loves your plans for an outdoor chapel and is considering donating to that project."

The little fat man's demeanor changes instantly. Right before my eyes he goes from grumpy to jolly in a second. Maybe he has a split personality?

"Oh! That would be wonderful! I've always wanted to have an outdoor chapel to hold services in nice weather!" The man nods enthusiastically. "My dream would be an overhead trellis covered with clematis vines to protect people from the sun!"

"What a great idea!" Nick grins. "You know, I am a botanist and the head of landscaping for the resort. I'd be happy to donate my time to plan that for you."

It's as if the ill-tempered man we saw moments ago

has undergone a complete overhaul in personality. The reverend beams and claps Nick on the back.

"I can tell you are a godly man, Mr. Woodfield! Godly indeed! What do you want to know?"

Nick humbly asks the man if he can tell us exactly what happened this morning. He's really good. Too good. Seeing him perform for the minister makes me wonder if he's been 100 percent sincere with me. I shove that thought aside. Nick offered to help. He wouldn't do that unless he liked me.

Or maybe he's just bored. Maybe I'm just a diversion for him. I stop thinking about that because that would suck.

"Well." The rotund reverend runs his hand through his thinning hair. "Let's see."

Reverend Blake walks over to the spot where I'm guessing he stood this morning. He indicates that Binny stand where Leilani stood and for me and Nick to take up positions as the bride and groom. I feel the heat from a serious blush warming my cheeks. Nick seems to go with it easily.

"We were all in these positions," the reverend says. "Miss O'Flanagan was playing, and I'd just said the last words, *husband and wife*." He points to the copse of bamboo trees about 20 yards on our left.

"Then this woman comes out of nowhere." He looks at Nick eagerly—hoping his information is what he wants to hear. I can see him building his garden chapel in his head, measuring out the area.

"She runs so fast I almost don't see her face. She runs behind the bride and groom." His index finger traces the route behind me and Nick and over to Binny. "And she runs up to the ukulele player and shoves her backward off the cliff!"

The man is perspiring now with the exertion of merely speaking. "The couple, a Mr. and Mrs. Parker, just saw the last part. They remained where you are now, while I"—the minister runs over to the edge of the cliff behind Binny—"ran to the edge of the cliff and looked downward." He looks downward very dramatically.

"I didn't see much, because of the overhang, you can't see the exact spot where she landed—before it occurred to me to look for the murderer." He shakes his head sadly. "But she was gone."

The three of us join him at the edge of the cliff. I feel Nick's hand on my back, as if he's trying to keep me from falling.

"She was gone?" Binny asks, looking around. "Did she go back into the trees?"

Reverend Blake shakes his head. "I have no idea."

"Where were the Parkers?" I ask. "Did they see where she went?"

The minister thinks for a moment. "I believe they followed me to the edge of the Overlook. They seemed just as confused as I was and also tried to spot the killer. I don't think they really got a good look at her."

"That's interesting," I say as I look at Nick and Binny. The Parkers were the witnesses who gave the police the description. A description that resembled me.

"Can you describe the killer?" Binny asks.

The reverend's demeanor changes, and he eyes us suspiciously. "Why do you need to know that? I thought this was all about young Woodfield here being questioned about the bamboo trees."

Nick gives an easy smile. "I just wondered about her size and such. The police want to know if anyone hid or could hide in the trees. It really would help me."

Reverend Blake's face is closed. He's done here. That's abundantly clear.

"Hey! I have an idea!" Nick gives a look of having a eureka moment. "I've got a great idea for an arbor-like altar for your garden!"

Whatever concerns the minister has melted away, and he once again becomes very animated and happy. "Inspired! Truly inspired! Keep it all natural." He smacks Nick on the back. "You are a genius, my boy!"

It's ridiculous that this actually works.

"I didn't get a very good look at her." The man frowns in concentration. "But she was tall—definitely taller than the musician. She had a stocky build. And she had long brown hair."

I let out a sigh. I'm the same height as Leilani. Maybe a little shorter—and I'm certainly not stocky. This is good news.

"The police interviewed me, but I guess I didn't tell them that. The Parkers told him what they knew. I guess I didn't see the point of getting involved since they had their testimony."

What? He didn't tell the police what he told us? Why wouldn't he do that? We have to tell the detective what Blake just said. How ridiculous that the minister didn't even try to help.

"Have you used this musician before?" Binny asks.

Blake nods. "A few times. I usually have Kua, but it's my understanding that he died recently. Leilani can be difficult. She's a bit hostile, so I don't usually allow her to do much more than play."

"Really?" Binny feigns dismay.

"Oh, absolutely. Last month, she practically destroyed the Sharpman wedding. The woman screamed at the groom because he requested a song she didn't think was appropriate. I agree that the theme from *Shaft* is an odd choice, but it was their wedding. Then she took a swing at the bride because she called Leilani an 'angry ginger.'"

Okay—I know it's wrong, but I wish I'd seen that.

He turns to Nick. "Do you know Ben and Barbara Sharpman? Lovely people. They're in my congregation. Nice folks. They've never upset anyone except that woman. I was worried Leilani would follow them to their car to continue the argument."

"Did she?" I ask a little too eagerly. Did the Sharpmans kill Leilani? That would be awesome. Well, not for them.

The reverend shook his head. "No. She did chew me out after they left though. I'm still not sure what the problem was in the first place. I wasn't going to use her again, but circumstances forced it with the Parker wedding. That woman is a menace."

Reverend Blake opens his mouth like he wants to say something. He closes it.

"Is there something else?" Nick nudges.

"It's just strange, is all." The Reverend nods his head. "Leilani was dressed oddly."

"What do you mean?" I ask a little too eagerly.

"She had a huge black dress on. And it seemed to me that the woman had put on weight." He shook his head. "I'm sure it's nothing. You just don't usually see a woman wearing black at a wedding."

The three of us thank Reverend Blake, and Nick promises to stop by to discuss the outdoor chapel. We watch as the minister waddles back to the parking lot.

"It's not me," I say finally. "I'm not taller than Leilani."

Nick nods. "And the Parkers didn't really see the killer."

"And the minister didn't tell the police what he knows," Binny agrees. "I think it's safe to say that you're in the clear, Nani."

My friend hugs me as Nick walks over to the copse of bamboo. He disappears into the trees and a few moments later, emerges, shaking his head.

"What is it?" I ask as we join him.

"There's nothing in there that would offer up any evidence." He frowns. "What does Detective Ray think I can tell him? That line of inquiry leads nowhere."

"I don't care," I say. "His calling you gave us a heads-up. Now we know something he doesn't. Now we can prove I wasn't there."

"And we have more testimony that Leilani wasn't well liked," Binny says as she pats me on the shoulder. "Which means more suspects, right?"

We agree, but it sounds like the Sharpmans aren't the kind of people to kill someone, even for ruining their wedding. Back at square one as far as other suspects went.

"Let's go down to the rocks and check it out," Nick says.

Binny shudders. "How gruesome. I'm not sure I want

to see where she died." She really is such a sweetheart. I could understand that. Like the Sharpmans, Binny wouldn't hurt a fly.

"You stay here," I say. "Check out the area, and see if you find something the police missed."

"Perfect!" Binny agrees, and Nick and I make the long trek to where Leilani breathed her last.

We don't speak. It's strenuous, difficult work. Like most of the trails in Hawaii, this one is muddy, slippery, and steep. Jagged rocks dot the path, which gives way in several places due to erosion. Several times, Nick grabs my hand when I start to slide one direction or another.

This is the thing about living here: while I was an avid hiker back in Kansas, I find the trails here to be far more dangerous. In fact, I haven't gone hiking in months. Which is ridiculous when you have the perfect, year-round weather we have on Kauai.

Nick grabs my hand one more time as we both slide on some slick rocks. I smile at him. It's nice to have someone when things are treacherous. And Nick is special. He's not like the other guys I dated in Kansas or in New York City. I can tell that right away.

Not that I dated many losers. Most of the guys I went out with were great. The problem was there was no spark. None at all. And while they were all considerate and thoughtful, none of them made me feel like Nick does.

That thought makes me stop, and as I do, I slip on a rock and fall. Aside from a few bruises, there are no injuries except for my pride. I'm losing my touch. Nick helps me up and brushes me off. I get all tingly where he touches me. It's exciting and scary all at once. He makes me feel clever and brilliant. I like feeling that way.

Am I taking things too fast? Is he? I just met the guy, and already it seems kind of serious. Not like, marriage serious, but like we are a couple. A real couple. I stare at his back as he moves along the trail. He really is quite graceful. I wonder if that's a botanist thing.

Really? A botanist thing, Nani? Now I feel kind of stupid. I liked it better when I felt smart. What is really making this relationship move so quickly?

Maybe it's the serious situation I'm in. The fact that I'm a suspect in two murders adds weight to our brand-new coupledom. I don't want to start a relationship based on stress and hardship. Those never work. At least, that's what Sandra Bullock said in *Speed*.

Reality starts to set in. I'm a suspect—possibly the lead suspect—in two murder investigations! How did this happen? How did I end up in this position? I barely knew either of the deceased. In fact, I think the last time I ran into both—at that festival—was the first time in months that I'd seen them.

What makes me a suspect? Detective Kahoalani said that Leilani indicated that not only did I argue with Kua, and not only were we alleged besties, I was also the last person to see him alive. The murder weapon could be my kauwila uke (inconveniently missing), and witnesses described someone like me actually pushing Leilani off a cliff (something I've fantasized about many times—but did not do).

The evidence is damning. The only thing we can disprove is the witnesses' testimony to the most recent murder. My ukulele was still gone. And Leilani can't be questioned any further to admit her statement about me and Kua was false. In fact, she started the whole thing by pointing the finger at me. Even in death, the psycho can accuse me. Doesn't seem fair, really.

We hit the beach and look up. It's hard to see the edge of the Overlook, because it hangs out over the rocks. And we aren't able to get too close to where the body landed because there are huge, sharp rocks and the crashing waves.

"Over there." Nick points. "That must be it."

The police tried to draw a chalk outline on upright, jagged rocks. It looked more like a blob than a person. Leilani would've hated that, which is why I find it amusing. Police *Do Not Enter* tape is attached haphazardly to the general area, with one long streamer flapping in the breeze.

"I don't think we should try to get any closer," I say, wrapping my hands around Nick's arm. I can feel the muscles tensing beneath his skin. There goes that little shiver again.

"Okay," Nick agrees. "I don't see how the police even got that far."

The tide washes up over the rocks, taking the last of the police tape with it.

"Didn't the detective say they hadn't found the body?" I ask.

Nick nods. "That's what Detective Ray said. See how the water hits those rocks? I'm guessing her body was washed out to sea."

"It'll probably show up on the beach soon," I say with no evidence to support that, but it makes me feel clever again. "If the tide took her out to sea, it should come back."

"Unless sharks get it," Nick agrees. "Let's head back. You okay?"

I nod, and we start moving. It's faster going this time because of memory. But it is all uphill, making it impossible to talk. The good news is that he goes first, so I get a first-rate view of his nice body as we climb.

I'm thinking too much. Whatever Nick and I have going on will just happen. I might give it a shove or two in the right direction…but he doesn't need to know that.

By the time we rejoin Binny, we are covered in dirt and, in my case, bruises.

"Did you find anything?" my friend asks.

"Nothing," I say, trying to brush myself off. I only succeed in making my clothes dirtier.

"Well, I found something." Binny holds out a piece of paper, pinching it gingerly in one corner between her fingers.

I very carefully take it from her, holding it in the same spot, same place. "It's resort stationery."

A message is scrawled on the piece of notepaper, just under the Aloha Lagoon Resort logo, *Parker Wedding at 10 a.m. sharp, Overlook.*

"It's a description of Leilani and the time and place she'd be playing the Parker wedding!" I tell Nick.

Binny agrees. "It looks like there was a hired killer and this was her instructions."

"Where did you find this?" Nick asks. "The police should've been all over the area."

"That's the weird part." Binny leads us to the edge

of the cliff. She gets down on her stomach looking over, and we do the same.

"There." She points to a spot of mud just beneath the edge. "It was stuck there. That's why they missed it."

I move back to where the reverend had been standing. "So the killer runs out of the woods"—I run to the edge—"pushes Leilani over the cliff, and loses the note? So she was carrying the note in her hand when she shoved Leilani? Who does that?"

"Seems like an amateur move," Nick mumbles. "Carrying the note with her as she does the job."

"We have to take this to Detective Ray," I say as I gently grip one corner of the note. "I think it's time he and I had a little chat."

EIGHT

"MISS JOHNSON." Detective Ray points to a chair across from his desk, and I sit.

Nick and Binny were told to wait in the lobby, which is good because there isn't any room for more than two people. This might be the messiest office I've ever been in. Stacks of papers, thumbtacks, and paper clips litter the floor and completely cover the desk. I have to remove three binders from the chair before I sit. It's like an Office Depot exploded in here. How does this man get anything done?

I fill Detective Ray in on our trip to where Leilani was murdered. I tell him what Reverend Blake told us, and the detective frowns. He doesn't say a word as I describe that the Parker couple couldn't have seen much of the killer and grimaces when I hand him the note. When I finish, he leans back in his chair, still frowning.

"This is a criminal investigation," Detective Ray says finally. "You are not a policeman. You have no idea what you're doing."

Well, clearly, neither does he. But I think I'll keep that to myself. And maybe I'll buy him a desk organizer. Or three.

I nod. "I know that, sir. I just want to help. I didn't kill Kua or Leilani."

Yes, it sounds weak. It sounds ridiculous. It sounds like something the killer might say. But I'm desperate. I need this off my plate so I can pursue happiness with a certain botanist.

"Miss Johnson," Detective Ray says at long last, "you will benefit from their deaths, right?"

"Um, well, I guess so, now that you say it." I fidget in the chair. Something feels like it's stabbing me. Did I miss a thumbtack? I wouldn't be surprised. A rotting sandwich covered with white fuzz sits on a bookshelf a few feet away with flies buzzing around it. Now *that's* a crime.

He nods. "You will now have more opportunities with them out of the way. Am I wrong?"

I try indignation. "That's a terrible thing to say! I would never kill someone just for a gig!" I might wish it, but I wouldn't do it.

"I'm just looking for motive." Detective Ray shrugs. He doesn't seem defensive. I really need to up my indignation game. Another time though.

"Don't you have any other suspects?" I ask weakly. "I mean, both of them must have other enemies in common."

"I'm not that far into my investigation." The detective sighs wearily. "So far you are the only common link to both victims that I've found."

"But what about the note? What about Reverend Blake's testimony?"

Ray says nothing. That makes me nervous.

My heart starts to pound. "Maybe the two murders aren't related! Maybe it's just coincidence that they were both murdered at the same time!"

"Calm down, Miss Johnson," the man says. "You are a suspect, but we don't have enough to arrest you. Yet."

A thought comes to mind. I just need to be careful how I phrase it in order to find out what I want to know.

"Is someone handling the funeral arrangements for Leilani?" I ask as innocently as I can. The body had disappeared in the sea. The minister said it hit the rocks before falling into the crashing waves. People still hold funerals without the body, don't they? I mean, obviously there's a body, or they wouldn't know it was murder, right?

"No. No one has come forward."

I stare at the detective. "But you don't have a body, right? How do you know she's dead?"

He gives me a pitying look, as if I'm ridiculous to think of this. "We found a lot of blood—her blood—at the scene. So much of it that the coroner felt she couldn't have survived the fall."

"How much is that?" I ask.

"I don't know," Detective Ray says with a frown. "But the coroner thought it was too much for her to live. And we found her shoes and a hank of her hair."

I almost expect the man to produce these things. It seems like it would be in his wheelhouse to do so.

"So no funeral then." I remember my earlier thought. "No family or friends to claim her…um…what's left."

"Not yet," the detective said.

My second hope was to find out who was closest to

Leilani. I read something once that said the majority of murders are committed by someone you know. Of course, that also backed up the theory that I'd been the murderer. But if I had some names, I could do a little interviewing…

"I must insist that you stop investigating. This is a police matter and my case." He tries to look menacing but only succeeds in looking a bit like a lopsided bloodhound.

"I'm just trying to help," I grumble. The man wouldn't even have the new testimony or note if we hadn't checked it out. That's gratitude for you.

Ray sighs again. I feel like a little kid in the principal's office.

The phone rings, and I watch as he answers. He gives a few grunts into the phone before hanging up.

"I need to do something quick." The detective stands. "Stay where you are. I'll be back." He walks to the door, pointing at me wordlessly before walking out.

There's a file on his desk with photos of Kua and Leilani on it. After glancing at the door, I stand up and attempt to read the open file. A list of names that reads *People to Interview who Knew Victim* is on top. I look toward the door and take out my cell, snapping an upside-down photo of the list. Footsteps outside make me sit back down, shoving my cell into my purse. I paste on a look of concern as the man once again sits down at his desk.

"Just stay out of this, Miss Johnson," Detective Ray says. "You can go."

I race out the door and into the lobby, where I meet

with Binny and Nick. It's not until we are in the car that I tell them all about the meeting, including the picture I took.

"I can't believe you did that!" Binny gasps.

"It's getting late," Nick says. "Let's pick up takeout and head to my house. Maybe we can divide up the list to interview."

Binny looks like she's going to explode with excitement. A mystery investigation and she gets to see the mythical Woodfield mansion? Unfortunately, it isn't going to happen tonight.

"I can't," I say. "I've got another wedding tonight at the Blue Hawaii."

My friend looks crushed. I silently vow to make it up to her. She's waited all her life—she can surely wait a little more, right?

Nick drops us off at our cars back at the Loco Moco, and I give him a quick kiss on the cheek before he drives off. I did it again! I chastise myself for being so shameless and then congratulate myself because he seems to like it.

Binny hugs me before jumping into her Jeep and speeding away. As for me—I'm in my house in ten minutes. Mom is passed out in the backyard, an empty pitcher of something sticky and sweet on the ground next to her.

The wedding tonight is kind of a big deal. The couple, some big mafia boss from Atlantic City, is marrying his girlfriend, a woman who isn't half his age so much as a quarter of it. They'd arranged this a year ago. And since Fat Mookie (the gangster, of course) paid a ridiculous amount of money in cash, it was priority number one. Pastor Dan was even tripling my fee for it. I'd been waiting all week for this because I was going to set the money aside for Mom and me to go on a little trip, like to Maui.

But now that I'm accused of another murder, I didn't really feel like going. *Suck it up, Nani—you have to keep Mom in muumuus and mai tais.* I throw on the pink dress with the ukuleles on it, because the bride's favorite color is pink, and slip into my matching sandals, and head out the door.

"You shouldn't pay her so much!" Mary Lou's voice stabs me in the head as I enter the chapel. I can only assume she's talking about me.

"It's none of your business, Mary Lou," Pastor Dan says, and I suppress a smile. That's before I really see the chapel.

Somehow, the bride managed to turn everything pink. Bright pink. Pink flowers swallow the altar and block the fantastic beach view from the windows. Swathes of pink satin are draped over everything. Pink velvet cushions hide the lovely teak wood of the pews. And pink light bulbs rain a Pepto Bismoesque glow on everything else.

"Whoa," I whisper as I walk open mouthed down the aisle. Maybe I should've bought a pink ukulele for this occasion.

"You're going to run this business into the ground, Dan!" Mary Lou obviously feels she is entitled to skip Pastor Dan's title.

"It's my business," he fires back. "I'll do what I want." A door slams, and I rush up to the altar and pretend I'm enthralled with the giant pink sparkly cross that dominates the window.

Pastor Dan emerges from a pink satin-covered doorway. He looks mad. He's wearing the 1950s Elvis costume. The one with the short shorts. I try not to stare.

"I swear, Nani," he says as he stomps over to me, "I'm going to fire her one of these days!"

I laugh. "You say that almost every time I see you. And you never do. I don't think you ever will."

He winks at me. "Look—I made the shorts longer, like you asked." He points to shorts so short he's in danger of flashing me.

"What, did you go a whole millimeter this time?" I tease but avert my eyes anyway.

Pastor Dan shakes his head and walks past me to the altar, where he begins rearranging his notes.

Mary Lou bursts out of the back, and I can't help but stare. She's wearing a pink dress and pink lipstick with a huge pink hibiscus flower in her hair. I step back, fearing the god of colors will smite her with a lightning bolt. Her outfit is too much, even for the Rainbow State.

"What are you staring at?" She's stopped in front of me and looks furious.

"That's a nice color on you, Mary Lou," I lie.

"Oh…well." The woman blushes and smooths her dress. "Thanks." She sneaks a look at Pastor Dan to see if he notices the compliment, but the man seems very intent on his notes. Too intent, if you ask me.

"I just bought this," Mary Lou says. "I wanted to look nice for Fat Mookie and Bambi."

I gape at her. "The bride's name is Bambi? Are you sure we aren't being punked?"

Oh sure, I know that there are real people with that name, but Fat Mookie and Bambi? Are we marrying a couple of cartoon characters? Maybe I should play the Warner Bros. theme for the ceremony.

Mary Lou returns to her old self. "How dare you mock our clients! This is a business, and we are professionals!"

"You're right," I beg off. "I'll behave."

Did I just hear a chuckle from the altar? I try not to grin.

"Aaaaaaaaaaaaaaaaaaaaaaaaaiiiiiiiiiiiiiiiiiio-ooooooooooohmygod!" A shrill voice squeals almost every vowel in a pitch I wish only dogs could hear.

This is followed by the tallest Amazon I've ever seen. Tottering in on seven-inch high heels, with hardly any pink material to cover her unbelievably voluptuous curves, comes what I can only assume is Bambi. The woman's long blonde hair has been teased within an inch of its life, and her eyelashes could brush the altar, 30 feet away, if she blinked.

"This is *amazing*!" Bambi shrieks.

She's followed by what can only be described as the skinniest, shortest man on the planet. He wears a three-piece suit, one that would probably only fit an anorexic eight-year-old, and a fedora. He takes the hat off to mop his balding head with a handkerchief (also pink) before replacing it.

"Fat Mookie!" Pastor Dan calls out as he makes his way up the aisle to shake the man's hand.

This is Fat Mookie? Maybe I got it all wrong. Maybe

he's Bambi and the barely dressed bimbo is Fat Mookie.
I wait to see who responds to Dan.

"Nice to see you again, Pastor," the man says as he
takes Dan's hand and shakes it. He pulls up his trou-
sers to show blue suede shoes. "We're matching. Bambi
wanted me to wear pink, but I stood my ground." Standing his ground against Bambi must be like a toothpick
in a tornado.

Fat Mookie joins Bambi at the start of the aisle. She
towers over him by at least two whole feet, and I think
one of her breasts weighs as much as he does. Mookie is
at least in his late 50s, and Bambi looks about 21.

I'd love to hear the story of how these two met. I'm
not sure whether I'm going to laugh or faint.

"Pick your jaw up off the floor!" Mary Lou hisses
while elbowing me.

I oblige her. What else can I do?

"This is Mary Lou—she'll be taking pictures." Pastor Dan waves his hand at her, and Mary Lou practically
shakes with delight. I wonder if that's the closest he's
come to complimenting her.

"And Nani Johnson is our instrumentalist." Dan
winks at me, and I smile and nod. "She's a classically
trained musician from Juilliard," he adds.

Bambi can't be bothered to take her eyes off the
waves of pink that are now undulating obscenely in the
breeze from the open windows.

Fat Mookie bows to both of us, removing his hat. I
like him.

"Ladies," he purrs. "So very nice to meet you."

I hope that Mary Lou won't explode.

"Such an honor, sir." Mary Lou actually curtseys. Who does she think this guy is?

"It's nice meeting you as well," I say. "Do you have any requests for the ceremony?"

Usually, the couples submit their music a week or so out, in case I need to learn it. Fat Mookie hasn't done this, so I'm hoping he'll want something I can play.

He looks longingly at Bambi, who is now giggling and spinning around in the long sheets of satin—her arms outstretched—like a slutty Maria in the opening of *The Sound of Music*. I almost reach for my ukulele and play *the hills are alive*...

"Whatever you think appropriate." Fat Mookie turns back to me and smiles. "I didn't get around to filling out the request form, and that's my fault."

I think I love him. No one is ever that nice about the music. No one.

Bambi suddenly notices us and stops spinning. "Ooooh! But can you play Beyoncé's "Single Ladies" for when I throw the bouquet?"

I nod. Weirdly, I have that in my repertoire. I had to play it at a nursing home's grand opening a couple of weeks ago. Not kidding.

"Great!" Fat Mookie slaps his hands and begins rubbing them together. "Let's get started!"

"Now?" Mary Lou looks stricken. She glances at Bambi's attire. "But what about your guests?" Nice save. I'm sure she was going to ask if Bambi wanted to change.

Bambi nods so vigorously I fear her head will pop off. "Oh yeah! We got a booze cruise in half an hour!"

I say nothing, instead taking my usual place off to

the left of the altar. Pastor Dan ushers the couple to the front and takes his place. Mary Lou blinks, then runs off for the camera.

I launch into a lovely little song written by Queen Liliuokalani. After a few bars, I strum softly for the perfect background music.

"Dearly Beloved, thank you very much!" Pastor Dan begins, and Fat Mookie respectfully removes his hat.

The ceremony moves along like they all do. All the same words that link all the same couples together. I watch as I quietly play and start to wonder what was going through Leilani's mind when she played that wedding earlier today. It had to be a shock when the murderer ran up and threw her over a cliff. I felt a little bad for the Parker couple. And for the shark that probably ate Leilani. The indigestion would be epic.

"We wrote our own vows, Reverend," Fat Mookie says as he and Bambi turn to face each other.

We're at the vows already? I need to pay more attention. I slow down the tempo and continue strumming.

"BamBoobs," Fat Mookie says, and it's all I can do to not burst out laughing. "I loved you from the day I met you."

He looks expectantly at BamBoobs after the shortest vows I've ever heard.

"Back atchya, babe!" Bambi snaps her gum and grins goofily at her husband to be.

I stand corrected on the shortest vows thing. No Shakespeare is wasted with these two.

"Do you have the rings?" Pastor Dan asks.

Fat Mookie pulls out a platinum band with a diamond as big as his head and says the usual words. Bambi pulls out a simple black-titanium band and repeats what Mookie said as she places the ring on his hand.

"I now pronounce you husband and wife." Pastor Dan grins. "You may kiss the bride."

I try to focus on my music, but I'm curious as to how they're going to pull this off. Bambi bends almost completely in half, and her new husband rises up on his tiptoes to kiss her.

Thank God I wasn't murdered by the ukulele killer before now. I'd have hated to miss out on this.

"Okay!" Bambi shouts as I play the recessional music. "Time to throw the bouquet!"

She suddenly produces a very large bouquet, from where, I don't know. "Play Beyoncé now, please!"

The bouquet is a riot of bright pink flowers with a horseshoe in the middle of it. I've seen that before with Irish weddings—they insert a horseshoe, open end up, for good luck. That has to be one heavy bouquet.

I do as I'm told and begin a rousing version of "Single Ladies," just as I realize that Mary Lou and I are the only single ladies present. And since I'm playing a ukulele and the requested music, I'm completely out of the running.

But that doesn't stop BamBoobs, who turns around and tosses the large bouquet over her shoulder. I watch as it soars, almost in slow motion, through the air. It's going to miss its target (that being Mary Lou) by a mile.

I underestimate the woman, as Mary Lou expertly hurdles two of the pews just in time for the clump of flowers to hit her hair-helmeted head and knock her out cold. I rush to her side and try to revive her, with no success.

"Ooops!" Bambi cries. "I'm sorry!" Tears actually start to stream down her cheeks, blending with non-waterproof mascara, creating two black lines on her face. She looks like a blonde female Alice Cooper.

"Is she going to be okay?" Fat Mookie bends over the unconscious woman.

Pastor Dan whispers to me, "Keep trying to revive her." He turns to the gangster and his bimbo. "No problem, really. She has a history of fainting spells."

I wonder if that history includes being bludgeoned by pink flowers every time, but say nothing. I tuck the bouquet into Mary Lou's hands. She would've wanted it that way.

"What about the pictures?" Bambi's crying jag has ended, and she chews on her enormous lips. "I really wanted that cool blue frame."

"I'll deliver the pictures to your hotel tonight," I say for some reason. "Where are you staying?"

Fat Mookie peels off hundred dollar bills from a roll as big as his fist. "At the resort. Ask for Mr. and Mrs. Stone."

He hands what looks like at least a couple thousand dollars to Pastor Dan. "Pay for her doctor, will you?" He tips his hat at me, and taking his new wife's arm, they walk out.

"What happened?" Mary Lou shouts as she sits back up. "Did I win? Did I get the flowers?" She doesn't seem to notice that they are in her hand.

I think about telling her she was the only one in the

running for the blossoms, but decide to be kind. "You won. Look!"

Mary Lou stares at her hand as if she's never seen it before. She might need more than a thousand dollars if she has brain damage that bad. Then she notices the flowers and screams with delight. Problem is, she doesn't stop screaming.

"Mary Lou!" Pastor Dan helps her up and cuts her off. "The couple's photos, please? Nani's going to take them to their hotel."

Mary Lou carries the bouquet proudly in front of her as she marches off to the office. She must be pretending it's her wedding to Pastor Dan.

"You're screwed," I tell Dan. "She's going to think catching the bridal bouquet is a sign."

Pastor Dan groans. "Great. And I have a date tonight."

I stare at him. "You have a date?" Okay, that might have come off badly. "I mean, great! Who's the lucky guy?"

"You don't know him," Dan says quickly as Mary Lou emerges with the usual envelope and monstrous frame.

"I'm feeling a little light-headed, Dan." She shoves the pictures at me and gives the gay man a moony look. "I think you're going to have to take me to the hospital."

He looks at me hopefully for a moment, and I consider volunteering because he looks so desperate. But he waves me off.

"Of course I will," Dan says finally.

Mary Lou brightens, and I realize this is her first real date with him. Granted, it's to the doctor because of a botanical concussion, but she doesn't look like she cares. Pastor Dan pays me more money than I've made in weeks…combined…and I race out the door with the photos and ukulele before he can change his mind.

The Blue Hawaii Wedding Chapel is next to the resort, so in no time I'm at the front desk, dropping off the pictures for the Stones. The night clerk assures me they'll get them.

I just want to get home and take a long, hot bubble bath. A glass of wine is definitely in my future. My stomach rumbles. I guess I need dinner too. I drive back home, wondering what I have in the kitchen. I still haven't been to the grocery store.

With luck, I find a bagel and a jar of peanut butter. Perfect. I toast the bagel while the bath is running and pour a generous glass of red wine.

"Nani?" Mom calls out from the lanai.

I join her with my dinner, trying to be mindful of the bubble bath that's currently running.

"This came for you," she says with a weak grin as she hands me a white envelope. "I'm going to bed."

She's not feeling well. It's the booze, I know. I wouldn't say Mom's a full-blown alcoholic—she can go days without a drink. I even make her mai tais extremely weak. But when she's on a bender, there's nothing anyone can do.

It all started when my father died. That's why I never say anything. Mostly, she just goes to sleep when she drinks. Then there's the few and far between days when I get a call from the police that Mom's standing on the roof, dancing the hula and yelling at the neighbors. Someday, when all this murder stuff is over, I'll have a serious talk with her about it.

Just not tonight. I toss the envelope on the counter, and in minutes I'm sinking into a swirling, soothing realm of bubbles. I keep my mind blank as I add more hot water when it turns tepid. I've been thinking too much these days.

I can feel my body relaxing and my mind going fuzzy. Eventually, I get out, towel off, throw on a nightshirt, and go to bed. I fall asleep thinking of Mr. and Mrs. BamBoobs.

NINE

"NANI! WAKE UP!" Mom shakes my shoulder violently.

"Stop!" I groan, flinging my arm over my eyes. "It's too early!" What's she doing up anyway?

"There's no *mea'ai*! No *kope*!" She shakes my shoulder harder.

"There's no what?" I shrug her off and sit up, wondering if she's had a stroke.

Mom straightens up with a proud smile. "*Mea'ai* means food! *Kope* is coffee! I'm learning the native language of our ancestors. They have a class at the community center."

Nope, not a stroke. Instead, my mother is going insane.

"Yeah." I shove the covers aside and get out of bed. "Well, I don't speak Hawaiian, Mom. Sorry about the food—I meant to go to the store. Give me a moment, and I'll go now."

"E 'olu'olu'oe, makemake au i ka makeke!" she says haltingly. She doesn't sound like a native. She sounds like a Kansas transplant whose voice is cutting in and out on a cell call.

"Come again?" I ask, glaring at her a little.

"I just said that I want some mustard!" Mom beams.

"Do you really want mustard?" I ask. Mom's allergic to mustard. She breaks out in huge welts if she even smells it.

Mom rolls her eyes. "Well, of course I don't! Really, Nani! Where is your head?" She storms out of my room, and I sigh heavily, wondering if I can survive this newest obsession.

I grab my phone and see the envelope from last night but decide to wait to open it. I'm hungry too. Maybe I'll pick up some *malasadas* (a sort of donut) to smooth things over with Mom.

The store is packed this morning, and I realize it's Saturday. As I maneuver through the lanes of overpriced imported food, I remember that I had something on my phone. The list! The list of people Detective Ray is going to interview! Or as I like to think of them—suspects. Okay, so I don't really know if they are suspects, but he's interviewing them for some reason. That could mean they are persons of interest.

I pull my cart aside in the breakfast aisle, and after making sure the coast is clear, I pull up the photo. There are five names. I don't recognize any of them. Who are these people? None of them have the same surnames as Kua or Leilani. Did one of these guys commit murder?

The thought of this is exciting. It's nice to know you're not the only one considered a killer. Maybe the six of us should get together and form a little club or something. I shove the phone back into my bag and continue shopping with a little skip in my step. Things are looking up! The lazy detective will interview these people and find that I'm not guilty.

Oh wait. Detective Ray missed the note at the Overlook. And he didn't interview Reverend Blake—who was a far better witness than the Parkers. He'll probably screw this up too. What am I saying? Of course he'll screw this up. The man is incompetent. My innocence is in the hands of someone with a messy office that should be condemned and who overlooks important clues.

Well, I can't have that, now, can I? Nick and Binny are right. We have to investigate. With the way the police are handling this, I stand a very good chance of going to jail. As I pack the groceries into the trunk of my car, I realize I've made up my mind to follow up on these leads. Because jail would totally suck, and I'm pretty sure they won't let me take a ukulele, considering that's the weapon I allegedly used to kill Kua.

After I get home, donut Mom, unload the groceries, and put them away, I'm going to call Binny and Nick. It's time to get started. The three of us are going to blow this case wide open.

An hour later, we settle on the lanai. It's a gorgeous day. I hardly notice. When you live here, it's like this all the time. We never have inclement weather. Enough rain to keep everything green, no snow—it's very different than back home. In Kansas it could rain for a solid week. And don't even get me started on snow. I don't miss snow.

"So," Nick asks, "how should we tackle this? Where do we start?"

Binny frowns. "Whatever we do, we should get started. After this weekend, I'm out for a few days. My mom just told me she wants me to go with her to visit her sister in Honolulu. Sorry." She looks pretty unhappy.

But her family is very close. If family calls, you have to drop everything and go.

"Okay," Nick says slowly, "I'm free this weekend but only evenings next week. We're doing a major overhaul on the south garden at the resort."

"I don't know any of these names," Binny says as she studies the list. "There are addresses here, but no phone numbers."

I look at the list. None of them live in or near Aloha Lagoon. Three of the names are from Lihue, and two are from Princeville. At least we could hit one of those towns this weekend.

"Okay," I say, "we should do Princeville today. Maybe we can knock out Lihue tomorrow?"

"Do you know if the police have contacted them yet?" Nick thinks out loud. "I mean, Leilani's murder was just yesterday. If they haven't notified the next of kin…"

I shrug. "No idea. But he told you yesterday, so I'd guess the word is out. Detective Ray said no one had claimed Leilani for a funeral—not that there was a body."

"And it seems that the detective moves at the speed of snail," Nick says. "We might be the first ones to talk to these people."

"How do we know if they're friends of Kua or Leilani?" I ask. "How do we know what to ask them?"

"We'll wing it," Binny says. I know she's hoping we can do this before she leaves for Oahu.

"Okay. But we should work out some sort of a plan. These people are going to be a little freaked out when three strangers just show up at their door."

Nick studies the list and opens his laptop, plugging

the names into Facebook. "These two." He points at the two names from Princeville. "Todd Chay and Pauli Keo, according to their profiles, look like surfers. My guess is they're friends of Kua."

"Let's start with them, then," I say, secretly hoping this will go well. The last thing we need are hostile interviews.

As we drive, I fill my friends in on the wedding the night before.

"BamBoobs? Seriously?" Binny breathes raggedly between giggles. "How did you not lose it?"

"It wasn't easy," I admit. "The whole thing was ridiculous, but I made a lot of money. So it was worth it."

"It's worth it for the story alone," Nick says. "I wish I'd been there."

I shake my head. "You probably wouldn't have been let in. Mob guys are known for their paranoia." I think for a minute. "Fat Mookie was nice though. I liked him."

"I still can't get over it." Tears are running down Binny's cheeks. "Fat Mookie and BamBoobs!"

"I know. I'm still not sure if I dreamed it or not."

Looking out the window at the paradise flying by, I wonder if this whole thing has been a dream. It certainly seems like one. It's a nightmare with the murders, a comedy with the weddings, and a good dream where Nick is concerned.

Binny is telling Nick a story about one of the times she and I went to Princeville. I have a soft spot for this northern town. When I arrived in Kauai, I thought maybe I'd live here. After all, they have some great resorts, and it still has a small-town feel. Unfortunately, no one there was interested in having a ukulele artist on retainer.

For a week, Mom and I knocked about the island until we came at last to Aloha Lagoon. With only one resort and three musicians, I should've fled. But there was something about this place that made me want to stay. That very afternoon I ran into Pastor Dan on the street. I was carrying my ukulele in its case. He stopped to ask me about it and promised me steady work. The next day, Mom and I found the fixer-upper cottage, and the rest is history. Okay, so it's only been a year, but that counts as history.

Binny and I met on the beach at the resort. I was just sitting in the sun, forgetting how strong it was here, and I was getting a nasty sunburn. Of course, I didn't realize this. It was Binny who walked by and noticed I was turning an alarming shade of purple. She struck up a conversation before driving me to the emergency room.

At first I thought she was just being nice. But we'd really hit it off. Binny is a kindergarten teacher and is absolutely brilliant at it. She has summers off, which is why she's free to run around with me right now.

One month into living here, my friend invited me to perform at a school assembly. The kids loved it, which is how I ended up with ten kids for private lessons. I seriously owe her one.

From that time on, Binny adopted me and gave me tours of her island. We've also done two weekends on the Big Island and Oahu. There's still so much more to explore. That's what I love about it here. Each island is dramatically different from all the others. I've been here one year and haven't seen even a fraction of everything. Kansas isn't like this. If you've seen one corner of the flattest state ever, you've pretty much seen the entire state. Nothing is different. Nothing.

Kauai is my favorite…and not just because I now call it home. It's the people. Generous and welcoming to the point they'd help out a complete stranger without batting an eyelash. It's the landscape. Where else could you visit the beach, a huge desert canyon, and a tropical rainforest in one day? I love the sunrise—I love the sunsets—and everything in between. Every day of the rest of my life will be spent in paradise. Who could ask for more?

Unfortunately, I haven't been travelling much lately. Mom and work have kept me home. And when school's in session, Binny can't travel much. I'm not really the type to check things out on my own. I love to hike, but going alone is extremely dangerous here.

Now I have Nick. If things keep going this well, I'll have someone to run around the island with. That would be great.

Why haven't I gotten to know more people? I've kept myself closed off—isolated. That's weird. I wasn't like that before Dad died. But then, I didn't have an alcoholic, borderline insane mother then either. Having people over is out of the question if they don't understand.

Mom is social. She's the queen of the community center. But if I'm totally honest, Vera Woodfield is the first friend she's brought home. She's been isolating herself too.

When I was growing up, my mother was on the PTA, my Girl Scout leader, on the church altar society, and helped Dad out in his business. She was wonderful, out-going—a social butterfly. My father's death had a huge and damaging impact on our lives.

I lean my forehead against the cool window and close my eyes. I'll have to deal with this at some point. Too bad I don't have siblings to help me. Especially an older sister or brother who could be candid with Mom.

Well, that's an impossible wish. Unless Mom adopts a respectable 30-year-old, that will never happen. I haven't really talked to Binny about this. The tradition of 'ohana means respecting your elders and taking care of them. She'd find my complaints disloyal somehow. I don't want her to think less of me. She knows my mom is a bit strange, but that's all.

Nick, on the other hand, understood without me having to say a word. And while I'd never consider Perseverance Woodfield on the same level of "odd" as Mom, I know that he deals with some of the same issues I do. It's comforting.

"We're here," Nick says as he parks the car on a street.

I look around. The first address, for Todd Chay, is a tiny bungalow across from the beach. The idea that he's a friend of Kua's looks more obvious now.

"Let's get this over with," I say as I open the door and step out into the sunshine. That's the great thing about living here. You think nothing bad could ever happen on a day this beautiful.

The bungalow is a bit worse for the wear, definitely broken in. I like it. It seems homey. Nick, however, is on his guard. With a deep breath, I lead the way to the door and knock.

"Ya?" a sleepy young man answers. Smoke billows through the doorway, and I realize this guy's stoned.

"Is Todd here?" I ask, plastering a sunny smile on my face.

Stoner shakes his head and points at the beach before slamming the door.

"We must look like narcs or something," Binny says.

Nick is already walking across the road to the beach on the other side. I run to catch up.

"How are we going to find him?" I ask.

The beach has only a few people with surfboards on it, but I don't want to be pushy. If this is a locals' beach, they won't appreciate our intrusion.

Fortunately, we have Binny. She's been surfing since she was a kid. She struts ahead confidently, knowing that this is her territory. With flip-flops, cutoff shorts, and a white tank top, she easily blends in. Nick and I fall back a little so she can do her thing.

Staying back far enough so we don't look suspicious, but close enough to run to her aid, Nick takes my hand, and we stroll along the beach, looking like a tourist couple. His hand squeezes mine, and I squeeze back. No one gives us a second glance. And I get to act like Nick's girlfriend—which is a total win.

They do, however, notice Binny. I watch as she casually walks up to a group of guys. In seconds they are laughing and flirting with her. It's amazing how she puts everyone at ease. She tosses her short bob a few times, and it has the anticipated effect. These men are putty in her hands.

"She's a natural," Nick says.

I nod. "She's been around surfers all her life. And she's Hawaiian, which helps."

I wish I had that talent. I make a silent vow that if I get myself out of this, I'm going to try to get to know the people of Aloha Lagoon better. There are so many people my age—especially working at the resort. There's no excuse for me not to make friends. And it's good networking too. Now that two of my competitors are gone, I could probably get work doing the big luaus at the resort.

Wow. I guess I really do look like a suspect when I put it that way.

"Hey, guys," Binny calls out as she walks toward us.

Behind her is a Hawaiian in his late 20s with a surfboard tucked under his arm. He doesn't look very happy. He probably thought he was making time with Binny, or he doesn't like nonlocals on his beach.

"This is Todd Chay." Binny stops in front of us, but Todd stays a few steps behind.

Nick thrusts his hand out. "Aloha, Todd. Nice to meet you. I'm Nick, and this is Nani."

Todd takes his hand and gives it one shake before dropping it. He says nothing.

Binny gives him a blinding smile. "Todd knows Kua. He's agreed to answer a couple of questions."

Todd shifts from one foot to another. His unease is making me nervous. It doesn't appear to affect Nick at all.

"Sorry to hear about your friend, man." Nick nods solemnly. "That's rough."

"Yeah." Todd relaxes a little. "Binny here says you're from Aloha Lagoon. Did they catch the guy who did this?"

I shake my head. "Not yet. I knew Kua too." We need a premise for this conversation. We'd decided on the way here that I'd pretend to be connected to the dead uke player.

"Some cop called," Todd says. "Says he's going to talk to me. Find out what I know. But he hasn't been here yet."

So Todd has a phone. Just because we couldn't find a number doesn't mean he's disconnected. I'd bet he has a cell and no landline. I wonder how Detective Ray found the cell number.

"He talked to me too," I say, leaving out the parts where he practically arrested me as the murderer. "He wanted to know if I knew anything. I just can't believe someone would kill Kua. Do you have any ideas?"

I held my breath waiting for him to answer. It wouldn't be farfetched for this guy to clam up. But if I pushed a little, maybe he'd give us something to work with.

Todd shrugs, his bland face revealing nothing. "He had a few enemies. Always going off on people if they weren't Hawaiian. Especially surfers."

I already knew Kua was prejudiced. It was good news that he'd pissed surfers off. That could take the heat off of me. If Detective Ray would get up here and interview people.

"Yeah, he had a temper," I nudge.

"I never had any problem with anyone who isn't native," Todd says. His expression softens now that he doesn't deem us a threat. Binny's attention might have something to do with that.

"To me," he continues, "anyone who surfs, even the

beginners, are paying homage to our ancestors and culture. Kua could be a jerk."

Still no mention of possible suspects. How could we get him to talk?

"How long have you known Kua?" I ask. "I've only known him about a year or so."

Todd looks off at the waves, possibly concerned he's missing out. "All my life. He's my brah. Well, he was."

Binny steps up her game, slipping her arm through his. "Do you know Pauli Keo? I think he lives around here."

Todd gives up half a smile. That's something. "He's not a surfer. Plays guitar at a coffeehouse. I don't think Kua knew him." Todd gives us the address.

So, Pauli must be connected to Leilani. We might kill two birds with one stone today.

"See those guys?" He points down the beach to a group of men standing and staring at the sea. "They are *pilau*. Bad sort. They had a big fight with Kua a few days back. Said he stole their waves for the last time."

I squint at the figures. We're too far to see them properly.

Nick speaks up. "Is that a gang?"

Todd nods. "Call themselves Sea Dogs. *Dogs* is about right though."

"You don't get along with them?" Binny asks. She gives him a dazzling smile. Good girl.

"No. They're bad. Get into trouble all the time. Like to beat up malihini just cuz they're not local. Not good."

So they're violent, which makes them suspects in my book. The only problem is, none of them know me enough to frame me for Kua's murder, and the probability that they'd know Leilani enough to want to kill her is zip.

It occurs to me that Alohalani is the only member of the Terrible Trio still alive. But he wasn't on the detective's list, so maybe he's not a suspect? No, I can't see it. He's the top musician on the island. He has no reason to kill Kua or Leilani. I push the thought out of my mind and try to focus on the business at hand.

"Gotta go," Todd says as he ambles away. He's either done with us or has figured out that Binny isn't actually interested.

"Mahalo!" Binny shouts after him. Hawaiian terms still trip me up. But Mahalo is so much prettier than "thank you."

"I wonder why he's on Detective Ray's list," Nick says. "He doesn't seem like a suspect."

"What are we going to do about them?" I point to the Sea Dogs.

"Nothing. At least nothing right now," Nick says. "Too dangerous. We can tell the detective about them, but I don't think we should investigate them on our own."

Binny nods. "Some of these surfers are bad news. They wouldn't talk to us anyway. Let's go check out this Pauli guy."

Ten minutes later we find ourselves in the coffee-house Todd mentioned. It looks more like a dilapidated bar. We leave the bright sunshine outside as we walk into the stale darkness of the tavern.

There aren't many people here. Just the bartender, a few locals at the bar, a couple of tourists at tables in front of a tiny stage where a lone guitarist sings folk songs.

"I'll get the drinks," Nick says, pointing at a table near the back. "You guys go sit down."

Binny and I sit at the table, and I turn my full attention to Pauli Keo. He's a young guy. Definitely part Japanese or Chinese, with long silky black hair and a slender but muscular body. He wears puka shells and an aloha shirt over khaki shorts.

His voice is rough, deep, kind of like a growl. It reminds me of a Russian singer I used to listen to. It's a great blend with the music. He sings in Hawaiian, a song that Binny translates to be about a girl who dies and the young warrior so depressed that he throws himself into an active volcano. Cheerful stuff.

"What do you think?" Binny asks over the din.

"Because Todd doesn't think this guy knew Kua and he's on Ray's list, I'd say he's a connection of Leilani's. But then again, Todd knows him, so he could've known Kua too." Which would be great, because he'd be a reasonable suspect for both.

Nick joins us with a pitcher of beer and a plate of *poke*, the popular raw fish appetizer. We dig in as we listen to the musician. I'm really getting into him. His unique voice and devotion to traditional music is hypnotic. That's a good thing—making it easy to stand out among the competition. The three of us sit there, saying nothing as we watch him finish his set.

"I'm going to take a short break," he says, running his right hand through his hair. "Mahalo."

We watch as the entertainer goes to the bar. The bartender hands him a drink and then points at us.

"I bought him a drink for when he got on break." Nick

winks at me. "I thought maybe he'd come to us." Nick is smart. If I don't go to jail, I'm definitely keeping him.

Sure enough, the singer smiles as he brings his drink over to our table and pulls up a chair.

"Mahalo, man." He shakes Nick's hand and gives us a warm grin. "Nice to have real music lovers at this dive."

This guy can't possibly be connected to either Kua or Leilani. He's just too nice. I notice that he gives Binny the once-over before sliding his seat a little closer to hers. My friend smiles and doesn't say anything. She neither encourages nor discourages him. It seems to make him more interested. I never understood that, but Binny has it down. She can tell what a guy likes just by watching him. And this guy is definitely interested.

We make introductions all around. For a split second, I think I see him frown when my name is mentioned, but it's possible I imagined that.

"Aloha Lagoon, eh?" Pauli grins. "I've always wanted to work there. They have that amazing little tiki bar on the beach...what's it called?"

"The Lava Pot," I say. "You should approach them. Definitely."

No, please don't, I think. I don't need any more competition. With Kua's and Leilani's deaths, there will be more work for me. As soon as I think this, I regret it. Good thing I didn't say that out loud.

"Especially now that we've lost two musicians in Aloha Lagoon in the last couple of days," Nick adds before taking a drink of his beer. Crap. Nick says what I'm thinking.

Pauli's eyes settle on Nick. He seems to be appraising him.

"I heard," Pauli says as he drains his glass. "Two ukulele players, right?"

Binny nods, bringing his attention back to her. "It's so sad. I heard they were both murdered." Her face falls, and I see Pauli take it in. Oh, she's good.

"That's a shame," he finally says. "Do they know who did it?" Again, I imagine his eyes are settling on me.

I shake my head. "No. At least, we haven't heard anything."

"You're a musician, aren't you?" Pauli catches me off guard with this comment. He looks completely calm—as if that's a normal thing to ask someone.

I sit back and smile. "Good guess. I studied at Juilliard."

"Really?" He looks interested, his eyes drilling into mine. "What instrument?"

I hesitate for a second. "I started out with classical guitar. How did you know I'm a musician?" I'm not ready to say that I play ukulele.

"You were watching my hands, not my face, when I played," he says, still focusing completely on me. "You still perform?"

I shake my head. "Not anymore." Not a lie. I don't play guitar anymore. I only play uke. Somehow I have the gut feeling that telling him this would be a bad idea.

"Right," Pauli says after a long drink. He doesn't believe me. "What brings you here from Aloha Lagoon? Scoping out the competition?"

Ah. So that's it. He thinks I'm just making sure he

won't take over my territory. Musicians are so territorial. Kind of like the mafia or drug lords, I guess. Only we slay with our music. Hmmm… I'd have to remember that joke. Maybe I could use it around Fat Mookie.

"Just out for a drive," Nick says smoothly. He points at me. "Nani just moved here a year ago. She's starting to get island fever."

Pauli nods. "That happens a lot. Not to me—I love it here. But I can understand mainlanders feeling that way. I once drove across the whole country in a week, from California to Maine. It amazes me that you can do that on the mainland."

"It's kind of like Europe," Nick adds. "And there, the countries are much smaller. You can go from Paris to Berlin in mere hours."

The two men start talking to each other very animatedly, so I lean over to Binny and whisper, "Island Fever?"

"It's something people who move here from the mainland get. Being confined to a small island gets a bit claustrophobic. Many move back within a year."

I sit back and think about that. I've never felt that way. Kauai is one big county with maybe 65,000-plus people. Just Wichita, in my home state, has six times that many people.

I guess I'd never thought of it before. Growing up in a small city, miles away from anything else, prepared me for living here. It makes sense that some folks find the ocean surrounding the island to be confining. But I don't. I look out at the deep blue and think of the places I could go.

"Isn't that right, Nani?" Nick is looking at me meaningfully. Uh-oh. What did I miss?

"Sorry," I say, feeling the heat creep up into my cheeks. "I was daydreaming."

Everyone laughs at that, so I relax. Maybe it wasn't something important.

"Nick tells me," Pauli says, "that you play the ukulele. Why didn't you mention that earlier?"

His eyes are on me. I'm being sized up as a competitor. I've never been comfortable with that. Perhaps it's time to fight fire with fire—find out why he's on the detective's list.

"I don't know," I say. "I've been so distracted lately. With two of my colleagues brutally murdered, I'm worried I might be next." I throw in a little shrug and hope he buys it.

"Scary." Binny nods. She looks at Pauli. "Did you know them? Kua Liu and Leilani O'Flanagan?"

The musician hesitates for a second, but I notice it. "Yeah. I knew both actually. There aren't a lot of professional musicians living on the island. You kind of run into each other now and then."

Pauli sits back. He doesn't give us enough information. He's probably on the detective's list for a reason, but for what?

"You knew both of them?" Nick asks easily, as if it is the most normal question in the world. "Were you close?"

I hold my breath because this could be the thing that shuts this suspect down. Pauli looks at each of us, lingering a bit too long on me. Does he think we are being too nosy?

"Kua and I played a couple of gigs in the same place. I met Leilani a couple of years back. She'd just come back from the Big Island after living there a few years. I don't think it went well."

I could barely contain myself. "What happened?" I thought Leilani had always lived here. I never heard about her living on Hawaii.

Pauli shakes his head. "She didn't say. I dated her for like…one minute."

My jaw drops. I couldn't help it. Someone dated that redheaded dragon lady?

"I'm guessing your experience with her hasn't been the best," he says, studying me. It feels like I'm under a spotlight.

"You're right," I admit. "Something about me rubbed her the wrong way."

Nick and Binny don't say anything. Why aren't they saying anything?

Pauli finally smiles. "Yeah, I can see that." He gets to his feet and thanks us for the drink. "I've got another set to do. Nice meeting you."

"Did he just slam me?" I say under my breath as the musician walks away.

"I don't know," Binny says thoughtfully. "I kind of took it to mean he knew Leilani could be awful."

Nick shrugs. "I have no idea. It could be either or both."

"So we have no idea why this guy is on the list." I sigh.

"Not necessarily," Nick says. "He performed at the same places as Kua and briefly knew Leilani. His history is more with Kua."

"Unless…" Binny brightens. "Unless he's throwing us off track and he really had more of a relationship with Leilani."

"I'd kill her too if I was him," I say. "But that could be a red herring. I can't tell if he was honest with us or not."

Pauli is back on stage, playing a slow ballad. This time, I study him. What's going on with this guy? He knew both of the deceased. He's a musician who'd love to play at Aloha Lagoon. That is a possible motive, but a bit extreme. Of course, Detective Ray thinks that's my motive.

It could be that there was bad blood between him and Kua. I didn't like some of the people I graduated with. I could picture Kua bullying Pauli because he saw him as a threat. Or maybe they dated the same girl?

Or he murdered Leilani because she was a complete psycho. He could've killed both of them. That would be very convenient. But is this man capable of that? I can't tell. Will Detective Ray think so? I'm not sure of that either.

"What do you think?" Binny asks. "Is he our guy?"

Nick shakes his head. "I don't know. And I don't think we're going to get anything more out of him today."

It's getting late, so we decide to head back. As we talk on the drive back to Aloha Lagoon, I realize we have nothing so far. Nick is convinced that Pauli is suspicious. Binny thinks the Sea Dogs did it. I've got nothing.

"I think this trip was a waste of time." I sigh as we pull into town. "We haven't really found anything."

"Did you think we'd show up and they'd confess?" Nick asks.

"Yes. That's exactly what I hoped would happen." I'm not kidding. That would've been awesome.

Binny laughs. "There's always tomorrow. We have three people to interview tomorrow. Maybe we'll get lucky."

Lucky. Right. If tomorrow goes like today—we'll be no further than we are, and I'll probably end up in jail.

TEN

WE SET OUT the next day with new hope. All night, as I tossed and turned in bed, I told myself to relax. It's early. Too soon to tell. And then I'd tell myself I was running out of time. If we didn't solve this, then I was going to be arrested. Needless to say, I didn't sleep well.

But the sun shines brightly in the sky today, and Binny has brought malasadas, so things are looking up. As we climb back into Nick's beater and head to Lihue, I note the three people we are going to see.

"Elizabeth Chen, Gina Perkins, and Bob Reed. These guys are our targets."

"I looked them up last night," Binny says. I wish I'd thought of that. It would've been more productive than tossing and turning and imagining myself in an orange jumpsuit.

"Elizabeth and Gina are roommates, so we can knock them out with one visit. Bob Reed runs a shave ice stand on the beach."

I stare. "How did you find all that out?"

"Facebook," Binny says. "You guys didn't think of that?"

Nick shakes his head. "No. It never occurred to me. I'm not on Facebook."

This time, both Binny and I stare at him. "You're not on Facebook?" I ask.

Who doesn't do Facebook in this day and age? My mom even has a page. She lists herself as single and "looking for men." She has four thousand nine hundred friends. All men.

Nick shrugs. "What? I don't think it's a big deal."

"How do you *live*?" Binny howls. "It's how I keep track of twelve aunties and uncles and forty-seven cousins. I'd never remember their birthdays if I didn't have that alert." She shakes her head. "Then there are all my high school and college friends, my surfer friends..."

"Almost every venue on the island has a page. It's how I find out if they're looking for talent," I add.

"I just don't think it's necessary," Nick says. "It's no big deal."

Binny's mouth opens and closes multiple times...like a gasping fish.

"Well, now you know what a good tool it is for investigations," I say.

Nick decides to change the subject. "So Gina and Elizabeth are roommates. It's possible that they know Leilani. Bob works on the beach, so he probably knows Kua, right?"

"We can't assume anything until we talk to them." But I do hope it's that easy.

It's noon by the time we pull into Lihue. We decide to start with Bob Reed. It takes no time to find his beachside shave ice stand. As I order, I try to sum him up like a detective.

Middle aged, balding, with a pot belly. Nice, friendly

smile—a normal sort of guy. No bodies in his cooler, no sign saying *I'm a Murderer*.

The sun is high, and people are crowding the stand. Binny grabs a picnic table, and we sit, sizing up our target as we eat.

"What do you think?" Nick asks.

"He's pretty old," Binny says.

"I'd say we don't beat around the bush this time," I mumble. "Let's try the direct approach. See if that works?"

Nick and Binny nod. We've got nothing to lose. After about 20 minutes, the crowd thins, and in another five, Bob Reed is alone.

"Let me try this on my own," Nick says. "I think these guys are clamming up with three people interrogating them."

"Fine," I say. "Binny and I will handle the girls." I'm actually relieved. I was starting to think the same thing. We got almost nothing out of the two men yesterday. I'd be intimidated if three strangers came up and started asking me odd questions about dead people.

"Aloha!" Nick calls out as he walks up to the man.

I watch as the two men lapse into what appears to be a comfortable discussion. Nick is really good at this. He's so comfortable in his own skin. I wonder if that's due to knowing who you come from and living in the same house for generations. There are no blank spaces in his family tree. He knows how they lived and what they wanted out of life. That's where his ease with people comes from, I'd bet.

Binny is staring at me. "What's going on with you and Nick?"

I tear my eyes away from the men to look at her. "What do you mean?"

"I mean, you barely know the guy. You haven't really had a single date. In fact, you've only known him a couple of days."

"Well, that's how all relationships start out. You get to know each other over time."

"Yes." Binny waves my statement away. "But he's already devoted a lot of time to you. And he's not freaked out that you are a suspect in a murder case. And he volunteers to spend his whole weekend driving two women he's never met before around the island, interviewing suspects. Does that seem weird to you?"

Yes, it seems weird. "Not really. Stranger things have happened."

Does Binny think it's weird that a man is interested in me? That can't be it. No one is nicer than Binny, and she'd go out of her way to make me feel better. So why the third degree?

My silence seems to upset her. "I'm not saying he isn't a total catch. I hope he is. I just want you to keep an open mind. Play devil's advocate."

"Okay," I say. "I understand that. You're just looking out for me. And this whirlwind…whatever…isn't textbook dating 101. But he seems sincere."

We look at Nick. He and Bob Reed are locked in a serious discussion. Did he get the man to open up? I feel the tingle of hope in my stomach.

"All right." I turn to my friend. "I'll try to keep my eyes open. And I promise to find out more about him. But really, don't you and everyone else in Aloha Lagoon know all about the Woodfields? If he's a serial killer, wouldn't it have come out by now?"

Binny gives in. "Just be careful. Promise me."

I nod, but this train of thought is bothering me now. I don't know anything about Nick. On the other hand, I'd like to think I'm a good judge of character, and nothing seems out of line. Ugh. I do not need this right now. All these murders must be getting to Binny. After all, she can't remember a murder ever occurring in Aloha Lagoon—and she's lived here all her life.

Why does my life have to be so complicated right now? In fact, why am I investigating these murders in the first place? The detective's list has five names. And the fact that Detective Ray hasn't arrested me yet must mean I'm not that much of a suspect, right?

In fact, I decide that after today, I'm going to give up on this. Nick and I can go on a nice date. I can hit up the resort for Kua's and Leilani's gigs. Okay, that seems a little harsh. It's probably a bad idea to start shooting for their usual jobs.

On the other hand, Pauli seemed pretty keen to work at the resort. Would he be there first thing in the morning to schmooze? If so, why shouldn't I give it a shot? What should I do?

Nick walks back to us, shouting "mahalo" and waving at Bob Reed over his shoulder. Binny and I wait until he's right in front of us.

"Let's get lunch," he says.

"What did you find out?" I ask, but he cuts me off.

"Not here. Come on."

We drive about four blocks and end up at a cute little

pizza place. Nick ushers us in, and we find a table. The suspense is killing me.

"Tell us!" Binny explodes first.

Nick grins. "Actually, I did rather well. You see those two girls over there?"

We follow the direction of his finger and see two young women, both with blonde ponytails, wearing waitress aprons.

"Yeah?" I ask. "So what?"

"That is Elizabeth and Gina. Bob told me they work here. I figure it's better to make small talk here than to just show up at their home."

Binny pouts. "But that was going to be *our* interview."

"He knows them?" I ask. "How did you find that out?"

One of the blondes comes over and gets our orders. I try not to stare openly as Binny orders us a round of soft drinks and a large pepperoni pizza. The name tag says *Gina*. She smiles thinly before heading back to the kitchen.

"I know that," Nick begins, "because Bob knew Leilani. And those two are her former roommates."

Leilani had roommates? *Human* roommates? I guess I always thought she lived in a cave with rabid bats as her only friends.

"Bob also said," Nick continues as he keeps his eyes on the two waitresses, "that he knew Kua."

"He knew both of them too?" I marvel.

Binny nods. "This isn't a big island, Nani. And it's even smaller if you move in certain circles...like surfers or musicians."

"What did Bob say about Kua and Leilani?" I ask.

Gina arrives and plunks down our drinks with some empty plates and napkins. She grins weakly at us before leaving again. I'm pretty sure she's hardly noticed us at all.

"Do you think she's upset about Leilani's death?" Binny asks. That's so like her to be concerned about total strangers.

"Bob says Kua played regularly in a bar not far from here whenever he was in town to surf. Bob likes music, so he would go hear him perform. Afterwards they'd hang out at the bar for a while. He liked Kua and has no idea who would want to kill him."

"Huh. I guess Leilani and I are the only ones he wasn't nice to," I mumble.

Nick continues. "Bob couldn't say enough about what a great guy Kua was. Our murdered uke player was very devoted to his mother. He worked every gig he ever got to pay for her nursing home. And he visited her every single day."

"Really? That's so sad. Who's looking after his mother now?" I ask.

Nick shook his head. "Bob didn't know. It's possible there are other family members on the island. Maybe they'll step up."

Binny looks like she's going to burst into tears. "I want to send her flowers or something. Can we go to the funeral?"

I nod. "I was planning on it. I read once that the murderer usually goes to the funerals of his victims. Gives them a little thrill."

"That is horrible!" Binny gasps.

"You realize that line of thinking could backfire for you," Nick says. "If you're a suspect and you show up, Detective Ray is going to wonder why."

I shrug. "He thinks I knew them. Leilani led him to believe Kua and I were close. Besides, the whole island is probably going. So I'm going."

Kua was nice to his mother. Well, of course he was! What did I think? That just because he didn't like me he was a soulless test-tube baby? Clearly he was liked by some people, like Bob.

"Did he say if he suspected somebody?" I ask hopefully.

Nick fidgets. He looks nervous. "Well, he did mention one person."

I sat straight up. Bob had a suspect in mind! This would take the spotlight off of me!

"Who? Who is it?"

Nick sighs. "Kua told him he only had one enemy. You."

"What?" I couldn't have heard that right. Did he say *me*?

"Kua told Bob that he had a hostile relationship with only one person. A 'haole' ukulele pretender from the mainland."

Yup. That sounds like me all right. Damn.

ELEVEN

I SLUMP IN my chair, dejected. If Bob told Nick, a complete stranger, that he thinks I killed Kua, he'll certainly tell Detective Ray that. And if the detective shows him a picture of me, Bob will mention that we came around asking questions.

I bury my face in my hands. "I'm so screwed."

Binny pats me on the back. "Not necessarily. It's just hearsay. The police can't use that as evidence."

I look up. Nick gives me a feeble smile. Totally screwed.

"Look, Nani," Nick says. I love it when he says my name. Although, I'd rather hear it on the beach at sunset than deciding whether I should just order all my clothes in prison orange from here on out. "We still have these two to talk to. Maybe they'll turn up something."

"I don't get it." I shake my head. "Todd and Pauli don't seem to be suspects. Why did the detective have them on a list to investigate? And Bob will implicate me when Ray does meet with him. The detective warned me off of investigating on my own. Maybe I should just go home and wait for him to take me downtown."

Nick rolls his eyes. "If Kua and Leilani were difficult with you, they had to have been that way with other people, right? And there's the Sea Dogs gang too. And I don't think we should rule Pauli out. That guy was definitely hiding something."

Binny nods. "And those two waitresses are former roommates. Pauli said he only dated Leilani for a minute. He knew what a pain she was. If these two are former roomies, chances are she was horrible to them too."

We are quiet for a few moments. Gina walks up and sets the pizza on the table. She gives us the same thin smile. Maybe that's just how she is? I shouldn't read anything into that. Still, how did Leilani end up with roommates that didn't kill her after a day or two? I wanted to murder her after seven seconds. Hmmm... I should keep that to myself.

I dig in, plucking a steaming, greasy slice of pizza and plopping it onto my plate. It's good. Really good. In fact, it's probably the best pizza I've ever had here in Hawaii. My friends must feel the same way, because they are tearing into it too. I hadn't realized how hungry the fear of a lifetime in jail could make you. I guess I'll be packing on the pounds from here on out. In college you have the "freshman fifteen" when it comes to weight gain. What do you call it in prison? The "felon fifteen"?

"That is the best pizza ever!" Binny moans as she throws her napkin on her empty plate.

Nick nods. "I didn't even know this place existed. How could I not know that?"

I shake my head. "You guys don't have a clue. Don't get me wrong. You do seafood and fruit and barbecue great and all, but you can't do pizza. Until now."

Binny throws a napkin at me, and Nick rolls his eyes. It feels so good to have people to hang out with instead of babysitting my mother at home. What's Mom going to do if I go to jail? She could live on the money Dad left for a while, and maybe Vera would keep an eye on her, but is that enough? I made a mental note to ask Nick— if things go south, can Mom stay with them?

"It's the sauce." We look up to see Gina talking to us. "Vito, that's the owner, he's from New Jersey. It's his mother's secret recipe." Her voice is flat, lifeless, and limp.

Nick stands. "Excuse me." He pulls his cell from his pocket. "I've got to make a call."

I watch him leave. To my surprise, Elizabeth joins us. And that's when I realize we are the only people in the restaurant.

"Sit down!" Binny urges the women with one of her dazzling smiles. "You have a moment. Take a load off."

The two waitresses look at each other, shrug, and sit. It can't be this easy, can it? Now all I have to do is get them to confess that they murdered Leilani. That shouldn't be too hard. These two look like they have the combined intelligence of a wet napkin.

"When did this place open?" Binny asks. Her smile is disarming, even on women.

From a distance, Gina and Elizabeth look like each other. Same height, build, and dishwater-blonde hair in a ponytail. But close up, I can see there are differences. While Gina has the palest blue eyes I've ever seen, Elizabeth's were brown, like mine. Elizabeth has full lips and plump cheeks. Gina is gaunt—almost as if she's aged too soon. Something I can understand if she lived with Leilani.

"Vito moved here six months ago," Gina says. "But we just opened last month."

"Did you move here with the restaurant?" I ask, hoping the question sounds normal. To be perfectly honest, these two are kind of creeping me out with their bland expressions.

This time Elizabeth speaks. "No. We've lived here about ten years. Before that we worked in Honolulu."

"Oh," I say. "So you're roommates?"

Gina and Elizabeth don't speak but do shrug at the exact same time. I kind of wish I had a cross or Bible or something in case they turned out to be demons.

"Well, I love the pizza! Do you have some flyers?" Binny asks. "We can take them home and let people know about this place."

"I'll get them," Gina says but doesn't move. It's like watching a toy run out of battery power. I suspect she won't move until she has to.

"Where are you from?" Elizabeth asks, startling me with her sudden initiative. Her manner is just as dull as Gina's. They're kind of reminding me of the twins from *The Shining. Nani, come play with us...*

"Aloha Lagoon." Binny smiles. Clever girl. She's gotten us to a point where we can get into the reason we are really here.

The women exchange a very long, curious look. At least, that's what I think it is. For all I know, they could be swapping recipes telepathically.

"Aloha Lagoon? Really?" Gina asks, but there's an edge to her voice.

"Yes," I say. "Have you been there?"

Once again, the two women look at each other. I wonder if they communicate telepathically.

"Leilani O'Flanagan was murdered there the other day," Gina says. "Did you know her?"

I nod. "Professionally only. She was a colleague of mine."

Gina and Elizabeth stand, their chairs flying backward. Gina points at me, her face a mask of horror. Whoa. We've gone from *The Shining* to *Invasion of the Body Snatchers.*

"You're that evil musician!" she screams. I half expect aliens to appear to replace me with a pod version.

"What?" *Evil? Seriously? Seems a little harsh since they just met me.*

"You tortured that poor, sweet, innocent soul!" Elizabeth shrieks. She is also now pointing at me.

Did she just refer to Leilani, the screaming psycho, as sweet and innocent? These two are crazy. They've gone from zero to harpy in two seconds.

"You're Nani!" Gina says my name as if it tastes bad. "We know all about you!"

"I don't understand," I start, but Elizabeth cuts me off.

"You teased and bullied our poor Leilani! And you killed her too!"

I teased and bullied a woman who once referred to my playing as the sound of a garbage disposal in its death throes?

"I did not!" I stand now, my face flushed with anger. "And Leilani was the bully! She treated me like dirt. She liked to pick fights with me and the other musicians."

My words might as well be in Dutch, because the

two creepy waitresses shake their heads violently, refusing to listen.

"Get out of here!" Gina hisses.

"I hope you get the death penalty!" Elizabeth cries.

We're out the door and back into the sunshine before we can even pay our bill. Binny turns back to do so, but Elizabeth locks the door, and Gina turns the *Open* sign to *Closed*. I grab Binny's arm and pull her toward me. Not only do they not deserve to get paid, but I kind of think my life might be in danger here, in Vito's parking lot.

"What happened?" Nick asks.

"Well"—I shift from one foot to the other—"we talked to them. And it didn't go well."

Binny and I climb into the car. From the window I see Gina writing down our license plate number. Great. When Detective Ray does interview them, Gina and Elizabeth will probably tell them I attacked them with a meat cleaver. To be honest, I really wanted to.

"I think we might be in trouble," I say. "And I'm afraid this is the last time we'll ever have that fabulous pizza. It might be the last time I have any pizza, if those two testify against me."

Binny fills Nick in on the conversation as I stare out the window. These women loved Leilani. How is that possible? The woman was evil and nasty, but either they loved those qualities in her or I'm the only target she ever had. My mind races back to all the arguments I'd ever had with the woman. I couldn't call them conversations. The words exchanged weren't civil.

Did I cause her hostility somehow? I couldn't remember ever picking a fight with her, Kua, or anyone.

Other people had to have had bad experiences with her. Pauli didn't date her long. Alohalani—the only other ukulele musician on the island now—understood how difficult she was.

I took in a deep breath and let out a sigh. No way was I imagining it. The only thing difficult to believe is that anyone got along with Kua and Leilani. And I need proof that they were rotten. I have to talk to someone who agrees with me.

"I think our next step is to interview Alohalani," I speak up. "He knows what those two were really like."

Nick and Binny are strangely silent.

"What?" I ask. "What is it?"

"It's just that…what I mean is… I don't mean to question you…" Binny fumbles.

Uh-oh. I have a bad idea where this is going.

"We're not questioning you," Nick eases. "Not really. But I think I need to point out that there are people who have a false impression of you and think you killed Kua and Leilani."

"You two don't think that I…"

"No!" Binny interrupts. "I'm sure those two were horrible people. We're just saying that it looks bad for you."

Nick nods. "This is something we need to be aware of. Something we need to counteract if we are going to prove you innocent."

Nick and Binny are right. When Detective Ray ever gets around to investigating the names on that list, he's going to come to the conclusion that I am the murderer. I have motive. I've been seen arguing with the two on several occasions. The alleged murder weapon is missing from my home. All signs point to me.

I'm starting to believe that I did it.

"Head home," I tell them as I rub my pounding head. "I need to sleep on this."

"Okay," Binny soothes. "We'll talk tomorrow."

"You're going out of town tomorrow, and Nick is going to work."

"What are you going to do?" Nick asks.

"I'm going to go see the only other ukulele performer left on Kauai. I'm going to see Alohalani."

And I'm going to make him agree with me. If he doesn't, clearly I'm from another dimension, and I should turn myself in. At this point it's the only thing I can do.

Mom is asleep when I get home. I do the dishes and put away laundry before going to bed. As I lay there, I think about Kua and Leilani. Somehow the two of them have managed to implicate me from the great beyond. It's a nice trick because I seriously doubt either one of them made it to heaven.

I hope, as I drift off to sleep, that Leilani got eaten by a shark after all. At least there'd be some poetic justice in that. Again, I feel a little sorry for the shark as I finally fall asleep.

The next morning I call Alohalani's office at the community college and make an appointment for 9:30. To my surprise, I'm patched through to Alohalani himself.

"Nani?" he asks as he comes on the line. "I was planning on calling you."

He was? "Oh? Why is that?"

"I have a theory on Kua and Leilani's murders, and I'd like to talk to you about it."

"Great," I say, a little confused. "I'll see you in a bit."

"Mahalo," the man says before hanging up.

This is very interesting. He wants to talk to me. Granted, it's about the murders, but that's okay because that's what I was going to talk to him about. This could be the beginning of a good relationship with the best musician on the island.

"Where were you all weekend?" Mom stands in the doorway, watching me brush my teeth. She's wearing her bright-pink muumuu—the one covered in green palm trees. In her right hand is a spoon. There's no plate, nothing she'd be using a spoon for. She's just standing there, holding it as if I were a cup of soup.

"Out with Nick and Binny." I mangle the words through a sudsy mouth. "We went to Princeville and Lihue."

A smile spreads across my mother's face. She kind of looks like a crocodile sneaking up on prey. Only the prey in this instance is poor Nick Woodfield and a wedding ceremony.

"Oh? You've been seeing a lot of him lately." Mom grins smugly.

"Yup. He's a great guy." I spit and rinse, then head to my bedroom to find my sport sandals. Mom follows.

"Why did you take Binny with you? You two should be alone." There's that grin again.

"I wanted her to meet him. It's important that she like him." Found the shoes, now to braid my hair.

"And does she?" Mom asks.

"Of course. We get along great."

My long brown hair properly plaited, I throw on some mascara and lip balm. I'm hoping khaki shorts and a nice T-shirt will be all right. Things are so casual here. I remember my surprise at seeing a group of lawyers in a meeting at the resort—all dressed like it was casual Friday at a strip mall. No one wears a suit unless it's a funeral or wedding…and even that's iffy.

"Are you meeting him today?" Mom asks a little too hopefully.

I'm sure she's already set the date and reserved the chapel. She's probably planning for all of us to live together at the Woodfield mansion. I wouldn't be surprised if she's already picked out her bedroom. I'm not sure Vera would approve of Mom's decorating habits. Somehow I can't picture forty coconuts in hula skirts appealing to the Woodfields.

I shake my head, disappointing her. "No. He's working. I'm going to meet someone at the community college."

"Oh?" is all she has to say. One word speaks volumes from Mom.

"I'm looking into teaching a class or two there," I lie. She shouldn't know about our little investigation. Mom has a tendency to say the wrong things to the wrong people at the wrong times.

But my mother is no longer there. I hear the blender going in the kitchen. Great. She's hitting the mai tais early today. I don't want to have to worry about her, but if she's imbibing this early, she'll be napping on the lanai by eleven.

I slip past her into the living room to grab my briefcase. The coconuts are gone. Now, a couple dozen pink flamingos are suspended from the ceiling. Someone (meaning Mom) has taken a sharpie to draw little black masks around their eyes. She tried to make little sunglasses for them. I worry that I know this without having to ask her. Is this what I have to look forward to when I'm her age? Maybe I should make a reservation for a senior living condo now.

It's a short drive to the college, and I try to think of what Alohalani wants to tell me and what I'm going to ask him. I have to be careful. While the man doesn't seem to hate me like the other two, he certainly isn't anything I'd call a friend. Maybe that will change with Kua and Leilani gone. Dare I hope?

The car behind me rushes past on a two-lane road, flashing me the chaka sign—thumb and pinkie extended, middle fingers folded into the palm. It doesn't bother me. People drive like this all the time. I look in the rearview mirror.

Two cars back is a nondescript white sedan. Something about the car nips at my memory, but I draw a blank. It's not surprising. A lot of people here buy white cars to cut down on the heat absorption. I shake the feeling something is off as I pull into the parking lot of building number two. I look for the car as I get out, but it's gone. I'm really starting to get paranoid. I wish this case was over. I'd like to go back to my normal self now, please.

The secretary for the music department is a bored-looking student in a tank-top dress and a messy topknot. She snaps her gum before giving me directions to Alohalani's office, then goes back to playing some game on her cell phone.

The teacher's door is covered with pictures of Alohalani through the years at various gigs. I can't help but grin at a photo of him with The Ukulele Orchestra of Great Britain from their last tour here. And is that Jake Shimabukuro? Wow! I have a little fan-girl moment as I raise my fist and knock.

"Come in," a voice calls, and I open the door.

Alohalani Kealoha waves me in. His office is amazing. The walls are covered with every kind of ukulele imaginable, from pocket ukes to cigar-box instruments. Where there aren't instruments, there are shelves filled with books on Polynesian music, composition, history, and instruments. A single open window looks out onto a vast expanse of green landscaping and large jungle plants. Breezes blow the scent of jasmine into the room. Sheet music of ancient Hawaiian songs are stacked in tidy piles on his desk. It's no wonder he's so proud of his heritage.

The office is pretty large. On his desk in front of him is a textbook on music theory. It occurs to me that I should take one of his courses someday. I suddenly feel very unqualified to even be on the island.

"Miss Johnson, aloha," Alohalani says genially. He's still smiling, and I realize it's sincere. Maybe outside of the mad competitiveness of performing, he's just a nice guy. Or he thinks (like everyone else) that I killed Kua and Leilani, and he doesn't want to make me angry.

"Mahalo," I reply as humbly as possible. "I appreciate you taking the time to see me, and I'm curious as to what you want to tell me."

He motions me to sit, and I do. My eyes skirt the perimeter of the room. There's so much history here—I could spend months in just this room.

"First of all, why did you call to make an appointment?" Alohalani asks. He's still polite, but now there's a bluntness I can't ignore. Is the nice guy gone?

Okay, I'll just dig in. "I know you've heard about Kua and Leilani." I leave the sentence hanging there to see how he takes it.

The man shakes his head, but I can't determine if it's sadly or not. "I've heard."

That is all he says. I'm just going to have to be up front with the whole thing.

"Do you have any idea who killed them?" I ask. It's a risk. He could throw me out. He could yell at me for being insensitive.

"The police seem interested in you," he says. No expression. None at all. Is this his idea about the murders? That I'm the killer? That kind of sucks.

"I have no idea why," I blurt out. "I barely knew them. I can't understand why this is happening."

"The police," he repeats, "seem to think you have motive. That you wanted them out of the way to get rid of the competition."

I shake my head vigorously. "Not true. I would never do that."

"And they believe that you fought with Kua and Leilani every time you were in the same room as them."

Okay, well, that's true. I can't deny it.

"Detective Ray warned me that I might be next."

My heart actually feels like it's stopped. "You're joking. They think I'm the killer and that I'm going to kill you? You can't believe that." Please tell me he doesn't believe that.

The older man looks at me in silence for a very long time. I'm desperate to know what he's thinking, but I feel like asking him directly would be the wrong move. The clock on the wall—a hula girl whose hips swing back and forth in keeping with the time—ticks so loudly it's making my head hurt.

"I don't think you killed them," Alohalani says at long last. "I don't think you will kill me. Or I wouldn't have allowed the appointment."

I sigh with relief. "You may be the only one who thinks so."

"At first," he says, "I didn't think the two murders were related. Now I do. I think the murders were committed by the same person."

Now we're talking. He's going to get to the reason he wanted to meet me.

I lean forward. "Really? Do you know who?"

"I have an idea," he says. "But I'm not sure of it yet. I didn't tell the detective my theory, and I'm not going to tell you until I know for sure."

What? He thinks he knows the identity of the murderer and won't tell me? That's how you get murdered in the TV shows! The victim confronts the murderer alone, with no back up, and the killer kills her or him.

"You won't tell me? You have to tell someone! What if you're next?"

He nods. "I've thought of that."

"And…"

"And I'm not ready to say."

"But," I say, "you wanted to talk to me about your suspicions. Right?"

He gives no reply. There's something in Hawaii called "island time." Things just move slower. People don't do stuff before they're ready. I've always admired island time. Until right now.

I sit there, gaping at the man. "Do you have it written down somewhere, or can you give me a clue? It's dangerous for you to play cat and mouse with a killer."

Alohalani considers this. He's a thoughtful man, I realize. Everything is perfectly thought out before spoken. The Hawaiian culture is big on saving face. You don't cause conflict. You don't accuse anyone of anything before you know for sure. There's a saying that the best way to save face is to keep part of it shut. And yes, that's a nice sentiment. But it doesn't fly in the face of murder. And apparently, Kua and Leilani thought this didn't apply to them, judging by their behavior.

"If you won't tell me your suspicions," I say, "you have to tell the police. They're this close to arresting me." I pinch my fingers together for emphasis. "And keeping it to yourself only helps the killer."

It's quiet for a long time. Is he thinking about it? What if he decides to keep it secret? I understand that revealing it is at war with one of the main tenets of his culture and upbringing, but what if it saves his life?

"Okay," Alohalani says at long last. "I'll give you a clue. And I will call the police after you leave, and tell them what I think has happened. I originally wanted to let you know I don't think you did it. And I have written down my thoughts on the matter. In fact, I'm pretty sure I know what really happened."

"Thank you for being one of only three people who thinks it's not me." I relax a little. "And you should call Detective Ray with your findings immediately. I don't want you to end up a victim."

"I am not worried about myself," he says. "I'm worried about you."

"Y…you're worried? About me?" I stammer in shock.

He nods. "You are not so bad. You are a decent musician, and I could maybe mentor you. Make you better."

I'm so startled that I don't know what to say. These are huge compliments from him. And a real acknowledgement of my talent. Okay, so it's a weak acknowledgement, but I'll take it! I'm finally on the inside. No longer an outsider. I imagine sharing the stage with Alohalani and Jake Shimabukuro. Things might actually be looking up for me! Granted, it's on the backs of two murdered musicians—which is sad, of course. But hey, I'll take anything.

"I'd love that," I gush. "I was thinking of taking one of your classes on the history of Polynesian music or something anyway."

Alohalani smiles cautiously. "Okay, I'll tell you what"—he reaches across the desk and grabs his calendar—"how about a week from now, same time and place, to discuss your future?"

My head spins with joy. "Yes! That's perfect! I'll be here!"

"It won't be easy," he cautions. "Bring a soprano uku-lele with you, and I'll see what I have to work with."

Okay, I know this is a backhanded compliment. I mean, I went to Juilliard—I'm not exactly a hobbyist. But instead of being outraged, I nod so hard my head's in danger of becoming unfastened.

"Absolutely! Thank you!"

He writes down the appointment in the book, one week exactly from right now, where he has my name for today. I'm in his book twice. This is huge! This is progress.

"So what's the clue?" I finally ask as he puts his cal-endar away.

"It's not what you think," the man says. "If you're looking at strangers, you're looking in the wrong place."

The office phone rings loudly, making me jump. As he answers it, I digest what he's just told me—turning the words over in hopes of finding some meaning there. *It's not what you think…if you're looking at strangers, you're looking in the wrong place.* What is he saying?

"Can you give me anything else?" I ask.

He waves me off. "I've got to run down the hall for a moment. One of my students dropped off her term paper in the wrong slot. I'll be right back."

I nod as he exits, wondering what he means by the clue. It's not a stranger. But does that mean a stranger to me, him, or the two murdered people? I'm definitely going to need more information. Somehow, when he gets back, I'll have to convince him to tell me more. How hard can it be? I talked him into taking me on as a mentee.

The trick will be to make sure he knows that this is

for his own good. I have to make him understand that the killer is still out there and could strike one of us at any second. The thought makes me shiver. I stand up and go to the open window to get a little fresh air.

The view is marvelous. But it's not perfect. Now that I'm closer, I realize I can see the parking lot—including my car. Next to it is a white sedan. I feel a little chill in spite of the warm breeze. Is that the same car that was following me earlier? Oh wow! Am I being followed?

Yeesh, Nani. Get a grip. Now you're seeing killers behind every corner. It's just a white car. Like so many others here. Stop being so jumpy! Alohalani will be back any minute. I'll get his theory out of him, and the case will be closed.

To distract myself, I turn to look at all of his books. He has an amazing assortment of out-of-print music. I've never seen some of these before. I gently run my hands over the well-worn spines of compilations of hula music. Perhaps he'll let me borrow one of them next week. I love traditional music. There wasn't much available at Juilliard.

I'm so excited about the possibility of working with this man. At long last, I'm getting some recognition here. I've worked hard and proven myself. Now I'll at last be in the "in crowd."

Ugh. That's awful. What am I? Fifteen?

There's a noise in the hallway. Alohalani must be coming back. I don't want him to see me drooling over his collection. Quickly, I take my seat and look hopefully at the door.

He appears with a large knife sticking out of his

throat, eyes wide and bulging. The dying man reaches for me before stumbling backward against the wall.

"Oh my God!" I shout as I run to him.

Alohalani collapses to the floor, and I fumble with my cell, attempting to dial 9-1-1.

"9-1-1. What's your emergency?" a female voice answers.

"Help! A man's been stabbed!" I shout into the phone. I give the address and beg them to come quickly. I'm shaking all over. Is the killer in the hallway? Am I next? What should I do?

Alohalani gurgles, bleeding from his mouth and throat. It only takes a second for his eyes to go glassy. He's gone. All that talent and musical history. Gone forever.

The bored student comes running down the hallway. She stops when she sees me leaning over her dead professor and lets out a horrific scream.

"What did you do?" she asks.

I think about telling her I was in the wrong place at the wrong time. I think about this, but I know this won't do any good. Because I look like a murderer. It definitely appears that I've killed Alohalani.

I'm now the last uke standing.

TWELVE

THERE'S BLOOD ON my shirt. Everything sounds like it's far away. But it's not. It's right in my face. All around me. I'm sitting where the student assistant was earlier. She's standing in the corner with a blanket around her, sobbing. A policeman is trying to take her statement, but she's too upset.

I've already given my statement—through numb lips and deaf ears. It's so quiet and noisy at the same time. I watch as the body is wheeled out of the room. I want to scream. I want to cry. But I can't.

How could this happen? He just walked down the hallway. The man was gone for, like, 30 seconds before he returned with a knife in his neck. I'd heard nothing to indicate a stabbing was taking place. Shouldn't I have heard something like that?

What does a stabbing sound like? I'm losing it. And I'm probably going to jail. The police all keep giving me surreptitious looks. It's like being in a room full of flounder fish, all gaping at me.

Think, Nani! What did you hear? What did you see? I have to pull myself together. Detective Ray is in the other room with the coroner. I have to be in my right mind when he questions me. I have to make him see that Alohalani didn't suspect me.

This is just perfect, isn't it? I'm the main suspect, I go to see the last living potential victim, and he's murdered while I'm there. No one sees it happen, but I'm in the same room, looming sinisterly over the dead body. I'm so screwed.

Okay, so what did I see? Alohalani walked out of his office because he got a call from a student who said she needed him to pick up a term paper. Okay. He left the office and walked into the hallway. I was at the window, then at the bookshelf, checking out his music. I heard a noise, and Alohalani came back.

The fog starts to dissipate in my brain. I have something to hold on to. What was the noise I heard? I strain to remember, but I can't. Was it a scuffle? Was it Alohalani struggling with his killer? It had to be.

When the police walked me to the front of the department's offices earlier, I noticed a long, bloody trail that started about halfway down the hall in the other direction, back to Alohalani's office. That had to be where it happened. He was attacked in that spot. But by whom?

The police will think this a pretty open-and-shut case. They had me, red handed, at the scene of the crime. This is it. I'm not going to be Alohalani's mentee. We are never going to play together with the ukulele greats. I wonder if they'll let me bring an instrument to prison? Unlikely, since they think I killed Kua with a uke.

"Is there anyone we can call for you?" A policewoman stands in front of me. Her face is soothing, comforting.

"Um…" I struggle to hold it together. "I drove here."

She shakes her head. "I don't think you should drive like this. You're in shock."

I am? Well that makes sense. That explains the fogginess. But who to call? Mom is probably three sheets to the wind by now. Binny is on a plane to the Big Island. There's only one person.

"Nick Woodfield," I say as I hand the officer my phone. My fingers feel too clumsy to dial it myself.

The woman nods and, after pulling the name up, dials. I barely hear her speak. It comes across as a garbled mumble. I stare at the wall across from me, trying to make sense of everything.

It all happened so fast. I think about the open window. Had the killer been just outside and thought he was going to be revealed? That might be something. And the white car from earlier. The one I thought I should know. Was that the killer following me here?

Which begs the thought—was I the target? Maybe the killer was going to take me out, but when he saw where I was going, decided to continue with the plan to frame me by killing Alohalani. If the killer was eavesdropping outside the window, he heard that Alohalani thought he knew who killed Kua and Leilani. The murderer then made the call to the teacher's office, asking him to come down the hall. And that's when and where he struck.

It was so easy to frame me yet again. I'd walked right into it. Led a killer to the perfect time and place for a murder. Why hadn't I thought of this before? I'm so stupid.

"Miss Johnson?" Detective Ray is standing there, looking down at me.

"Nani!" Nick appears in the doorway.

He rushes to my side. "Are you okay?"

That was awfully quick.

"Mr. Woodfield." The detective narrows his eyes. "Would you take Miss Johnson down to the police station? She's not under arrest, but I do want to talk to her."

Nick nods and helps me to my feet. We leave before the policeman can change his mind.

"What happened?" Nick asks once we're in the car. "I got a call from the police telling me to come to the community college because there'd been a murder."

I tell him everything. All of it, leaving nothing out. It's like a rehearsal for what I'll tell Detective Ray later. About the clue. About the professor wanting to take me under his wing. Everything.

Nick pulls off the side of the road and stops the car. He throws his arms around me, holding me close. He's just come from work and smells of grass clippings and green things. It's nice. It's soothing. And I just melt into him.

After a few minutes, he pulls away and searches my face. "Should I call your mom?"

"What? No!" I croak. My voice is breaking. It's all too much. "She'd just show up and make it worse."

"Binny?" he asks.

I shake my head. "She's on her way to a family thing."

Binny would drop everything and come back if she knew. But it isn't necessary. She could visit me in prison. Wow. My thinking has gone from zero to bleak in seconds.

Nick starts the car again and pulls away from the

curb. "I'll be there for you. And I think you should tell the detective everything. Absolutely everything. I can't bear the thought of you getting hurt."

I nod because he's right. We should never have taken it this far. Alohalani is dead because of me. Because I went to see him.

"This might not be the right time to tell you," Nick says. "But Kua's funeral is tomorrow morning. Leilani's is the next morning."

"And Alohalani's is going to be soon." I feel awful. That poor man. I'll never get that image out of my head.

"Do you want to go?" Nick asks gently. "You don't have to. Nobody would think badly of you if you don't."

"What will people think if I don't go?"

"We shouldn't worry about that."

I throw my hands up. "It doesn't matter anyway. I won't be able to go. I'll be in jail in a few hours."

"No, you won't," Nick says. "I already called our family attorney. He's ready in case they do arrest you."

I turn to look at him. "Why would you do that? You barely know me?"

Nick smiles. "Because I like you. I like you a lot. And I want to help."

I let his comments percolate. I hope it's true. But what if it's not? What if Binny's right? I hardly know Nick. I just met him only moments after finding out Kua was dead. And he's been by my side ever since. It does seem weird.

Okay, so he's moving too fast. Does that make him a bad guy? I really like him. He just came into my life at a crazy time. He shouldn't be punished for that.

I lean back against the seat and close my eyes. I give up thinking for now. Let someone else do the thinking. Pretty soon, I'll be at the police station. A place I probably won't be leaving. Might as well enjoy my freedom as much as I can for the minutes I have left.

So much for Hawaii. So much for paradise. I should've stayed in Kansas.

"We're here," Nick says, and I feel the car stop.

I open my eyes and see that we are parked at the coffee shop across from the police station.

"I thought you might like something to eat and drink before you head over to talk to the detective," Nick says. His eyes are searching mine, looking for what he can do to help.

I nod, and he gets out of the car and runs inside. I'm just about to slip into sleep when he climbs back into the car, holding a bag and two steaming cups of Kona coffee. The aroma is intoxicating, and I hear my stomach rumble. I haven't eaten anything since this morning.

"Actually I'd like a *Get Out of Jail Free* card, please," I say as I open the bag. Donuts! Real donuts! The kind I'd get back home. I might have to skip from liking Nick to loving him.

"I'm so sorry this happened." Nick frowns. "I should've gone with you to interview Alohalani."

I shake my head. "He would've been uptight if you'd come. Going alone was the only way. The only thing that might've changed is, and this is if the killer was following me, Alohalani might be alive—if I didn't go see him."

"Whoa, hold on there." Nick shakes his head. "This isn't your fault. None of this is your fault."

"I think the Terrible Trio—now the Dead Trio— would disagree with you."

"If you think I'm letting you see the detective with that attitude, you're crazy," Nick insists. "Besides, Alohalani told you he wanted to see you. It's not all on you, Nani."

"I'll tell him that. Like you said—I'll tell him everything. All of it. From the white car to the dying professor."

We eat in silence for a few moments. My brain begins at last to clear. I'm a little more focused on a full stomach. This isn't good—but it is better.

"What was it about the white car that made you notice it?" Nick asks. He looks so nice. Like a white knight in shining armor on Christmas Day. I'll miss that in prison.

I shrug. "I don't know. It was too far behind me to see the plates or the driver. It just made me think I'd seen that car before."

"Do you know anyone with a white car?"

"Lots of people. Maybe a dozen or so. It's a common color here."

"That's true. You said the window in Alohalani's office was open. And you think the murderer was listening outside?"

"I have no proof. There's no way of knowing if that happened. It's just a theory."

"It's a good one," Nick muses. "In fact, I think that's exactly what happened. The killer followed you. Hid under the window and heard the professor say he knew who killed Kua and Leilani. Maybe something in the clue he gave you tipped the killer off. And he had a perfect chance to frame you for this murder too."

I groan. "So now the murderer will either kill me next or continue to frame me. I'll end up dead or on death row. Neither of these are good options for me."

Nick thinks. "I wonder if the detective will let me sit in with you."

"No idea, but I think it's unlikely."

"I'm at least going to try." Nick tucks a stray strand of hair behind my ear. "I convinced you that we needed to investigate on our own."

Detective Ray pulls up at the station across the street and gets out of his car. He glances our way but makes no effort to acknowledge us. I watch as he goes in.

"It's time." I undo my seat belt and step out of the car.

Nick nods. "Let's go."

An hour later, the detective leans back in his chair. I'm seated in front of him, and Nick is standing, crammed into the back corner. He has to stand because of the lack of chairs. He doesn't seem to mind or even notice how insanely messy this office is. Maybe it's a guy thing.

"That's quite a story, Miss Johnson," Detective Ray says.

But does he believe it?

"It's the truth, I'm afraid. I feel terrible that this happened." And I do. I wish more than anything that Alohalani was still alive. And not just because his murder implicates me.

"So the professor was going to tell me who he thought

killed the other two?" The detective frowns as if he can't get his head around the idea.

I nod. "That's what he said."

"And his clue to you allegedly was"—he looks at his notes—"'it's not what you think. If you're looking at strangers, you're looking in the wrong place.'"

"That's what he told me." I feel like a parrot, repeating the same thing over and over.

"Any idea what it means?" the detective asks.

I shake my head. "None at all. Why would I make up some stupid clue to cover my tracks if I'd killed him? And why would I invent that he wants to mentor me? I've wanted that ever since I arrived on Kauai. Why would I kill him if he offered that?"

"I don't know," Detective Ray says. "It doesn't make sense. But all the circumstantial evidence points to you."

At least it's circumstantial. He doesn't really have anything on me. Nothing to prove I did it. So why do I feel so miserable?

"My gut reaction is that you didn't do it," the detective explains. "But everything points to you."

Um…yay? "So, what are you saying?"

"I'm still not arresting you. Not yet," Detective Ray says. "But the knife is in the lab, and if there's one fingerprint of yours, that's it. You're going to sit out the rest of the investigation in a cell."

I nod. "I didn't touch the knife. Not at all." Wait…no. I'm sure I didn't touch it.

"Did you recognize it?" he asks.

"No, but I didn't look at it that closely either." A chill rushes through me beneath my skin. What if it's one of mine? That's what this killer does—finds a way to frame me.

"Mr. Woodfield," the detective says. "I'll need to warn you off investigating. I tried to do that to this woman." He points at me, and I slink a little lower in my seat. "But that didn't work. So I'm counting on you to nip this in the bud."

Nick nods but says nothing. Which means he's planning to keep investigating.

"I'm letting you go for now. I still have some folks to interview. But I mean it when I say do not leave the island."

I jump to my feet. "I promise. Thank you, Detective." I grab Nick's hand, and we are out of there before Detective Ray can change his mind.

"So what now?" I ask as we get into Nick's old green beater.

He turns to me, and the look in his eyes says I'm not going to like the answer.

"Alohalani said he'd written down his suspicions, right?"

"That's right! I forgot about that!" I should've told the detective. Why didn't I think of it earlier?

"How do you feel about doing a little breaking and entering?"

"Well of course, that's what I was thinking after narrowly escaping arrest—let's give him a real reason to haul me away. Are you crazy?" I shout. "I'm one tiny step away from being arrested! Getting caught breaking into somewhere would definitely land me in jail."

Nick considers this. "What if I can guarantee we won't get caught?"

I think he's teasing, but those lovely brown eyes are definitely serious. That's it, I'm falling for a man who has no idea how things really work. Wait…did I just say I'm falling for Nick?

"You can do that?" I sound a little skeptical because I am.

Nick holds up his fingers and starts ticking them off. "One, we'll wear gloves and hats. Two, we'll be very careful. If it looks too dangerous, we won't do it."

I roll my eyes. "Oh, well, as long as we have hats and gloves, there's no way we'll get caught."

He ignores me and continues. "Three, and most importantly, we're going where no one else will be."

"And where, pray tell, is that?" I fold my arms over my chest, unconvinced.

"We will break into Alohalani's office at the college." Nick grins triumphantly. "He's dead, and the police have gone through the office, so no one should be there."

"Won't the police still be at the college?" I ask.

Nick shakes his head. "I don't think so. You didn't tell the detective that Alohalani wrote down his thoughts. And Kahoalani doesn't have the resources to guard it. But like I said, if anyone's there, we won't attempt it."

I say nothing. Mostly because I have no idea how to respond to such a suggestion. I'm dating (well…sort of dating) a crazy person. Is Nick really interested in me, or is he just after the buzz he gets from all of this?

Nick puts a hand on my shoulder. "We can do this. I know we can."

"We've already pushed things too far by interviewing those five people," I say at last. "The detective is going to find out we were there questioning them. He won't be happy with that. Especially when he realizes I copied the list on his desk. That has to be a jailable offense."

"Okay." Nick considers this. "Then this is our big chance to prove you didn't do it before he finds out we talked to his list of witnesses."

I lean back against the seat and close my eyes. Do I want to take this step? Become some sneak thief in the night? If we get busted, I might as well go on the run. I hear Greenland is nice this time of year...

"Think of Nancy Drew." Nick's voice interrupts my thoughts, which now involve getting used to prison food. "I'm sure you read her books when you were a kid. She always did stuff like this."

That seems like a low blow—involving Nancy Drew in this. I open my eyes and look at him. "She was a fictional character with cute clothes, a blue convertible, and whose dad was a big-shot attorney. There's a difference." And how does he know about Nancy Drew anyway?

"Okay, consider this—what choice do we have? And if we find his notes, we'll be able to prove that the professor didn't think you killed Kua and Leilani."

He's right. I know he's right. It's not that I mind that—it's just I have an aversion to breaking the law and getting caught. It's almost like I'm running head first into a cell to save the detective some time and trouble.

"All right," I say finally. "When do we do this?"

Nick starts the car. "I'll drop you off at home and pick you up at ten tonight."

"Ten. Fine. Let's just get it over with. I'll be ready," I agree.

The problem is, ready for what?

THIRTEEN

HOURS LATER, I look at myself in the mirror. My long brown hair is tied up in a bun. I'm wearing a black T-shirt and black cargo pants. In my hands are a pair of black rubber gloves and a black stocking cap, and I'm wearing black sport sandals. I look like a deranged ninja.

I've spent the last few hours trying to talk myself out of this (by the way, I lost the argument). I can't believe we're going through with it. My stomach is twisting into knots that would make a sailor nervous. Why does Nick think we can pull this off? Has he ever broken into a building? I haven't. The man is overly confident. He's going to have to make this happen. I don't even know where to look in Alohalani's office. It was packed with stuff. How could we hope to find a needle in a haystack?

I can hear Mom's TV show blaring in the next room. Hopefully, I can sneak past her and...

"Nani!" Mom shrieks as she rounds the corner, wine in hand and sloshing over the edge of the glass. "Where are you going dressed like that?" I can hear the plastic flamingos clacking together in her wake.

"Oh, um, Nick and I are going to a costume party," I lie.

"Dressed as what?" Mom asks.

If I say burglars, she'll remember that and possibly let it slip to the wrong people.

"Merchant marines," I somehow come up with. "It's a naval theme."

She looks at me for a moment, her eyes narrowing. "I just can't understand why you'd want to go to a party with a man looking so…so masculine? Couldn't you be a slutty marine?"

"*Mom*!" I cry. Slutty marine? Is she kidding me?

My cell buzzes, and I look at it. "Nick's here. Gotta run!"

I make it out the door before she can say one more word. Huh. It isn't Nick's ancient Cadillac in my drive. It's a new black SUV. I squint through the passenger window and see Nick waving me inside.

"Where did you get this?" I ask as I get in.

"I wanted to go totally incognito. I borrowed it from someone and changed the plates to some we had in the garage. They're at least a decade old. Untraceable."

Nick is dressed like a mirror image of me. All we need are little black masks, and we could rob banks in the 1940s.

"How are we going to get into the office?" My stomach is doing flips, and I worry that I'm going to vomit. This had better pan out.

"I figure we can try to get in through Alohalani's office window."

"You think it'll be open?" I ask. "That's just too much to hope for."

"Stranger things have happened. Besides, the building has one unlocked entrance, and there might still be a student at the front desk. If the window doesn't work, we can try that."

"Dressed like this? Why would anyone in their right mind let us in?"

Nick is already racing down the freeway toward the college. "We have to try. The man told you he had notes. It's up to us to find them."

"I don't know...it still seems like a huge risk." But Nick seems steadfast on this idea, so I'm just going to go with it. At some point, this will all be over, and I'll be home. Hopefully, without dropping DNA everywhere.

"Here." Nick tosses me a black ski cap. "Put it on. I don't want you dropping any telltale hairs."

"Why not just go with a ski mask?" I ask, even though I go ahead and put it on.

He's right. A long brown hair would certainly implicate me in a break-in—which is exactly what we're doing. If caught I'd actually be guilty.

We pull onto campus and find a parking spot next to several other cars. A huge banner announces a visiting artist concert. I can't help but wonder who it is. Then I remember that I don't care, because I don't want to be here.

"This way." We get out of the car, and Nick leads me back around the building where Alohalani's office is. The two of us cling to the walls, ducking under windows as we move. I don't see any cameras, but I'm not too surprised. Who's crazy enough to break into a community college? This girl, that's who.

"Here!" Nick whispers.

I look up. It's the window all right. I can tell by the view from where we're standing. I'll never forget that view. Only instead of thinking about it in wonder, it'll be a bad memory. Shortly after I saw it, Alohalani appeared in the doorway with a knife sticking out of his throat.

"You're not going to believe this," Nick says. He's standing, looking into the darkened office. "The window is open."

I stand up. "What? You're joking."

Sure enough, the window is wide open. That's weird. Maybe the cops screwed up. Or maybe the dean wanted to air out the stench of death before giving it to some unlucky professor. Whatever the reason, we are going in.

Nick boosts me up, and I slip through the window, landing on the floor. He lands next to me. It's dark. Really dark. And that's when I realize I didn't think to bring a flashlight. I had all that time at home and didn't think to bring a flashlight. Nancy Drew would be appalled.

"Use the app on your cell," Nick says, and I nod so he doesn't think I'm an idiot because that didn't occur to me. I humbly turn on the app and am almost blinded by the beam.

"How are we going to find his notes in all of this?" I whisper as I sweep the beam around the room. There was paper everywhere—from the piles of sheet music to the books on the shelves.

Everything is here just like it was before the office owner died. I stare longingly at the shelf full of old music. The professor was going to mentor me. I was going to have access to his collection of Polynesian music. It would've been so amazing to go through those shelves.

Nick stands over the desk, shining his light down on

it. "I don't know. We'll just have to look through everything." He gently sifts through the papers with his gloved hands.

My hands are starting to sweat inside the latex gloves. Okay, if he's got the desk, I'll look into the filing cabinet. I pull open the top drawer and start running through it. Student files. Names I don't recognize. There's nothing here with my name, or Kua's, or Leilani's. I close the drawer carefully and go to the next one.

More music! Each file contains yellowed sheets of music, all from Hawaii's past. I want to study them. I want to take one of his ukuleles off the wall and start playing (which I am smart enough not to do right now). What will happen to this stuff? Would it be weird of me to call and ask if I could buy it?

I shut the drawer and open the third one. This time, I find a box inside. Opening the lid, I see it is filled with photos. Could there be something in there? Very gently, I pull the box out and set it on the desk. I remove the lid. Nick looks up for a moment but then goes back to work. He's going through the desk drawers now.

The pictures seem to be pretty old. Mostly the teacher and his students. It makes me think of Juilliard. I had some amazing professors there. I wish I'd taken photos. I sift through the first 20 or so pictures before coming to one of the Terrible Trio.

It had to have been taken a while ago. The three of them are standing under a banner that says, *Aloha Lagoon Music Festival.* We had a music festival? There hasn't been one since I've been here.

In the photo, Alohalani is standing in the middle,

smiling almost imperceptibly. Leilani is on his right. Her face is twisted and mean, and her arms are folded across her chest. Her red hair is pinned up, and she looks like she just ate a cockroach.

Kua stands on the professor's left. The only one who isn't empty handed, he's cradling a baritone ukulele. Where Leilani looks disgusted, Kua's expression can only be described as arrogant. His chin is raised, and he glares at the camera.

Who took this picture? Were they surprised at the level of hostility shown by the performers? I flip the photo over, but there's nothing on the back. I put the photo back and continue going through the box.

"Anything?" Nick asks after a while.

I shake my head. "Nothing really. I've got one more drawer to go through, but nothing so far. You?"

"I'm not sure," Nick says. "Let's keep going."

As I go through the last drawer, I wonder what he means by that. Is he keeping information from me? Did he find something important? Am I just being paranoid? Maybe he just doesn't want to talk too much. It might alert someone that we are here.

The bottom drawer has nothing but files of receipts. Nothing special. A total waste. I stand and stretch, looking around the room. Alohalani's entire life is in this one room. I don't know anything about him. Was he married? Did he have children? I couldn't remember seeing a ring on his finger—but some musicians don't like playing with jewelry on. I scan the walls for personal photos—something with a woman or kids. There's nothing there.

I feel the dull pain of regret. I should've reached out and persisted in getting to know him. Instead of avoiding Alohalani, I should've tried harder to find out what he was like. Now I'll never know. My last memory of him is his face, grimacing as he died.

There are four ukuleles on the walls and two on the floor, sitting on stands. I run my finger over a beautiful soprano. No dust. He took really good care of his instruments. I drool over the pristine Lanikai koa-wood ukulele. This is a $1,000 instrument. It's so hard not to take it down and strum. He has a beautiful Kamaka pineapple uke just begging to release its mellow tones. There's a lovely Pono rosewood tenor ukulele shimmering in the moonlight. The last ukulele intrigues me. It's a cigar-box uke, and it looks like perhaps Alohalani made it.

I check out the two ukuleles on the floor. They're both vintage, from the 1930s, when ukuleles made a comeback. Not worth a lot of money but full of sentimental value to their owner, I'm sure. I lift one up automatically and once again consider playing, when I remember that I can't. We have to maintain silence, or we'll be discovered.

I'm just about to put the uke back on the stand, when I hear something rattling inside. That's odd. Why would there be anything inside the uke? Very gently, I turn the instrument upside down, and a folded piece of paper falls into my hand.

After replacing the ukulele, I start to unfold the paper. Is this garbage that somehow got tossed inside? Or was it put there on purpose? I take the paper to the desk and smooth it out. Nick sees what I'm doing and shines his flashlight on it.

It's a photo of the Overlook, where Leilani was murdered. The words are clear, as if written only yesterday. In black ink, scrawled in a masculine hand, is the word *ki'i'lua.*

"What is ki'i'lua?" I ask Nick.

"It means *deceiver.*" He draws the photo closer to his face.

"This doesn't seem like it could be his notes on the murders. He must have more than this, right?" I ask. Okay—so I was expecting a well-written tome on who killed Kua and Leilani and how. A girl can dream...

Nick shrugs. "It doesn't look like notes, but it might be a clue."

I fold up the photo exactly as it was and shove it into my pants pocket and begin going through the sheet music on the shelves. There's some really rare stuff here. I'm very careful with the old manuscripts.

That's weird... I pick up a new piece. "Ukulele Lady?" You've got to be kidding me. Among all this amazing music is this 1925 standard written by mainlanders. Why would he have this?

My thoughts are interrupted by the sound of the doorknob turning. We freeze. Uh-oh. We never checked the door to see if it was locked. The knob twists one way and then the other. It is locked. That's a relief.

Until the first blow shakes the door in its frame. Someone is trying to kick the door in.

Nick shoves me toward the window, and I dive through, huddling beneath the window as he lands be-

side me. There's a splintering roar, and I can hear someone moving around the office now. Whoever wanted in
certainly got their way.

"Should we see who it is?" Nick whispers so slightly
I barely hear it.

I'm paralyzed with fear. Light bursts through the window, puddling on the grass. Whoever is in there is rooting
around like a wild boar. I cringe to think of those pre-
cious instruments and ancient music manuscripts being
flung around like rags.

"Nani?" Nick is staring at me. Oh right, he asked me
something.

I shake my head. "Too dangerous."

Nick looks up at the window. I can tell he's torn between wanting to see who is inside and running. I, however, am not. I start to creep along the wall, standing up
once I clear the window. Nick does the same. We turn
the corner, and Nick pulls my arm back. He points at
the woods across from the window.

"We might be able to see something without being
observed," he whispers in my ear.

I can't tell if I'm tingling because of his close prox-
imity or because I'm terrified. Probably terrified. Nick
has strange ideas about dates.

"Okay." I nod. The foliage is thick, and we're dressed
in black. We should be able to move around unseen.

It seems to take forever for us to cross to the woods
and then move very slowly so as not to disturb the foliage as we work our way to being directly across from
the window. It's a ways away. But we can just make out
a human shape moving around in the office.

"Can you see who it is?" I ask shakily.

Is this the murderer? The thought makes bile rise in my throat. Has he come back to get something? And if so, is that something why the Terrible Trio was murdered?

"I can't see anything," Nick says as he peers through the branches.

We watch the dark shape move back and forth in the window. Whoever it is, he's getting angry now. A book flies through the air, hitting the wall with a crash. This is followed by a frustrated shriek. Whoever is there didn't find what he wanted.

"Hey!" a man's voice shouts off to our right.

We shrink into the greenery. The light goes out in the office.

"Campus security!" a man shouts. He's closer now. Is he yelling at us or the guy in Alohalani's office?

A man in uniform comes running across the lawn toward the window. We see a shaft of light as the intruder opens the door and disappears. The security guard shines his flashlight through the window, then turns and runs around the side of the building.

"That was close." I shudder.

Nick puts his arm around me and pulls me against him. I welcome it. I feel a little safer now. We stay for another five minutes, then shed our gloves and hats in an attempt to appear more normal (I'm pretty sure the merchant marines costume-ball thing won't work here), and then we emerge from the woods and run for the SUV. The minute we are inside, Nick pulls out of the parking spot and drives away. I look behind to see if anyone is following us.

"I think we're in the clear," I say in a normal voice for the first time in what feels like hours.

"Are you all right?" Nick asks as we pull out onto the freeway and soon blend with all the other cars.

"I think so," I say slowly. "Yeah. I guess I am."

"That was close." Nick whistles.

I nod. "I can't believe we did that."

"When the guy was breaking down the door, I thought we were goners," Nick admits.

"Do you think it was the killer?" I wonder.

Nick nods. "It has to be. He must be looking for those notes Alohalani told you about. If you're right, and the killer was eavesdropping, then he knows that something in that office will implicate him."

"This is crazy," I say. The adrenaline is wearing off, and for some reason I start to laugh.

Nick laughs too. "That's a fact. Definitely the most dangerous thing I've ever done."

"Me too." My laughter fades. Now I feel like collapsing. I'm overcome with a fatigue that won't let up.

At least I still have that photo of the Overlook. The killer didn't get that. Not that I have any idea what it means…

"The sheet music!" I snap my fingers, which, when wearing rubber gloves, sounds like two balloons rubbing together.

"What are you talking about?"

I shrug. "It's probably nothing. But I found some music that certainly didn't belong there." I tell him about finding "Ukulele Lady."

"Do you have it? The notes might be in there," Nick asks hopefully.

"No. I dropped it the minute I heard the doorknob turning." Damn. How did I let that happen? The killer probably has it now.

"It's okay." Nick pats me on the back. "I think we should check out Leilani's house."

"What? After that? You've got to be kidding!" I protest. The last thing I want to do is go through this all over again.

"I'm not. Remember, this killer broke into your house too. Now Alohalani's office. Maybe he tossed Leilani's house too."

I shudder. "I don't think going to Leilani's will help. Besides, if the killer has already been there, we won't find anything. Not that we know what we're looking for, that is."

"Then maybe he dropped something or missed something."

I stare at him. "You're really enjoying this turn as a cat burglar, aren't you?"

Nick grins. "Come on. I know it sounds crazy, but I have a gut feeling we should look there."

"I'm not sure your gut is qualified to make a decision like that."

He shrugs. "Nevertheless, I'd like to check it out. It's not very far from here. And we know the owner isn't coming home."

Ugh. Do I really want to search a dead woman's house, just because my so-called boyfriend has a hunch? And what's next? We break into Kua's and Alohalani's houses?

"I know it sounds crazy," Nick says. "But it's just a short distance from here. It can't hurt to try."

"How do you know it's close by?"

"I looked it up," Nick says.

I look at him. It doesn't make any sense to go there. But Nick is convinced we should try. And what if he's right? What if we find something? I have no idea what that could be, but on the other hand, no one lives there, so why not?

"All right," I decide. "Let's go now before I change my mind." And then be done with it. After tonight I promise never to break into anywhere again. Nancy Drew be damned.

FOURTEEN

It TAKES US a few tries to find Leilani's house. The cottage isn't visible from the street, but we find a dirt road that gets us there. Tucked in behind some banyan trees, the house is hard to find. Especially in the dark.

"This is good," Nick says as he turns off the car. "No one should see us up here."

"I'm not sure 'good' is the word I'd use." Shadows move against the house. It's definitely freaking me out. But I get out of the car and quietly close the door.

The house is tiny, but that isn't too unusual. Hawaiians spend most of their time outside, so a small house isn't a big deal like it is on the mainland. Nick turns on his flashlight, and I can see the cottage is painted lime green. It's completely dark inside, which makes sense since the owner is deceased and she'd split with her roommates.

"This feels so wrong," I murmur. "Disrespectful too."

Nick whispers, "We'll give it a quick once-over and get out. I promise."

He leads the way to the front door and tries the knob. Locked.

"You take the right side, and I'll take the left," he

says. "If there's a window open, text me. If not, meet me at the back door."

I do that cartoon gulp. You know the one I'm talking about. And it's loud. But I agree. As Nick goes one way, I go the other. There are two windows on my side, and I slide a gloved hand over each one. Neither one budges. I don't hold out much hope for the back door being unlocked but proceed on anyway.

It's eerily still outside. No rustle of animals in the undergrowth nor the sound of birds in the trees. The moon that illuminated all those shadows earlier has disappeared behind some clouds. If it wasn't for Nick's flashlights, I'd be stumbling over everything.

Leilani didn't have much of a garden, but she didn't really seem like the type. If she did grow anything, I'd imagine it would be hemlock or belladonna. I slip around to the back and see Nick at the door, waiting for me. He twists the knob. It doesn't yield.

I spot a mat on the steps and yank it up. A key gleams in the flashlight beam. Nick picks it up and inserts it into the lock. We hear the telltale click. We're in business.

Once inside, I close all the curtains while Nick turns on his flashlight. We're in a tiny but very clean kitchen. The walls are citrus yellow, and the table and countertops a lime green that match the outside paint job. No dirty dishes sit in the sink—nothing to indicate it has even been used.

The kitchen is open on one side, leading into a dining room. The table is covered with sheet music, packages of replacement strings, electric tuners, and a few capos and straps. Three ukuleles hang on the wall, inside their cases. The table and chairs are simple oak. A tile floor is the only other hint of décor. We violate a strict code by not removing our shoes when we entered. No way am I leaving a pair of shoes behind if we have to run. Besides, it isn't like anyone lives here anymore. I think about that. Leilani's roommates had split with her and were living in Lihue. I wonder why they didn't come here to live with her. But then, that would be pretty far from where they work.

"You check out this room," Nick whispers. "I'll sweep the rest of the house."

I nod and start to go through the music on the table. It's nothing special—certainly not like the museum-quality music Alohalani had. In fact, most of it is junk—the same-old, same-old stuff we usually get as requests: "Lovely Hula Hands," "Ain't She Sweet," "Somewhere over the Rainbow"—not a lot of imaginative stuff. In fact, it's a pretty cheesy collection. It only shores up my conviction that Leilani had no imagination.

Why would she keep this cheap music around? Didn't she have it all memorized by now? No matter how many sheets I go through, it's all the same. Nothing interesting. There should be some contemporary and classical music here, but if there once was, it's now gone.

I look around. If I didn't see her ukes in here, I'd think she kept her more important music somewhere else. But her instruments and accessories are all in this room. Why would she put anything anywhere else?

"There isn't much else to the house," Nick says, making me jump about three feet in the air. Okay, so it was more like a few inches.

"Just the living room, a bathroom, and a bedroom. No basement or attic," Nick says.

"Any music or any instruments anywhere else?" I ask.

He shakes his head. "But you should go check it out yourself."

No time like the present. I don't want to stay here one second more than I have to. I step into the living room and look around. There's a small flat-screen TV on the wall opposite a shabby love seat and two club chairs. The coffee table has a remote on it but nothing else. Something strikes me as weird, but I can't put my finger on it. It may be the stark emptiness of the room. There are no pictures on the walls. No tchotchkes of any kind. No personal effects.

Everyone has some personal keepsakes in their homes. Don't they? Even if it's just one or two things. But there's nothing here to even say Leilani lived here. Were there family members who already came and got her things? I inspect the walls, but there are no faded spots where pictures once hung...not even any holes where nails might've been.

The bathroom is very small. A stall shower, sink, and toilet. One sad towel hangs near the sink, and there's a bar of soap in a dish. Nothing else. The medicine cabinet has a bottle of aspirin and a jar of face cream. That's it.

Last, but not least, is the bedroom. Apparently Leilani loved the color orange, because absolutely everything in the room is a bright, glaring version of that color. The walls, carpet, and bedspread look like a bunch of orange popsicles melted onto everything. There is one dresser that's a darker burnt orange, but everything else holds on to the neon theme. It almost hurts my eyes to look at it.

Again—there are no photos or personal effects. In the dresser there's nothing but socks and underwear. I move to the closet and look. A couple of T-shirts, skirts, and two dresses are the only occupants. One pair of flip-flops sits on the floor. A harness and some coiled rope suggest that Leilani actually did stuff outside. She must've tried rock climbing. It was odd to think of her with a hobby. But then, she'd always been pretty fit. She had to get that way somehow.

Had someone come here and started packing up? The fact that things are still on hangers and in drawers make me realize that whoever it was will probably be back. As I close the drawers on the bureau, something thuds. I find an envelope taped to the back.

"What's that?" Nick asks behind me, causing me to jump one more time.

"You have to quit sneaking up on me!"

"Sorry. What is it?" He points to the envelope.

I turn my attention back to it. The seal is broken, so we won't tip anyone off if we open it ourselves. I pull out a single photo.

"Oh, wow" is all I can say.

"What on earth?" Nick says.

There's a photo of Kua, but I get the impression that he didn't know he was being photographed at the time. There are other people in the background. They kind of look like the Sea Dogs we saw when we met Todd in Princeville.

"Why would she have this? Leilani hated Kua. And why hide it?

Leilani was following Kua and took a picture of him. But why? Was she obsessed with him? Did Leilani have feelings for Kua? If so, it never, ever showed. It didn't make any sense.

No writing on the back of the photo. Weird.

"Maybe she was blackmailing him?" Nick asks.

I shake my head. "He's not doing anything worth blackmailing." For all I knew, Leilani just took the picture to practice voodoo on him.

"We'd better put it back," Nick says, and I agree.

There seems to be no reason to take it with us, and if a reason turns up later, we can always drop hints to the police on where to find it. I fasten the envelope back on the drawer and turn it back against the wall.

We work our way back to the kitchen. This is a total bust. We've broken into her house for nothing. Nothing at all. The only thing I've gotten out of this mess is the knowledge that Leilani didn't have a torture chamber in her bedroom or a scary dungeon filled with alligators in the basement. I must say—I'm pretty surprised. Leilani was somewhat fairly normal.

"We should check the kitchen before we leave." Nick looks at his watch. "It's getting late. Let's do it quickly." He backtracks, making sure we didn't leave any trace of our visit before joining me in the kitchen.

I nod and start pulling out drawers as Nick goes through the cabinets. We find nothing but flatware, cups, and plates. I shove the last drawer shut a little too hard and something flutters out.

"It was stuck under the drawer," I say as I retrieve it. From the back, I can see it's another photo.

Nick looks out the window. "I see headlights at the bottom of the hill!"

I stuff the photo into my back pocket just as he grabs my arm and shoves me out the back door, turning off the lights before he joins me. We run like we're on fire and scramble into the SUV. Nick tears out of the drive the opposite direction from where we came. Is there anything at the other end of this road?

He turns off the lights and pulls off the road, plunging into a grove of banana trees. Nick shuts off the engine, and we wait.

"Maybe it's someone who lives up here," I say quietly.

"I hope so," Nick breathes.

A flash of light hits the road behind us, and we both duck down. We wait, but no one passes. After about ten minutes, Nick eases the SUV back onto the road and drives up the hill, continuing in the opposite direction from whence we came. There are no other houses. In fact, the road ends with a huge sign that says, *Kapu! Trespassers will be shot.*

"We have to go back down," I whisper. "And that means past her house."

"Or we could wait up here all night." Nick gives me a look.

Much as I'd love to hang with him all night, I'm far too worried about whoever made that sign and being discovered by whoever's at Leilani's house.

"Maybe it's her family coming to get the rest of her stuff?" Nick asks.

I glance at my watch and shake my head. "At one o'clock in the morning? I doubt it."

"What if it's the same guy from Alohalani's office? Maybe he's worried that Leilani had ideas on who killed Kua? Or he could be lying low here, knowing that Leilani isn't coming back."

I think about that for a moment. If the Terrible Trio were all killed by the same guy, what could they have that he needs?

"I think we should go," I say finally. "I'd rather drive and be discovered than get trapped here, waiting for someone to kill us."

Nick agrees and turns off the headlights, proceeding back down the dirt road. We hold our breath as we pass Leilani's house. A white car is sitting in the driveway. The lights in the house are out, but we can see a flashlight beam bouncing around inside.

"Whoever it is definitely isn't supposed to be here, or they'd turn on the lights," I say.

"Didn't you say something about a white sedan earlier?" Nick asks.

I nod. It looks like the same car I saw following me to the college. It's quite a coincidence, but it's too dark, so I can't be sure. We pause for a moment, wondering what to do.

"Maybe we should check it out?" Nick asks.

I really want to know who's been following me all day, but I'm completely beat, and my nerves are shot.

"I don't know if that's such a good idea…"

"Aren't you curious?" Nick asks.

I shake my head. "Quite frankly, I'm terrified."

To my surprise, Nick jumps out of the car and walks up toward the house. Whoa. I thought we were acting as a team! Is he ignoring what I think about this?

Before I can complain, Nick jumps back into the car, and we pull out.

"What just happened?" I ask a little crankily.

He smiles. "I got the license plate number. Just in case."

"We could hand that over to the detective!" I get it. Okay, I'm not mad at him anymore. That may be the smartest thing we've done this whole evening.

Nick continues to drive. It's very slow going. Without moonlight, the road is hard to see. After a couple of minutes, Nick turns on the headlights and drives faster until he meets the highway. We ride in silence, each wondering what just happened, until Nick pulls into my driveway. The lights are off in my house, which means Mom's asleep. That's the best thing that has happened all night.

"Hey." I sit up and look at Nick. "You said you found something in Alohalani's office! What is it?"

Nick snaps his fingers and pulls out his phone. He pulls up a photo and shows it to me. It's a birth certificate belonging to one Lori Finnegan. She was born in Canada to Irish immigrants.

"What is this? And why did Alohalani have it?" I ask.

Nick shrugs. "I don't know, but it seemed so out of character that I took a picture of it."

"What did you do with the original?"

"I put it back on the bookshelf. It was sandwiched between two sheets of music."

A heavy sigh escapes my lips, and I slump into my

seat. "I have no idea if we got anything we can use. Was it all for nothing?"

"I don't think so," Nick says. "We know that someone else was at both places, looking for something tonight. I think that's because the guy who followed you to Alohalani's this afternoon is following us now to see what we're doing. That's significant. We found out that Leilani had an unnatural obsession with Kua."

"But we're in a different car. That vehicle followed me when I was in my car. How did they know we took this SUV?"

Nick frowned. "They must've been watching us. They think we know something. And we do. You found a clue."

The photo I found in Leilani's kitchen!

I pull it out of my pocket and turn on the overhead light.

"What the..." I whisper through chattering teeth. I'm shaking. Is it because the adrenaline is gone? Or is it the fact that I'm looking at a photo of myself.

Leilani took a picture of me and hid it in her house. A picture of me sitting on my lanai with a ukulele—it's difficult to see because of the distance from which it was taken.

Why would she have this, and what was she doing sneaking around my backyard?

FIFTEEN

"NANI!" MOM'S IN my doorway again.

It's early. Earlier than I normally get up. I can tell by the soft lavender sky outside my window. And since I didn't get home until three thirty or four in the morning, I need more sleep.

"What?" I groan and throw the covers over my head.

"I'm out of rum," Mom says.

I peek out from under the blankets. "Are you serious? No liquor store will be open at this time." I look at my alarm clock. "Six a.m. I'll get up in a few hours and go."

I turn away from her, intending to go back to sleep.

Mom's not having any of it. "There's that twenty-four hour place on the other side of town."

"Great," I grumble. "I'll go in a few hours."

"But I want it now! Vera and I are going to go golfing, and she's coming here for a quick cocktail first!"

This gets my attention. "You? Golfing? Since when do you golf?"

Mom narrows her eyes. "I golf."

"Because I've never, never, ever seen you with so much as a golf club," I start. "Because I've never known you to play golf. Because I'm pretty sure you think the ball is made of cheese."

Mom puts her hands on her hips. "Are you going to go get the rum, or shall I?"

That gets me out of bed. Last time she went shopping, she started drinking as she went. By the time she got to the checkout, she tried to pay with Tic Tacs and told everyone that aliens had landed.

"Fine. I'll go. But next time, you have to give me more notice than this."

I swing my legs over the edge of the bed and yawn.

"Well!" Mom puts on her shocked act. "I had no idea I'd need rum today! I can't predict the future, you know!"

"That's not what you told everyone at the farmers' market when they sold all the eggs before you got there. You said you were going to run for office and make every chicken on the island lay twice as many eggs."

It occurs to me I shouldn't let Mom go out much. Maybe I should nix this golfing trip. Nah. Let Vera deal with her. It's just golf. She's not likely to decorate the country club with pink flamingos or coconuts. I've got bigger problems than that.

Unfortunately, I'm out of cash. I track down Mom's purse in the living room. The flamingos are gone. Instead, in the middle of the living room is a huge wooden tiki god. At least that's something I can put in the garden when she's tired of it. I would wonder where the coconuts or flamingos went, but I discover that I don't care.

On my drive over to the store, I think about last night. And the photo. I'll never forget the photo of me in my own backyard.

Why in the name of all that is holy did Leilani take a picture of me? And why in that setting? It couldn't be blackmail. I wasn't doing anything. Well, okay, I was doing something, but I wasn't doing anything abnormal or illegal.

I get out of the car and stomp sullenly into the store. A 24/7 box store, it has everything you could ever need at any time of day or night. I pick up a bottle of rum and head to check out. Why is the line so long so early in the morning? There are four people in front of me. In Aloha Lagoon at sixish in the morning, that's a stampede.

"Excuse me," a man's voice says. I swivel to see Robby Lugosi standing behind me. His wife is nowhere to be seen. A little shiver runs through me. This is quite a co-incidence. Is this guy following me? Weird.

"Aren't you that musician from the other day?" he asks with more animation than he'd had at his own wedding.

"Yes, that's right." I hide the bottle of rum behind my back. "How's the honeymoon going?"

"Oh, okay," he says. He's holding a container of whipped cream, duct tape, and a package of pencils. That's a weird combo for so early in the day. Hell, that's weird for any time of day. But I couldn't say much with a bottle of booze behind my back.

"Do you know the area very well?" Robby asks.

Great. The man was a blob at his wedding, but now he wants to make small chat.

"I've only lived here a year," I answer apologetically. Yes, I know the area well. No, I don't want to get roped into being some kind of tour guide for the Lugosis.

"It's just that I was thinking of trying surfing. Up in Princeville. Do you know anything about that?"

I look him up and down. This is the last person on earth I'd ever picture on a surf board. And it sounds like he isn't taking his new wife with him.

"There are beaches down by the resort. They even have instructors, so you don't need to go all the way to Princeville."

I turn back to face the register. I hope he gets the hint.

He doesn't. "I've heard about a dangerous gang called the Sea Dogs. I hear they aren't too happy with beginners. Surfers, that is."

"I'd stay away from them then." I turn only halfway to face him. "In fact, I think they usually surf in Princeville. So you really should stick to Aloha Lagoon."

Secretly I will the checkout clerk to go faster so I can get away from this guy. Either that or I'll have to break out the rum and start drinking now. Mom wouldn't like that.

"Did you know those two ukulele players who got murdered?" Robby says. This guy really can change the subject at the drop of the hat.

"Three." I step up to the checker. Finally.

"Excuse me?" Robby asks behind me.

I pay for the booze and pick up the bag. "Three. There have been three murders here—all ukulele players." Now why did I tell him that? It's so early I can't think straight.

"Sounds like you're in a dangerous line of work." Robby stares at me with a blank face.

I get the distinct impression that he's not joking. Pastor Dan should start screening couples for weirdness or insanity.

"Nice seeing you." I nod as I race out to the car.

I start the engine and hit the gas. I can't get away fast enough. What was that all about? The man wouldn't shut up. Maybe he's just lonely, and with a wife like that I'd believe it. But talking about the Sea Dogs and recently deceased? I...

An image pops into my brain. I pull into a parking lot and turn around, full steam ahead for Nick's place. I need to talk to him. Right now.

Vera answers the door. "Nani! How nice to see you! I'm just heading over to your house."

"Here." I shove the bag with the liquor into her arms. "Mom needs this. Is Nick home?"

"Nani?" Nick steps up. He looks like he's ready to go to work. "Come in!"

Vera excuses herself and takes the bag with her.

"What is it?" he asks.

I tell him about my strange encounter in the store with Robby Lugosi.

"That is weird," he says. "But I don't get what you're doing here."

"The Sea Dogs! Remember that photo we found behind Leilani's dresser? The Sea Dogs were in the picture!"

Nick's eyes grow wide. "That's right. I remember that now."

"Well, maybe Leilani was blackmailing Kua for his involvement in that gang! Maybe he was running drugs or something!"

"That might explain why Leilani's dead," Nick agrees. "The gang could've killed Kua to cover up their activities and Leilani to keep her quiet...permanently. But it doesn't explain why they framed you or killed Alohalani."

"But it may explain the break-in at Leilani's house last night!" To be totally honest, I'm a little excited that I might've figured something out.

"We'll have to think about that." He kisses my forehead. It's nice. So nice, that I am still standing there. Like an idiot.

"I'm sorry, Nani." Nick frowns. "But I've got to get to work. We're getting some new plants in from Maui today, and I've got to be there."

"Oh." I try to hide my disappointment. "Right. You go. I'll give this more thought."

Nick stops and looks into my eyes. "Why don't you head over to the resort and talk to Julia Kekoa, the activities coordinator. With the Terrible Three gone, she'll be desperate to book someone for the big luaus and on-site weddings."

"You don't think that's a bit tasteless?" I ask.

He shakes his head. "I don't. They'll need someone fast. Besides, that guy we talked to in Princeville, Pauli, might score the job before you do."

"That's not a bad idea..." I say. "Okay. I'll run home, grab my résumé, and head over."

Nick grins. "Then you can meet me for lunch. Say noon at the Loco Moco? I'll buy to celebrate our little breakthrough on the case."

I can't help but smile. "It's a date."

Mom and Vera are gone by the time I get home, thank goodness. I need to get organized. Hitting the resort now would be a good idea. They'll need someone soon. The resort always seems to have big events on the weekends. I change my clothes, check myself in the mirror, toss my résumé into a briefcase, and head out.

On my way over, I practice what I could say to the activities coordinator that doesn't sound like I'm a total weirdo and possible serial murderer.

I guess you need a new musician now that the others are dead...

Sorry to hear about Kua and Leilani—but the good news is I'm available to fill in...

Ugh. It's no use. I'll just have to wing it and hope Ms. Kekoa doesn't call the police.

I pull up to the front of the resort and get out. I love this place. It's beautifully designed and has some of the most picturesque views of the ocean on Kauai. The architect must've been a genius. Almost every room has a view of the ocean. That's not easy to pull off.

"Hello." Roberta Lugosi is standing on the lanai.

"Mrs. Lugosi, isn't it?" Why am I running into them today? And why aren't they together?

The woman nods. "That's right. You did our wedding the other day."

"I hope you're enjoying your honeymoon." I've got nothing. Her husband burned through all my small-talk material earlier.

"It's nice," she says absently. "My husband... Robby... he's sick with the flu. I'm going to check out the surfing lessons here."

Um...her husband just told me he was going surfing. This couple is definitely weird. And she certainly didn't look like the type who'd take up surfing. Or any new sport.

"Good luck." I try to end the conversation. "There's an instructor here at the resort."

Roberta looks at me curiously, as if I just spoke to her in Swahili. After a few seconds she nods and walks away. What is with these people? I definitely need to talk to Pastor Dan about screening couples. I shake my head and walk inside to the lobby.

"Is the activities coordinator in?" I ask the front desk. The man behind the counter nods politely and disappears into the back room.

Okay. Showtime. A young woman about my age with a pleasant smile walks up to me, holding out her hand. I shake it.

"Hello, I'm Julia Kekoa. How can I help you?" she asks.

I like her immediately. Something about her seems so friendly and approachable. *Please let me land this gig!* I'd love to work for sane folks.

"I'm Nani Johnson. I'm a professional ukulele musician. I thought maybe you'd have an opening?"

Oh my God. Why did I say that? What's wrong with me? She's probably pushing a panic button under the desk.

"Come on back." Julia leads me around the counter into the back office. She sits and motions for me to do the same. Well, at least I got in the door. And Detective Ray isn't in here waiting to pounce with *Aha! I knew it!*

"I'm sorry. That probably sounded bad," I say. "I'm aware of the horrible murders. This probably isn't the best time…"

She waves me off. "It's okay. Really. I know what you meant. And we do desperately need someone for the luau this weekend. Are you available?"

I nod. "Absolutely." I hand her my résumé. "I assume you'll want to check my references…"

"You went to Juilliard?" Julia asks as she looks the document over. "Impressive. And you've been teaching lessons and working at the Blue Hawaii Chapel. That's really all I need to know. Can you start immediately? Would you be interested in teaching lessons here?"

"Really? That's great!" I sound like a moron. And I haven't answered her question.

"Yes! I can start right away."

She rises from her chair. "I'll pass this on to our HR division, and we'll get in touch with you about the luau. I'll make a copy for Alexander—our leisure groups co-ordinator—in regard to the lessons."

"Thank you!" This went better than I hoped. "I look forward to hearing from them!"

She leads me back to the lobby and shakes my hand again before the front desk calls her over. I'm in! I can't believe it. I thought it would take years. Instead it took three murders.

What is wrong with me? Couldn't I show a bit of humility? I certainly didn't want it to work out this way.

"Hey." Pauli Keo walks up to me. "I know you."

"Aloha." I paste on my biggest smile. Did I get here before him? Was Nick right about him moving into my territory?

"You gonna be working here too?" he asks with a careful grin.

I nod. "Luaus and maybe lessons. You?"

"Three nights a week."

"Great!" I feel like I'm acting a little over the top. "I'll have to check you out." I can feel the blush rising in my cheeks. "I mean check your music out."

"Okay," he says. "See you around."

Pauli walks off, and I watch him. Does he wonder if I killed three performers in order to get their gigs? Hmmm…did *he*? This idea has some merit. I mean, if he can think it, so can I, right?

"So you got the job! Congratulations!" Nick joins me at a table at the Loco Moco for lunch. "I'll get to spend more time with you."

Nick's wearing the resort polo shirt and khakis, and he makes the uniform look good. It feels like we've been seeing each other for months, not days. Murder is a strange matchmaker.

"This is going to be great for us, Nani." His eyes seem to drink me in. Nick is definitely intense.

There's that nervous feeling again. He's coming off a bit too eager. Oh, for crying out loud! Stop being so suspicious, Nani!

We order, and I fill him in on how it went. I leave out the embarrassing parts. I'm not stupid. I just act that way occasionally.

"You're going to Kua's funeral after lunch…" Nick says. "Remember that sometimes the murderer turns up at the funeral of his victim." Now he looks a little worried. Which is really sweet. I'm worried too.

I nod. "I'll keep an eye out. Leilani's funeral is tomorrow, so I'll look for someone who goes to both."

"Good idea," Nick says as the food arrives. "Just be careful. Don't make any citizen's arrests or anything. If you see something suspicious, you should let the detective know."

"I will," I promise. It's nice to have someone other than your crazy, alcoholic mother worry about you.

I'm famished and tear into my burger. Being a suspect in three murders is exhausting. I don't want our relationship to be just about death, so we make small talk until he has to go back to work.

"Did Detective Ray stop by to talk to you yet?" I ask as Nick pays for lunch

"He's coming this afternoon. Maybe I'll find out something. I'll let you know." Nick smiles.

"Why don't you come over after work?" I ask. "I'll throw steaks on the grill, and we can share what happens this afternoon."

"That sounds perfect."

Nick kisses me on the lips, only for a moment. But I feel my body respond to him. I go all squishy inside, giggling like a schoolgirl as he walks away. He kissed me. Not on the forehead, but on my actual lips. Maybe tonight we'll just relax. Not talk about the case. Act like a man and woman on a sort of date.

Now, I just have to go to the funeral of a man I loathed. A man who people think I murdered. Piece of cake, right?

My cell rings as Nick disappears from view.

"Binny." I sigh. "I'm glad it's you."

"Who were you expecting?" my friend says.

"I'm always expecting the police these days. How's it going? When do you get back?"

"I'm at your house, waiting to go to the funeral with you."

It feels like a boulder has been lifted off my shoulders. "You cut your trip short to go with me?" Once again today, I'm happy for something I shouldn't be. When all this guilt catches up with me, I'm probably going to have a stroke.

"It's all right. Mom doesn't need me. But you do."

She's right. I do need her. More than she suspects.

SIXTEEN

ON THE WAY to the services, I tell Binny about Alohalani's murder. My best friend's mouth drops open as I describe the scene. She's horrified. For a moment, I think she's going to freak out, but she keeps it together. I don't know what I'd do without her.

Kua's funeral is held beachside, not far from the resort. It's my first since I've moved here, but Binny has filled me in on proper protocol. Tradition dictates that after the ceremony, the friends and family paddle out on the ocean—in a boat or on surfboards—and scatter the ashes.

Leis are placed around our necks as we arrive. Binny whispers to me that after the thing with the ashes, we will throw our leis into the sea. As the ceremony starts, I look around to see who is here.

I don't know most of the people. It seems to be a lot of family, but I'm not sure. I'm not surprised to see Todd Chay from the interview list here. He told us he knew Kua. I am surprised to see some of the gang members from the Sea Dogs present. But then they surfed with him, so maybe it's not that weird. I'd have to ask Binny about that later.

Detective Ray makes eye contact with me, and I try

to act casual. He's a respectful distance from the rest of us. It makes sense that he'd be here. Like Nick said—the murderer sometimes comes to the funeral of his victim. Of course that implicates me, but maybe I'll get lucky and the detective will overlook that.

The minister alternates between the Hawaiian language and English. I don't understand much of it, but I nod when everyone else does. In fact, I'm just starting to get the hang of it, when I see her. A woman standing on the other side of the crowd. At least, I think it's a woman. She's wearing a large black hat with a veil that obscures her face. Her dress is black and billowy, hiding the shape of her body. She shows no reaction. She just stands there, observing. Like she's the only star of a weird art film.

Who is she? Besides being someone who doesn't want to be recognized, that is. I can just make out the outline of oversized black sunglasses beneath the veil. Maybe she's a love interest or maybe a family member whose mourning runs very deep. I can't tell. The woman just seems out of place here. But since this is my first Hawaiian funeral, it's possible that the woman's presence is part of the tradition.

Binny nudges me, and I realize that people are climbing into a large boat. I follow her lead and take my seat with the others. Detective Ray doesn't join us. Neither does the lady in black. A couple of elderly people also remain on the shore. My guess is that it isn't mandatory to participate in this part of the ceremony.

As we row out to sea, I can't help watching the detective on the shore. His eyes are on the boat and probably on me. Is he waiting for me to come back so he can take me in? I look for the woman in black, but she's vanished.

The Sea Dogs and some other surfers paddle out to sea on surfboards. Does the detective suspect the gang of Kua's murder? I know it's wrong to hope for that, but I do. I want the suspicion off of me.

The minister says a few words in Hawaiian, then nods to an old woman at the front of the boat. Could it be Kua's mother? She lifts an urn and empties ash into the ocean. All at once, everyone removes their leis and tosses them overboard. We sail back to the beach in silence.

"What do you think?" Binny asks as we walk to my car.

We'd decided not to go to the dinner announced by the family. I'd feel like a fraud being there, and I'm fairly certain Kua wouldn't want me to go. It's the least I can do for him.

"Did you see the Sea Dogs?" I ask. "And Todd Chay was there too."

Binny nods. "I noticed. Do you think they killed him?" She turns and looks out at the ocean where the men are still sitting on their surfboards.

"I don't know. They seem too reverent about the whole thing to have killed him."

"I see what you mean." Binny's eyes are still on the surfers, who've now formed a circle and are clasping hands.

"The good detective spotted me." I put my seat belt on. "But he didn't approach me. I thought he would."

Binny shakes her head. "It can't be that bad. Not yet."

I change the subject. "What was the story with the

woman dressed all in black? Is that part of the ceremony?"

"I've never seen her before." Binny frowns. "My guess
is she's family, but it's weird that anyone would come
dressed like that."

We drove back to my house, and I filled her in on our
nocturnal burglaries the night before. Binny says nothing, but she looks freaked out. I guess if she told me
she'd been breaking into strange places in the middle
of the night, I'd feel the same way.

Mom isn't home. She left a note—something about
going to a luau in Hanalei with Vera. I'm secretly relieved. It means that Nick, Binny, and I can speak openly
about our little investigation.

I'm happy that Mom has found a friend in Vera. Maybe
being part of a twosome might make her a little less crazy.
Perseverance Woodfield might be the best thing that's
happened to me. Well, except for Nick, that is.

The steaks are sizzling on the grill, and Binny and I
are lounging on the lanai when Nick arrives. He'd gone
home and changed out of his work clothes and now looks
ridiculously hot in a fitted black T-shirt and khaki shorts.
He runs his right hand through his dark hair, tousling it
boyishly. Nick adds a sly smile and a wink, and it makes
me tingly inside. Brandishing two bottles of wine, he
joins us.

It's a warm Kauai night. Not too hot, not chilly.
Breezes come and go, and I begin to unwind. The sun
is low in the sky, giving the flowers in my garden an
ethereal glow. This really is paradise. I know that sounds
cliché, but it's true. Even with all my problems, it's im-

possible to be depressed. And even though it won't be easy, I'm determined to stay here and make Aloha Lagoon my forever home.

"How did it go?" Nick asks as we set the table.

Binny and I fill him in on Kua's funeral. It feels strange and kind of disrespectful to talk about it. I know I didn't kill him, but other people's perceptions tainted my appearance at the ceremony, and I felt guilty.

For some reason, when we're through, Nick seems interested more in the Sea Dogs and Todd Chay than the lady dressed in black.

"Maybe Todd did it." He sits, unfolding a napkin in his lap. "I didn't get the impression from him that he and Kua were close."

"I don't know," Binny says. "It could have been one of the Sea Dogs."

I shake my head. "I didn't get a vibe off of any of them. The Sea Dogs even performed their own private ceremony after." A memory pops into my head.

"Did I tell you I ran into the other Lugosi this afternoon?"

"What are you talking about?" Binny asks.

I tell the two of them about both encounters with the bland couple. "Robby was interested in the Sea Dogs. You might be onto something there, Binny."

Nick shakes his head. "Then this investigation is over. Those guys are dangerous. There's no way we should get involved with them."

I think about this for a moment. "There was the lady in black…"

"That was weird," Binny agrees. "She was covered from head to toe. We couldn't describe her if we had to."

"She was definitely hiding something. Who goes anywhere dressed like that in this day and age?" I ask.

"There's no way to find out who she is unless she turns up again," Binny says.

"Do you think it's one of Leilani's former roommates—Gina or Elizabeth?" I ask. "I just couldn't buy that they loved her that much. Leilani was too horrible."

Binny nods. "It would be the perfect cover up. Act like they loved her, but secretly, they killed her."

I agree. "If I was her roomie, I'd want her dead. That woman was toxic."

Nick sits back, his plate empty. My mother would call him *a good eater.* Even though she doesn't cook, she appreciates people who eat well. It's one of her many, many peccadillos.

"We should definitely consider Elizabeth and Gina. Remember Alohalani told you that things aren't as they seem? If you're right about them lying to us, that would fit their behavior perfectly." Nick shrugs.

"But that doesn't explain Kua. Or Alohalani." I chew my lip.

"Then perhaps the murders are unrelated," Binny answers. "The Sea Dogs killed Kua, and the roommates killed Leilani, then Alohalani because he knew too much."

"But why frame me? I'd never met Gina or Elizabeth before now."

"Leilani probably complained about you so much"— Nick is getting excited—"that they pegged you as the perfect patsy."

We sit quietly with our thoughts as the sun sets and the solar lights come on. Sure, these explanations might work. But it doesn't feel right. Like a puzzle piece that almost fits but not quite. You shove it into the one remaining hole, but it isn't seamless. That's how this feels.

"My missing ukulele hasn't turned up yet," I think out loud. "Why frame me with my own instrument and have it go missing? Seems to me the killer would want it found."

Nick shrugs. "Maybe he's going to use it again. Or it's a mistake. That could explain a lot with this whole mess."

"I don't know…" I run my hands through my hair. "I'm beat. And we've got Leilani's funeral in the morning."

Binny and Nick help me clean up. It's late before they finally say good-bye. Binny leaves first, promising to come over in time to head to the funeral. Nick looks into my eyes before kissing me. There's that tingle again. This man has definitely lowered my defenses. I press up against him, kissing him back.

"I should go," Nick says finally.

I don't want him to go. But my life is absurdly complicated now. Once the case is solved, maybe we should do a weekend trip to Maui. Get to know each other. Or, if things don't work out, maybe the prison will have conjugal visits.

As I put away the dishes, I notice something on the floor. It's an envelope. Oh right. Mom said this came for me the other day. It must've fallen on the floor. I'd totally forgotten about it. The envelope is completely blank except for my name typed across the front.

The back of the envelope is sealed with tape. That's odd. Maybe the glue didn't work or something.

"I'm home!" Mom shouts from the front door.

"In here," I call out, my eyes still fixed on the envelope.

"Oh, you haven't opened that yet?" Mom asks as she dumps her purse on the counter.

"Where did this come from?"

Mom stares into space. "I don't know. It just showed up somehow. I don't even remember picking it up."

I stare at her. "You don't think that's a little strange?"

"I'm sure it was just in the mailbox or something." Mom rolls her eyes. "By the way, who was just here?"

"Nick and Binny came over for dinner. But they left a while ago."

My mother shakes her head. "No, the car I saw pulling out of the driveway before I turned in."

I shrug. "Maybe it was just someone turning around to go the other way?" I didn't hear a car pull in, but then, I'm pretty distracted.

"That must be it." Mom takes out her earrings and plunks them on the counter. "I just thought it was weird. But maybe not—after all, there are tons of white sedans on the island."

It's as if I've been frozen instantly. I can't move or speak. A white sedan? Could it be coincidence? It couldn't be. In the year I've lived here, I never had so many encounters with one type of car.

"I'm heading to bed. Night, kiddo." Mom doesn't notice that I've turned into a statue. She just kisses me on the cheek and leaves the kitchen.

Maybe Mom's right. There are so many white cars on the island. It's just coincidence. Whoever it was just used our driveway to turn around. That has to be it, or I won't sleep a wink tonight. For a moment, I consider calling Nick or Binny, but they'd be worried and want to come over. I need to get some sleep. That wouldn't happen with Nick here. My chemistry would be all off, and I'd just be keyed up.

Instead, I might as well open this envelope. Sliding a fingernail under the tape, I pry it open and extract a single sheet of paper. It has just one sentence on it: *Back off, or you'll be next.*

Well, that can't be good…

SEVENTEEN

BINNY LOOKS AT me skeptically. "Well, it could be a prank…" We're in her car, driving to the funeral of someone I never liked, possibly even hated.

I shake my head. "Who would prank me? Mom? Vera? You? Nick? I barely know anyone else."

"Do you think Nick left it?" Binny asks. "I've already told you that I think it's weird how he shows up out of the blue and bam, you've got a relationship already."

She has a point. But I don't want it to be true.

"Do you really think Nick's involved somehow?" My mood darkens as I think of that kiss from last night.

Binny shrugs as she pulls into the parking lot of the Presbyterian church. Leilani may be half Hawaiian, but she is also half Irish. It makes sense she'd have a more traditional funeral.

I can't stop thinking about what Binny said. Nick's arrival at this bizarre point in my life could mean something sinister. Or it could be a coincidence.

"All I'm saying," Binny whispers as we sign the guest book, "is, be careful around him until we know a little more."

"There is something else…" I tell Binny about the

white sedan Mom saw coming out of our driveway last night.

Binny's eyes bulge out of her head. Really? The note didn't worry her, but a random car does?

"I think you and your mom should come stay with me for a couple of days."

"Oh. Well, that's very generous of you, but I don't think there's any room." And I don't think Binny would like Mom decorating her house with random things found in Hawaii.

"I have a guest room in my apartment." Binny frowns. "The killer is stalking you. Isn't that obvious?"

I shake my head. "Stalking and listening, yes. But killing me won't help him. He needs me to take the fall for these murders."

"I don't like it." Binny looks around before turning her attention on me. "I don't think you're safe there."

"I'll be extra careful, I promise. Just don't tell Nick yet. I don't want him freaking out."

"If he isn't involved, then he'd want to protect you too. You could stay at his house. I'll bet that place has a dozen guest rooms."

I nod. "Mom would love that. But I'd feel weird asking him."

Binny doesn't like this answer. "I'll keep it from him for now. But if one more 'coincidence' happens, I'll put you in the federal Witness Protection Program myself."

"It's a deal." I nod, glad to end the conversation. "The funeral is about to start. We should go in."

The church is almost completely empty. Elizabeth and Gina sit up front by a very large blaze-orange coffin. Both are crying. I don't see any family—but then I wouldn't know what they looked like. I'd never heard the woman so much as mention parents. I always thought she was raised by rabid hyenas.

"Where should we sit?" Binny asks.

"Not too far up," I plead softly.

Gina and Elizabeth already think I had something to do with Leilani's murder, so there's no point in giving them a physical target. We sit in the middle pews. I look at my watch. The service should start in a few minutes. Where is everyone?

I hear footsteps behind us and notice Todd Chay and Pauli Keo walk in. They see us and head over. To my surprise, Todd sits on Binny's right, and Pauli sits on my left. It's like they're flanking us so we can't get away. We nod to the men but say nothing because now the organ is playing. Out of the corner of my eye, I see Detective Ray walk in and sit down in the pew opposite us.

So this is it? This is the sum of Leilani's life? Six people? That is so sad. I almost feel bad for her. Even if she did bring it all on herself.

The minister steps up to the lectern and motions for us to stand and sing from the hymnal. We make our way through "How Great Thou Art," but I can't help but think this is the strangest funeral I've ever been to.

"Friends, family, and loved ones," the minister says, "we are here to say good-bye to our beloved Leilani O'Flanagan."

I'm guessing he never met the woman, or he wouldn't have said the word "beloved." Gina and Elizabeth burst into loud sobs. Are they acting—or did they really care about her?

"So they must've found her body," Binny breathes in my ear so Todd and Pauli don't hear. She motions to the casket.

"I guess so." I wonder how much of it was left when it washed ashore. Then I stop wondering, because that's nasty.

We sit through the ceremony, singing three more hymns and enduring an extremely long reading from the book of Psalms, when I hear a snort of disgust behind me.

I turn my head to see the lady in black, several pews away. Her arms are folded over her chest, which tells me she is not happy. Maybe she didn't like Leilani either. She's wearing the same clothing, hat, and heavy veil. I can't even begin to make out who she is.

For a moment, I wonder if it's Alohalani's wife, if he had one—which is something I don't know. That would make some sense. If he was married, the wife probably knew Kua and Leilani. She would've met them at concerts or something. My guess is that Leilani wasn't any nicer to her than she was to Alohalani. She could have decided to come to these funerals out of professional courtesy. But why did she completely cover herself? Maybe she's disfigured! Or maybe this is how she mourns.

I decide I like that idea, and I turn back to the proceedings. The minister has just asked people to come up and share their memories of Leilani. I'm not surprised to see Elizabeth jump up and race to the lectern.

"She was a wonderful person and close friend," she sobs. "And her talent was beyond compare. No one on this island came close to her musical talent." She glares at me. "No one."

I decide not to react. It's Leilani's funeral, and I don't need to defend myself against a dead woman. I notice Pauli tense up and wonder what he really thought of Leilani. I'm going to ask him once the funeral is over.

Gina gets up next. She tells this weird story about how Leilani once loaned her a sweater, then told her she could keep it. Gina tells us she's wearing it right now, to honor her friend. Then she says almost exactly the same thing that Elizabeth does—about how kind and thoughtful their late roommate was.

I feel like I'm being punked. How is it possible that these two loved someone as cruel and contemptuous as Leilani? I guess it takes all types. Or like Nick said the night before, they killed her and are acting like this to throw off the police.

I can't tell if it is an acting job, but then I never met these two women until after Leilani was murdered. And if they loved her so much, why did she move out? And if she was out of their lives, why kill her? Maybe it was over that sweater Gina is wearing.

Gina leaves the podium, and the minister asks for someone else to come up. Besides the detective and the creepy woman in black, it's up to the four of us. Binny didn't know her, but Todd, Pauli, and I did.

The silence is getting uncomfortable. Neither Todd nor Pauli makes a move. The minister doesn't seem to realize that now would be a good time to end the funeral. He just stands there, waiting. Elizabeth and Gina finally turn around from the front pew. Their eyes settle on me, and I can feel their hostility drilling into my skull. If hatred could kill, I'd have died the moment I met Kua and Leilani.

Without thinking, I rise to my feet and walk up to the front of the church. Why am I doing this? And worse—what am I going to say? The dead woman hated me. She never said a nice word to me. All she did was put me down.

But my stupid conscience is making me go up and say something. I stand there, looking out at the few people who came to Leilani's funeral, and feel a wave of sympathy for the woman. Everyone in the church is staring at me. The lady in black leans forward as if I'm about to impart some warm, fuzzy story about Leilani.

"Leilani was, as her roommate Elizabeth said, a gifted musician," I say at long last.

Then it occurs to me that I need to say more.

"I've had the good fortune," I lie with as much conviction as I can muster, "to hear her play on many occasions around the island. And each time, I was impressed by her talent and professionalism."

Okay, no need to lay it on that thick. But I can't stop myself. I'm overwhelmed by pity. No one should have such a poor turnout at her funeral. And after the testimonies of Elizabeth and Gina, I realize there must have been something good about her. I have no idea what—maybe she didn't kick puppies more than once, each time.

"I wish I'd gotten to know her better. I'm sure we all wish that now."

What am I saying? I feel like a ventriloquist's dummy. Words I haven't been thinking are coming out of my mouth. Before I go too far, I should wrap it up.

"Aloha, Leilani. Aloha," I finish and step down to walk back to my pew.

Detective Ray has a blank expression—which either means he's good at poker or has the personality of a cow. The lady in black stands and exits the church.

The minister decides he's gotten all he's going to get and steps forward to announce that there will be a short ceremony graveside. He steps down and walks over to the roommates to comfort them. This would be an excellent time to leave.

"Wow," Binny says as we stand to leave. "Just...wow."

I nod. "I know. I think I've been possessed by demons."

"I wondered about that." Binny smiles as we follow Todd out of the pew.

Pauli has gone the other way and is no longer behind me. The detective doesn't move, making me wonder if he's been murdered as well. We head out to the cemetery for probably the shortest graveside service ever recorded in the history of mankind. It basically consists of the minister saying a prayer before the casket is lowered into the ground. It took longer to drive there.

Only Elizabeth, Gina, Pauli, Todd, Binny, and I made the trip. The detective and the lady in black are absent. My heart aches a little for Leilani. No matter how mean you are, people should show up to your funeral, to say the least. If you think I'm feeling a little guilty—you're right. Binny and I just came to see if the murderer would make an appearance. If I wasn't a suspect, I probably wouldn't even be here.

I don't like myself very much for thinking that.

The ceremony ends with the minister walking away. He just up and leaves. We all look at each other, startled by this. After a second or two, the tiny crowd breaks up and heads to the road. By the time we get in my car, I'm completely spent. And it's only ten o'clock in the morning.

"I need a drink," Binny says.

"It's a little early," I say. I just want to go home, take some of Mom's Xanax, and follow it up with a long nap.

Then I see what she sees. Todd and Pauli are heading to a bar down the block.

"But it's always a good time for a drink," I agree. Intel first, drugs and nap later.

This time, we walk in and sit with the guys. They acknowledge our appearance with nods.

"That was an interesting ceremony," Pauli finally says.

"Why didn't you two get up and speak?" I ask.

Todd frowns. "I'm not much for publicly stating my feelings."

Does that mean he had feelings for Leilani?

"Me neither," Pauli says. "You did a nice job for all of us."

The waitress stops by. Binny and I order mimosas, while the guys order a pitcher of beer to split.

"Do you guys know those other two women?" Binny

asks. Her smile puts the men at ease. She'd be a great detective, I think. It's probably a little less dangerous than teaching.

Pauli shakes his head. "Never heard of them before today."

Todd shifts uneasily in his chair. "Elizabeth and Gina are just looking for attention. They didn't *really* know Leilani."

"But you did?" I ask.

He looks angry but answers. "Better than them. Leilani only lived with them a couple of months."

"Oh?" Binny asks, eyes wide and innocent. "I thought they were practically family—the way they carried on!"

I nod. "Seemed like that to me too."

"I'm telling you," Todd snarls. "They didn't know her! They were always on her back over this or that. Those two never cut her a break. They just used her for her share of the rent."

Whoa. Todd is seriously defending a woman I thought was more honey badger than human.

"That's too bad," I sympathize.

Todd looks at me. I'm hoping that from what I said at the funeral and how I'm acting now that he'll let his guard down.

"Elizabeth and Gina are just attention whores. They like that Leilani's death makes them important, but they had no idea what she was really like. I probably knew her better than most," Todd admits.

"But you said, the other day at the beach, that you weren't close," Binny says.

He shakes his head. "My feelings are too personal

to share with complete strangers. I know that Leilani rubbed some people raw. My friend Kua hated her. But she had her good side too."

Pauli studies his friend. I wonder if they really are friends or just rode down together. It seems as though Pauli didn't know how close Todd and Leilani were.

"I'm sorry for your loss," I say. If they were a couple, I'll know by his reaction.

"Mahalo," Todd says.

So it's true. Leilani and Todd were together. I wonder why he doesn't seem to be more upset. I'd think he'd be in tears or close to it. But maybe, like he said, he doesn't express his feelings publicly. Still, it's a little weird that he isn't acting more crushed by her death.

"Has anyone heard if they caught whoever murdered her?" Binny asks. Nice. She brings the conversation back to the mystery at hand. She should definitely consider a career in law enforcement. She'd be better than Detective Ray.

Pauli shrugs. "I heard that they thought it was you." He looks at me and gives me a little wink.

"I didn't kill her. I've never killed anything bigger than a mosquito."

Binny nods. "Nani wasn't there. I heard that the killer disguised himself to look like her though."

Todd stares at his glass of beer. He's avoiding eye contact. Does he think I killed Leilani? No, he wouldn't be sitting with me if he did. Unless he's going to stab me with my own cocktail umbrella.

"I don't think they know who killed her or the other two," I say.

"I don't see how they aren't related," Pauli says. "All three were ukulele musicians. Another reason to suspect you."

Really? That's how he's going to play it? Repeat that I'm a suspect over and over until it becomes true?

I sigh. "Someone is going to a lot of work to frame me. They even broke into my house and took one of my ukuleles. And it's the one they think killed Kua."

Todd looks up at this, eyes alert. "They think he was killed by a ukulele?"

"Well," Binny says, "they haven't found the weapon yet, but they think that's what it was. It hasn't been confirmed as far as I know."

Pauli leans forward. "You two sure know a lot about these murders."

Binny responds smoothly, "How can we not? You guys live in Princeville. But in Aloha Lagoon, it's all anyone talks about. Small towns are like that."

Are they buying it? I adopt my most innocent look. I'm hoping I look sympathetic, but suspect I look more like a constipated kitten.

"Huh." Pauli drains his beer. "That detective sure moves slowly. He called me a few days back saying he wants to meet—but I haven't talked to him yet."

Todd grimaces. It can't be easy to hear that the police aren't making his girlfriend's murder a priority.

"At his pace," he says, "it'll take years before this is resolved."

"I hope not!" Binny insists. "I'm worried that Nani will be next. There's a theme here among the murders, and she's the last ukulele performer in Aloha Lagoon."

I can't help but admire my friend. She does such a great job of controlling the conversation. I try to look frightened. Actually, I should be frightened. Whoever it is could come after me next. On the other hand, why would they?

"You'd better be careful," Pauli says. "Doesn't sound like the police are up to the task of protecting you."

He throws some money on the table and stands. "Ready to go, Todd? I've got to get back."

Todd nods and joins him. Binny and I watch them as they exit the bar.

"That was strange," Binny muses as she takes a swig of mimosa. "I didn't get the impression that they were close when we were in Princeville."

Through the window, I see the two men walk around the corner and out of sight. A few moments later, I see a flash of white pass by with Todd at the wheel.

I shrug. "Who knows with guys? I'm not even sure what's going on with Nick and me."

Binny looks at me. "I know you like him, but I still think you should be careful until you know more about him."

Again with the *killer as bad boyfriend material* thing?

"You don't honestly think he's the killer, do you?"

She shrugs. "I don't know. I can't think of a connection between him and the victims. But he's awfully familiar with you. Seems a little too soon."

"Great. I finally meet someone who's hot, funny, and likes me, and he might be framing me for murder."

Binny laughs. "You don't believe that. I'm not sure I do either. I just want you to be careful."

"Fine." I stand and add a few dollars to the tip. "We should go. I've got a lesson this afternoon."

We're on the road five minutes before I say something. "At least we know more about Elizabeth, Gina, and Todd and about their relationships with Leilani."

"Do you still think the roommates did it?" Binny asks. "According to Todd, they didn't like her as much as they let on."

I nod. "Which would mean their behavior at the funeral was all an act. That definitely moves them up, in my estimation."

"But it doesn't answer why Kua or Alohalani was killed. Or why someone broke into his office."

"Maybe the break-ins aren't related. Maybe they killed Kua and Alohalani just to frame me. Leilani probably let them know how much she hated me."

"That's true. I've heard of that happening before. The murderer kills several people, but there's only one truly targeted victim. The other bodies are to throw the investigation off."

"And the break-in could just be a burglary. Alohalani had very expensive music and instruments."

"I wish I'd been with you guys that night," Binny says.

I laugh. "Oh no you don't. You are way too nice to break into someone's office or home. You would've talked us out of it."

"Maybe." She looks off into the distance. "But I would've done surveillance or been the lookout. That's not illegal."

"We're no closer to finding out who did this."

"That's not true! You know more than Detective Ray. You have clues in the Alohalani case, and you know the real story about the relationships Leilani had."

I shake my head. "But we know nothing about Kua's murder. Nothing at all. I thought maybe the Sea Dogs were behind it, but after the funeral yesterday, I'm not so sure."

We drive on in silence for a few minutes before I say something.

"What do you think about that weird lady in black who was at both funerals?"

Binny waves it off. "It's probably just some freak. There are enough crazy people on this island that when one of them appears, I don't think anything of it."

I'm not so sure, but I don't say this. Binny's right—Hawaii has some very colorful characters. At least, more than I ever knew on the mainland. But I always chalked it up to the weather here. People from all over the world move here for the sunshine and temperatures. It makes sense that there'd be some eccentrics too.

For all we know, the lady in black could even be a man. But could whoever it is be the killer? I'd never seen anyone dressed like that in Aloha Lagoon before. But then, these were my first funerals here. It could be a crackpot who goes to all local funerals this way.

Binny and I say good-bye at my doorstep, and I'm not home five minutes before my lesson arrives. Johnny Milton is one of my favorite students. At five years old, he's mastered the chords and picked up fingerstyle like a pro. Teaching him is way too easy, and I feel a little guilty taking his parents' money. I lead him out onto the lanai for the lesson. It's too nice outside to stay in.

The child works through his scales flawlessly. His freckled face grimacing in concentration. Most of my students are just taking lessons for something to do. Johnny actually loves the instrument and wants to be here. He's so good, he'll probably take my place before he hits puberty.

"Miss Johnson?" Johnny asks in the middle of the lesson. "Did you kill those people?

"What? Of course not! Where did you hear that?"

I'm not totally surprised. Binny wasn't kidding when she told the guys at the bar this is a small town and the gossip flows like beer after an AA meeting. However, hearing it from one of my kids is a bit of a shock.

He shrugs. "My friends at school were talking about it. But Mom and Dad say it's ridiculous."

"That's right," I say, a little relieved. "I didn't kill anyone. Thank your parents for believing in me."

We finish our lesson, and as I see him to the door, I'm surprised to see Twila Grant's mother on the front lanai. Johnny runs to his mother's car and leaves.

"Mrs. Grant?" I ask.

Wringing her hands, the woman looks even more jumpy than normal. And she's here alone. Why?

"I just want you to know… I don't think you killed those musicians," she says.

"Uh, thanks?" This isn't good.

"But my husband thinks we should cancel Twila's lessons…at least until you're acquitted."

I'm pretty sure my jaw is resting on the tops of my

feet. This was something I hadn't expected. It never occurred to me that my students' parents would suspect me.

"Oh," I say quietly. "That's okay, Mrs. Grant. I didn't do it, but if you feel better waiting until this all blows over, that's fine with me."

The woman gives me a watery smile before running back to her car and speeding away. I stand there staring after her for a few minutes. Did that really just happen?

What could possibly be next?

EIGHTEEN

"So, LET ME get this straight…" Mom asks after she comes home. "Twila's mom is cancelling her lessons because they're worried you might be a murderer?"

I nod. "Not only Twila but half my students."

I got four more phone calls that afternoon—all cancellations.

"Huh," Mom says.

She doesn't say that it's ridiculous or even that these parents are wrong. She just says *huh*.

"And that letter," Mom asks. "It said 'back off, or you're next'?"

"Yup."

"Huh," she says again.

"Mom, you could at least act like you think I'm innocent," I protest.

"Oh, for crying out loud, Nani! I don't think you killed anyone. I just think you need to release a public statement saying you didn't."

"Seriously? Like a press release? You think I need to do that?"

Mom nods. "Yes. To the local newspaper."

"Mom, that rag only comes out a couple days a week and consists mostly of ads. I hardly think I need to contact them and plead my innocence."

"Look, kiddo. I know you're innocent. But some of my fellow mahjong partners at the senior center think you're guilty. I could lose my status there."

"Status? As what?" The weirdest alcoholic ever?

"Just think about it." She ignores my question.

"It's not going to happen, Mom." What else does she want me to do? Make a video for YouTube?

"Whatever." Mom dismisses me.

She pours a mai tai and heads into the living room to watch TV. I walk into my bedroom to find the giant tiki statue leering at me. That means she's getting ready to decorate the living room again. I'm too exhausted to go find out what we have in there now.

I'm losing students. I love my students. Would they even come back after this is all over? And would the women's correctional facility let the kids come to jail for lessons? I doubt it.

On the other hand, I've now got a gig this weekend playing a luau at the resort, and Ms. Kekoa said there'd be more to come. And Pastor Dan hasn't dismissed me. This is just a small setback. I am, however, considering calling Detective Ray and insisting he get on with the investigation.

I reach into my dresser and look at the anonymous typed note for maybe the one thousandth time tonight. Who wrote this? Was it the murderer or someone who just wants to spook me? If so, they are doing a good job. I haven't left the house since Johnny's lesson.

I pour a glass of iced tea, grab a uke, and step out onto the lanai. Dusk has settled, and a hush falls around me. That's when I realize this is the first time I've had to myself in days. I settle on the wicker love seat and stare out into the darkness.

I'm a little surprised I haven't heard from Nick. Either he's working late or he's coming to his senses and has decided it's not a good idea for an important pillar of the community to date that community's resident multi-murderer.

It doesn't really matter. Being alone is kind of nice. Soothing really. I pick up my little travel uke and start plucking at the strings. I'd read once that Sherlock Holmes plucked at his violin when he was deep in thought. It's an interesting comparison. Well, not because I'm as smart as Sherlock Holmes—that much is obvious.

The music eases my mind a little, and I close my eyes, allowing my fingers to improvise on the strings. I don't really consider my travel uke to be one of my performance instruments. I'd never play it in concert. But it's light enough to mess around with and small enough (I know, like a tiny instrument needs a smaller version) to carry with me.

I start playing chords now—C, then A, then F, then G, over and over. This is my favorite combination—it begins low and ends high. I play without thinking, moving between strumming and fingerstyle. As I do, the facts of the case stack up in my head.

Here's what I know…

Kua was murdered on the beach with something made of kauwila wood. My kauwila uke is missing. The main suspects we've even considered are a surfing gang named the Sea Dogs. They are dangerous. And Mr. Lugosi from the Blue Hawaii wedding was interested in them. Mrs. Lugosi said she wanted to learn to surf. Both of them lied to me about where the other one was. I'm not sure if the couple's bizarre behavior is even related to Kua's death, but I leave it there. Detective Ray interviewed Leilani—who implies that she and I were close—even though we weren't. During his murder, I was at home, alone. No alibi. His funeral is well attended, and the Sea Dogs are there. So are Todd Chay and the lady in black.

Leilani was murdered at the Overlook in the morning of the next day. I was at home then also, with no alibi. She was playing a wedding, and someone dressed as me ran out and pushed her over the cliff onto the rocks below. The police hadn't found a body but did find enough blood to indicate she couldn't have survived. There was a huge casket at her funeral, so they must've found her remains. Leilani had two roommates who claim to adore her, but according to Todd, really didn't get along with her. She was romantically involved with Todd Chay—who was friends with Kua. Someone (besides us) broke into her home—right after we did. We found pictures of Kua surfing and a photo of me in my backyard. Her funeral is sad, attended only by a few people, including Pauli and Todd.

Alohalani was murdered within several feet of me. My alibi is terrible in this case, because I was the only one with him after he was stabbed. I have very little to go on. I haven't interviewed anyone who knew him. He'd intimated to me that he had notes that implicated the real murderer. Nick and I searched his office and found a photo of the Overlook with the Hawaiian word for *deceiver* written on it.

Part of me wants to give up. This is too overwhelming. We've only really looked into Leilani's murder. We haven't done much with Kua's or Alohalani's investigations. The list of people on Ray's desk had people who knew Kua and Leilani. The person with the least number of people who cared about her is the one we've investigated the most.

If we wanted to investigate Kua's or Alohalani's murders, we'd have to invest more time than I want to. I'm tired. Exhausted. I don't want to do this anymore.

On the other hand, the police are doing little to nothing. And I'm losing students—half of them already—to the suspicion that seems to be attached to me like a shadow. If I don't look into this, who will? Detective Ray is taking his time. Do I have the luxury of waiting for him to follow through?

I feel like screaming, but that would alarm the neighbors and probably bring Mom running. I don't need any more attention on me. Instead, I just sit there, in the dark, wondering what to do next. The picture Leilani had of me pops into my head, and I wonder if someone is watching me right now. There's something odd about that photo, but I can't put my finger on it. I'm just sitting on my lanai outside, playing my ukulele…

My cell vibrates, and I look at it, grateful for the distraction. It's from Pastor Dan. *Can you come by right now? I'd like to discuss something with you.*

Great. He probably wants to fire me too. This day just gets better and better. I go inside and see Mom asleep on the couch. No point in waking her. I slip quietly out the front door, trying to ignore the many jiggling hula-girl statues Mom has placed around the living room. Just think—when I'm gone, she'll be free to decorate the whole house like this.

I drive to the chapel, pull into the parking lot and turn off the engine. That's odd. I don't see Pastor Dan's car. But the lights are on inside. Maybe he walked or hitched a ride or something like that. I might as well get this over with. If I'm going to lose this job, I'd rather deal with it now. Putting it off until later would just add to the torture.

"Hello?" I call out as I walk into the lobby.

It's eerily silent. The chapel is completely empty. He must be in the back office.

"Dan? Mary Lou?" I shout as I walk into the back room.

But there's no one here either. Huh. Did he step out-side to do something? That might be it. The man is al-ways puttering with stuff. He isn't very handy, but he's never let that hold him back. Once, he bought a huge Elvis head on eBay and tried to attach it to the front of the chapel. It fell off the next day, breaking his foot, but that didn't stop him. I stick my head outside and look, but he's not there either.

What's going on? Why would Dan text me to meet him when he isn't here? Maybe he's losing it. Granted, he's not that old, but early onset Alzheimer's can hap-pen. Could that be it? The door was unlocked, and the lights are on, so he must be here somewhere.

"Dan? Dan Presley?" I call out.

There's no answer.

I walk through the facility one more time, but still don't find Pastor Dan. All right. He must've just stepped out for a moment. Clearly he's expecting me, so I'll wait. I sit in a pew near the back.

It really is a lovely chapel, especially now that Bam-Boobs' endless pink decorations are gone. It's back to its simplest form, which is my favorite. I really do love it here. Dan's always saying he's going to leave it to me when he dies.

I indulge in a little fantasy and allow myself to think about what I'd really do with this place if it were mine. First thing I'd do is fire Mary Lou. That woman is insane. She wouldn't help me unless it was into my grave. No, she'd be the first change I'd make.

Second, I'd get rid of the tacky blue plastic frames. I'd need a photographer, but I'm sure I could find someone who'd help me part time. The resort has used photographers before. I could check with them, now that I'm on the payroll. I still feel a little rush every time I think that.

Third, I'd have to decide whether or not to keep the Elvis theme. The name Blue Hawaii Wedding Chapel isn't bad. It's kind of sweet actually. But without Pastor Dan and his impersonations of the King, it wouldn't be the same. Yeah, I'd definitely lose the theme but keep the name. Maybe Mary Lou is a little right in thinking there should be some blue in the décor. I'll never tell her that though.

Ouch!

Something has bitten me on the back of my neck. Stupid mosquitos. What really sucks is that mosquitos didn't exist here until the first missionaries brought them on their ships. Now we battle mosquitos all year long, when this island would truly be an epic paradise without them.

I rub the back of my neck, thinking that Pastor Dan had better get here soon. I'm tired. Actually, the day's depressing activities have taken more out of me than I thought. It's probably a good thing Nick is AWOL. I'd pass out on him the minute he arrived.

Whoa. When did the room start bobbing around like the Elvis bobblehead in Dan's office? My head is throbbing too. Am I having a stroke? The room begins to spin violently before going blurry, then black altogether.

It's so quiet. I feel like I should open my eyes, but my eyelids are so very heavy. Sensations slowly come to me. I'm lying on something hard—so clearly I'm not in my bed. My fingers curl around something I don't recognize at first. I think maybe I should open my eyes so I can get back in bed. Memory comes back to my fingertips, and I realize I'm holding a ukulele. I must've fainted out on the lanai or something.

It hurts to open my eyes, but I do it anyway. Bad idea—my vision is flooded with bright light. Am I dead? Is this heaven? Wait…why do I even think that? And it couldn't be heaven, because I'm pretty sure it wouldn't hurt to be there. It'd be more like clouds or something.

I force myself up onto my elbows. Oh. I'm at the Blue Hawaii Wedding Chapel. Something vague dances just out of reach in my mind. That's right. I came here for a reason. I close my eyes to think. Not that it helps. Oh right. Pastor Dan texted me. He said he needed to meet with me.

Carefully, I get to my feet. My legs feel like wet pasta. And I'm still holding the uke. I'd better get a grip. I'm in the chapel but halfway up the aisle. I remember sitting in the pews. That's right—I was waiting for Dan.

But I didn't have a ukulele with me. I study the instrument I'm still gripping. There are a few moments of foggy recollection. It's the kauwila uke. My missing uke! How did it get here? Did I find it before I passed out? It was probably here all along. I sigh with relief. I'd never thought to look here. Of course, I don't remember bringing it to the chapel, but who knows?

There's something on the edge of the instrument. It's red and sticky. Is that human hair? Oh no. No, no, no, *no*! This is the murder weapon. This is the uke everyone's looking for—the one that killed Kua! I'd better call Detective Ray. No more messing around. This just got super serious.

A distant sound resonates, making me think I should do something right now. What is that? Again, I close my eyes to concentrate. Sirens! It's the sound of sirens. Like the police use. Huh. I've lived here for a year and never heard them before. I wonder what's going on.

The noise stops abruptly, and a few seconds later, Detective Ray bursts through the door of the chapel, followed by two police officers in uniform.

"Miss Johnson," the detective says. "Put the ukulele down and put your hands up."

"Sir?" one of the uniforms ask. "You should look at this."

The men stare at something behind the last pew. I walk over, overwhelmed by the urge to run. It takes all the self-control I have to put one foot in front of the other.

"Miss Johnson, you are under arrest," Detective Ray says as he takes the instrument from my hands.

I arrive at the spot where they are looking. On the floor, unconscious and bleeding, is Pastor Dan.

"Why did you do it?" one of the uniforms asks me.

"I didn't!" I kneel down to examine my friend. "Someone..." I try to explain, but I've got nothing.

When did this happen? I was out—I didn't see a thing.

"He's still alive." Detective Ray has his hand on Dan's neck. "Call an ambulance!"

The detective points at me and says to one of the uniforms, "Arrest her for the murders of Kua Liu, Leilani O'Flanagan, Alohalani Kealoha, and for the attempted murder of Dan Presley."

NINETEEN

As the only person in the one jail cell in all of Aloha Lagoon, this isn't too bad. Okay, so it's terrible. They should hire Mom to decorate. And I'm *not* using that toilet, at all, ever.

Not only am I in here for crimes I didn't commit, but also no one will tell me how Pastor Dan is. In fact, they haven't offered me my phone call or even a drink of water. I glance at the toilet. Even if they had a sink in here, I wouldn't drink the water.

My mouth is so dry. And there's a strange taste on the back of my tongue. It doesn't make sense. None of this makes sense. I would never hurt Dan Presley. Yes, I was sitting in the chapel, thinking of all the things I'd change if Dan was dead and left it all to me, but that's not a motive, is it?

No! I would never hurt him to get the place. Never! It was just boredom that made me come up with that. Fortunately, the police don't know what I was thinking. They just know that when they walked in, I was holding the murder weapon and Dan was unconscious on the floor. It doesn't look good.

And just why did the police come to the church? I never called anyone. In fact, no one even knew I was there. Just Pastor Dan. He'd texted me. Asked me to come over. And yet, he wasn't there. Not when I was looking for him anyway.

Someone hit him over the head with my ukulele and set me up, or I've started sleep-homicide walking. Somebody—most likely the murderer of the Terrible Trio—framed me. They must've forced Dan to text me. But how did they knock me out?

The mosquito bite. I touched where I was bitten. It isn't swollen or itchy. It wasn't a bug bite. A hypodermic needle? That would explain the unconsciousness…the exhaustion…the bad taste in my mouth. I was drugged. I need to tell the detective as soon as possible.

But right now, I'm alone and in jail. I'm in jail. I have to admit—the killer did a really good job setting me up. It's impressive. Dan's cell will show that he texted me, and my phone will concur. The police arrived just in time to find me holding a bloody uke. My fingerprints are all over it. If I ever get it back—which seems unlikely—I'm going to burn it like a medieval witch.

This is very bad. If Dan is in a coma or dead, he won't be able to clear me. Tears prick the inside corners of my eyes. Please, please, let Pastor Dan be all right. Not for me…not to clear my name. But because I care so much about the man.

I'm still struggling to keep composed when an officer comes to take me to an interrogation room. He sits me down at a small table with two chairs and leaves the room. Detective Ray comes in and takes the chair opposite me. No one has handcuffed me to the table. I'm going to think of that as a good sign.

"How is Dan Presley?" I ask, rubbing my itchy tear ducts. "Please tell me he's going to be okay."

"He's in a coma. The doctor has no idea when or if he will wake up."

"I know how this looks." My voice shakes as I speak. "But I've been set up. I didn't kill or even hit anyone. And I haven't seen that uke until tonight!"

Detective Ray looks at me. His hound-dog face is completely blank. I have no idea what he's thinking. And it scares me.

"I'm pretty sure I was drugged." I show the detective the spot where I believe I was injected.

He shrugs and pulls my cell phone out of the pocket of his aloha shirt, sliding it to me. "You have one phone call."

I stare at the cell for a moment before picking it up. I only get one chance to ask for help. And I call the one person I trust.

Back in the cell, I pace like a caged animal…which, in fact, I am. If I get out of here, I'm going to devote every second to finding out who did this. The police don't care, because they've been handed the perfect scenario complete with killer (me) caught in the act (unconscious Dan) holding the murder weapon (kauwila uke) that I (allegedly) used to kill Kua.

My fear is turning to fury now. This is my home! Well, not this jail cell. No matter how the Terrible Trio tried to run me off (even though they're all dead), this is where I'm staying. I'm going to fight tooth and nail to get out of here, and then I'm not going to sleep until I catch this killer.

"Miss Johnson?" asks the same officer who took me to the interrogation room.

Who else would I be? I'm the only one here, in the only cell you've got! But I don't tell him that.

"Your attorney is here." The policeman unlocks the cell. "Your bail has been posted, and you're free to go."

Attorney? I don't have an attorney. And I don't know how much the bail is, but I assume it's more than Mom or Binny can pay.

I'm led to the lobby, where Nick is standing with my best friend and a well-dressed man I've never seen before. I'm so confused that I just stop and stand there, gawking. Nick bailed me out? I called Binny, not Nick. She said she didn't exactly trust him. Why did she call him?

"Nani Johnson?" The man I don't know steps forward and shakes my hand. "I'm your attorney."

Nick nods almost imperceptibly. Binny flings herself into my arms.

"Okay," I respond. And that's all I say as I walk out the door with my best friend, my possible boyfriend, and my lawyer, whom I've never met before.

"What happened last night?" Binny asks. "Why didn't you call?"

I shake my head. It's hard enough for me to get my brain around what happened. I'm still not sure I can even talk about it.

"Let's get you home," Nick says soothingly. Binny nods.

In the car, Binny chatters about the weather. I like it. It drowns out the thoughts in my head. I lean back and close my eyes. Before I know it, we're at my house.

Nick waves and points to the strange attorney. "I'm going to check him into the resort. I'll pick you up tomorrow for breakfast, and you can tell us what happened."

Binny, on the other hand, follows me inside. Mom appears and looks worried, but Binny waves her off.

"You go take a long, hot shower. Then you hit the hay. I'll stay overnight."

"Thank you," I groan as I walk into my room and shut the door. Although, I don't know what defense Binny can put up should the killer arrive. But I'm too tired to care.

My mind starts to wander to the events of last night, but I shut it out. After a hot shower I climb into bed and, to my complete surprise, fall asleep.

"Wake up!" Binny stands over me, holding a cup of tea. "Nick called, and we have to meet him and Mr. Bones in half an hour."

I open one eye, which is all she's going to get right now. "Mr. Bones?"

She nods. "Your attorney."

My attorney is named Mr. Bones? That can't be good. I sit up and stay that way for a few seconds. Then I climb out of bed and get dressed. I'm just brushing my teeth, when Binny pops in again.

"Ready?"

She looks like a million bucks for someone who probably spent the night on my couch.

"What about Mom?"

My mother still has no idea what happened to me last night. She's either worried sick or halfway through a pitcher of mimosas. For the first time in a year, I kind of hoped it was the second one.

"I told her you had a little trouble last night and that everything's fine." Binny winks as if we're involved in a major conspiracy operation.

We get into her Jeep, and she drives us to the resort for breakfast. Nick and Mr. Bones (I'm not at all confident I can say his name without giggling) are waiting for us. We sit down and order breakfast. I'm a little nervous about what happens now. I've never needed a lawyer in my life. Okay—we had one after Dad died, but technically that attorney wasn't mine.

When the waitress walks away, I tell them what really happened, and then I tell them what the police think happened last night and about being drugged. Binny's hand covers her mouth the whole time, and Nick looks worried. Mr. Bones just looks lawyerly.

"I wish you'd come to me sooner," Mr. Bones says. He's a tall, thin man with gray hair and one of those pencil-thin mustaches. He looks serious. Really serious.

Nick shakes his head. "We weren't worried about Nani getting arrested before." He turns to me. "Bones here has been our family's attorney since my grandfather was alive."

"You didn't have to fly in your lawyer, Mr.…er… Bones," I say. "I don't know if I can afford him." I look at the attorney. "No offense."

Nick shakes his head. "I'm covering this one. I have a huge trust fund, and I should use it for something."

"I don't know…" This is just too much. I can't let Nick pay for this.

"I won't take no for an answer, Nani. Besides, you

need him. You're out on bail, and that means they are suspicious enough to set bail in the first place."

I sigh heavily. I don't deserve this kindness. And what is Nick expecting in return?

"I don't expect anything," Nick says as if he can read my mind. "You owe me nothing."

"Ahem…" Mr. Bones clears his throat. "So after what you've just told me, Miss Johnson, I've got my work cut out for me. I'd like you to have some blood drawn so we can find out what you were injected with. Do you know where the nearest lab is?"

I nod. He's right. The blood work could help my case.

"You should go right away. Whatever it is won't stay in your system too much longer. I'll see what I can do. And Mr. Woodfield gave me the license number on the white car. I'll run the plate." He stands. "I'm going to make a few calls. Excuse me."

"What about breakfast?" I ask. "You just ordered."

He nods. "Just have it sent to my room." Mr. Bones gives Nick a slip of paper and leaves.

"Huh," I say.

"What?" Nick asks.

"I just thought there'd be more to it than that." I take a drink of orange juice.

Binny takes my hand. "I can't believe you went through all that last night!"

Our food arrives, and we stop talking. No point in adding to the gossip in town. Once the waitress gets instructions for the delivery of Mr. Bones's breakfast, she leaves us alone.

I devour my food, probably looking like a rabid warthog. Nick and Binny eat in silence. They are waiting for me to make the first move. I slow down, taking my time with the eggs, toast, and bacon. I have no answers for them. Just questions.

"So." Nick wipes his mouth on a napkin and replaces it on his lap. "What are your thoughts?"

"I don't have any. Just questions," I say. "We haven't even looked into Kua's and Alohalani's murders. Just Leilani's."

"No," Binny disagrees. "We went to Kua's funeral. And we've suspected the Sea Dogs."

I shove my plate away. "I don't think it's them. They hardly know me. Why frame me?" Besides, if a gang of thugs had broken into my house and stolen my uke, I think I'd know it.

"You think it's the work of one person," Nick muses. "Why?"

"I've never seen the Sea Dogs before now. Not once in Aloha Lagoon. It's hard to believe they could be involved." That, and I didn't want to start investigating them. I'm a lazy detective. I could give Detective Ray a run for his money.

"And I'm sure these murders are all linked. They all have two things in common. One"—I tick off my fingers—"they're the only ukulele musicians on the island. And two—I'm the only common denominator."

"You could be the next victim." Binny tries to comfort me, but somehow her words don't help.

"No," Nick says. "They didn't kill you last night. They framed you. Whoever it is wants you in prison for this."

Binny tries another tactic. "If you could tell the police who you think did it, who would you say? Right now?"

I think about this for a second. "It has to be one of Leilani's people. All five on Ray's list were connected to Leilani. Gina and Elizabeth are blatant liars, and they don't seem to like me. They pretended to love Leilani, but Todd says they didn't get along. And they lived with Leilani, so they'd know about me."

"What about Todd?" Binny asks. "It's obvious he and Leilani were an item."

"I don't know about him," I answer.

Nick pulls out a piece of paper from his pocket. "I did a little digging on Alohalani."

We turn to him, jaws on the floor. Is that where he's been?

"I talked to a couple of people who know him. Turns out Leilani owed him a lot of money. Kua too. Both were students of his, back in the day. They borrowed money from him. Apparently, they wanted to just play music without the inconvenience of a day job. He set them up, helped them get gigs, and took care of their expenses so they could establish themselves as professional musicians."

I shrug. "Okay, so how does that information help?"

Nick grins. "The professor was broke. He'd been demanding the two of them pay him back for months now. I guess he had a bit of a gambling problem."

"I still don't see how this helps," I say. "It only implicates Kua or Leilani in the murder, but they were both dead before Alohalani was killed."

"I think it's significant somehow," Nick says. "Maybe

he owed other people money too. Bad people. Someone who would've broken into his office to find the loan contracts."

Binny asks, "He made contracts with them when they borrowed from him?"

Nick nods. "He did."

"But," I insist one more time, "Kua and Leilani are dead too. They couldn't have killed Alohalani."

I want to believe this information is helpful. I really do. But it just doesn't add up.

"Was he married?" I ask. "If so, did you talk to her?"

Nick shakes his head, "Yes, he was married, and no—I didn't talk to her. She took his body to Oahu for cremation and his funeral. But I don't think she did it. According to my sources, she's only five feet tall and very frail."

"So who are these sources?" I ask.

"Students." Nick grins. "His work-study students, including the one you met at the front desk. Turns out they're pretty devoted to the man. It also turns out that he confided in them."

"Do you think one of Leilani's friends killed him?" I ask.

"Then why would they kill Leilani?" Binny asks.

"This is all too twisted. No wonder the police are anxious to arrest me. I'm the easiest way to connect the murders. For all I know, Fat Mookie and BamBoobs did it."

Nick frowns. "I forgot about him. He's a gangster, right?"

I nod. "From Atlantic City. Although they're more normal than the Lugosis. Something's weird about those two. But I don't think any of them murdered the three musicians."

"I think you're right. From what you've told me about the Lugosis, I think they're investigating something. I just don't think it's connected with this case at all," Nick says.

"Maybe they're investigating Fat Mookie? Or the Sea Dogs." I shake my head. "But that doesn't get us any closer to the truth in this case."

"What about Leilani's roommates?" Binny says. "I still think they're high on the suspect list."

"I guess." I'm not sure. "They could've killed Leilani because she was evil. Then killed Kua and Alohalani to deflect the spotlight from them onto me. Maybe. I just don't know if they're smart enough."

"Well then"—Binny stands up—"let's go talk to them one more time."

Nick frowns. "I have to work today."

"All right." I stand too. "We can do it at least to rule them out."

Nick kisses me on the cheek, and Binny takes me to Metro Lab. The blood draw is quick, and I give them Mr. Bones's number. They tell me it will be a few days. I try to explain that we need the results immediately, and they promise to do what they can. I hope they find something, and soon.

The drive to Lihue is quiet. Binny and I decide we needed to prepare what to say to the two women so that we don't spook them.

"I know!" I snap my fingers. "I'll tell them I borrowed

one of Leilani's ukuleles once and need to know if she has any next of kin to return it to!"

Binny chews her lip. "Won't they wonder why you didn't just call?"

"We can once again offer our condolences." That doesn't seem too farfetched.

We agree on this plan as we pull into the parking lot for the women's apartment. I ring the doorbell, and we wait. And that's when I see it.

"There's a white car over there," I whisper to Binny. Why didn't I get the plate number from Nick? I should've thought of that.

She squints. "It's so far away. Do you think it's the same one?"

I shrug. "I can't tell, but it does seem suspicious."

The door swings open as if it's been kicked in. Gina stares at us, and Elizabeth appears over her shoulder, looking like the Revenge of the Two-Headed Roommates. They do not look happy that we are here. I wonder if that's a sign of guilt.

They do not invite us in. "What do *you* want?" Gina says the word *you* as if it has a bad taste.

"We were visiting a friend in Wailua and thought we'd stop by to offer our condolences one more time." Binny gives her best sympathetic smile.

"You two were awfully distraught at the funeral," I add. "We were kind of worried about you."

Gina softens a little. "Well, that's nice of you."

"But we prefer to mourn in our own way and in private, thank you," Elizabeth snaps.

"One more thing," I say quickly. "I borrowed a ukulele from Leilani once and never got around to returning it. Do you know how we can contact her next of kin?"

The women look at each other earnestly. It's obvious they are trying to communicate telepathically. I can't help but wonder if they truly are.

"I'm sorry," Gina says as she starts to close the door. "We don't know of anyone."

I put my foot in the door. "She didn't have any family?"

Gina looks at my foot and then at me. She sighs. "No. She was estranged from every relative she ever had."

I could definitely understand that.

Elizabeth cocks her head like a bird. "There was this one aunt Finnegan, I think? She lives on the mainland."

Gina nods. "But she hasn't been here to see Leilani in years."

"Wait," Binny asks. "What about the lady in black?"

The roommates look genuinely confused. "Who?"

I speak up. "At the funeral. In the back of the church. There was a lady covered from head to toe in black. Was she related, do you think?"

Elizabeth shrugs. "I guess I didn't see her." She looks at Gina, who shrugs also.

"So what should I do with the uke?" I ask. I'm hoping they don't want it, because I didn't want to give one of mine away.

Gina says, "Keep it. We don't want it." She kicks my foot out of the way and slams the door.

"That was weird," Binny says once we are back in the car.

"Weird that Leilani didn't talk to her family, or weird that they acted so strange?"

"Both. Who cuts off every single member of their family like that?"

"You didn't know her." I grimace. "She was so mean that even a dog wouldn't like her. That must be why this aunt Finnegan isn't in the picture."

"This might mean it's a family member who killed her," Binny says. "Didn't you say she's half Hawaiian?"

"She told me that many times, mostly to rub my face in it."

"Then"—Binny bites her lower lip—"she must have family in the islands somewhere."

I sit up a little straighter. "That's true. But why weren't they at the funeral?"

Binny shakes her head. "No idea. 'Ohana traditions are pretty strict. You don't miss weddings or funerals, no matter what."

"I wonder why we didn't think of this before now."

"What can we do about it? We don't know Leilani's mother's name, or we could check it out." Binny goes back to biting her lip.

"We're in over our heads," I say. "There are just too many factors we can't figure out without a hard-core private eye." I slouch back against the seat.

"It was fun being a detective though." Binny smiles. "You made a great sidekick. Like Dr. Watson."

I wiggle my index finger. "Oh no, I'm Sherlock Holmes. You're the sidekick."

Binny laughs. "All right, you win."

"I guess we should just put all of our efforts into my defense case."

We drive the rest of the way back to Aloha Lagoon,

rehashing the same details over and over with no new ideas. As Binny drops me off in my driveway, I realized that we have nothing. Nothing at all.

"Mom!" I call out as I enter the house. "I'm home."

I walk to the kitchen and pour a glass of water. The kitchen is kind of a mess. Leave it to my mother to trash the place and expect me to clean it. I put some dishes in the sink and spot a pan in the middle of the floor. Great, I think as I stoop to retrieve it. She's wasted. That's all I need.

"Mom!" I shout. "You could've cleaned up after yourself."

No answer. The woman is probably asleep on the lanai or in the living room. I walk outside. Nope. Not here. I head back into the house and make my way toward the living room. I can hear the TV on. She's probably passed out.

The room is empty. No, it's worse than empty. It's chaos. Furniture is turned upside down, and the TV is facedown on the floor. Even the little hula dolls are scattered and broken—which kind of seems unnecessary. The couch cushions have been flung to the four corners of the room.

"*Mom*?" I call out as I run to her bedroom.

It's been trashed too. The bedding is on the floor, and a mattress wobbles unsteadily against the wall. Every dresser drawer is open, and clothes are strewn about as if a typhoon has hit. I run to my room only to find it is also trashed.

My heart is pounding. What am I supposed to do now? I race to the kitchen to grab my cell phone and am about to call 9-1-1 when I see it. A piece of paper is taped to the microwave.

It says, *Keep your nose out of my business, or something terrible will happen to your mother.*

This is bad. This is very, very bad.

TWENTY

I DIAL 9-1-1, and when the dispatcher answers, I explain what has happened. Ten minutes later, Detective Ray and two officers are at my door. And for once, I'm happy to see them.

"Are you sure she didn't just go out?" he says as he walks through the house.

I stare at him. "You must be joking. Why would she trash the house and write me a threatening note?" I mean, Mom is crazy, but she's not insane.

Ray says nothing. He just pokes around each room, as if my mother will jump out from behind a door, shouting "Surprise!"

"You see now that I'm being framed, right?" I ask in an attempt to get him to speak.

"Maybe," the detective says. "You could've taken her to a friend's house, trashed the place, and written the note yourself."

I lose it. "You can't be serious! Why would I kidnap my own mother?"

"To deflect suspicion from yourself," Detective Ray says calmly.

I notice one of the officers fingerprinting furniture. The other one pokes around but doesn't really do anything. This is getting nowhere.

"I called you because I need to find my mom," I say through gritted teeth.

"Or you called us as a red herring," Detective Ray says.

I throw my arms up in the air and scream. It has no effect. None whatsoever. I take out my cell and dial Nick. He should be home now. Maybe Vera knows what happened to Mom.

"Nick!" I quickly tell him what's happened. "Has your mom seen mine?"

I can hear Nick talking to someone in the background. I strain to try to hear, but it's no use.

"She's not here," Nick says. "She was supposed to meet my mother an hour ago, but she never showed."

"Oh no," I barely whisper.

"I'm coming over," Nick says before hanging up.

I can't protest, because what could I say? I shove my cell back into my pocket and tell the detective what Nick said.

He shrugs.

Pretty soon I'm going to become a real murderer.

I call the community center and a few other places, but no one has seen my mom today. Nick bursts through the door without knocking and wraps me in his arms. I give in because I need it. I refuse to cry, because what good would that do?

"I can't find her, Nick." My voice cracks a little. "She's not at any of her usual haunts."

This seems to get Detective Ray's attention. "She really is missing, isn't she?"

I wonder if I can say *Duh* without coming off as rude or sarcastic.

"Of course she's missing." Nick pulls away, and I can hear anger in his voice. Nice.

"If you'd done your job since the beginning, this wouldn't have happened!"

Wow. Nick is mad. I kind of like it. And he's right.

The detective looks from me to Nick. "We'll wrap things up here and get back to the station. I'll let you know what we find."

The two other officers magically appear and follow Detective Ray out the door. I close it behind them and hang my head. I really don't want to cry, but it's all been way too much. More than I can bear, really.

"Nani." Nick lifts my chin. "It's going to be all right. I promise you."

I shake my head. "I doubt it. I don't think anything will be all right ever again."

Okay, so I'm being dramatic. My mom's been kidnapped, and someone is framing me for murder. I deserve a little self-pity.

"Do you have your cell with you, in case she calls?" Nick asks.

I nod.

"Then let's go see Pastor Dan in the hospital. Maybe he's out of his coma. Maybe we can get something out of him as far as who did this."

That's a great idea. I need to see him to make sure he's all right anyway. Nick locks the door behind us, and we drive to see my boss.

"How is Pastor Dan Presley?" I ask the nurse at the front desk.

"He's starting to come out of it," she says. She looks stern. A very large woman with a name tag that says *Doris*, she's not someone you could mess with easily.

"Can we see him?" Nick asks.

"I'll have to ask his wife," she says. "Hold on." Doris disappears down the hall.

His wife?

"I thought you said he's not...he doesn't..." Nick struggles with what to say.

"I did. He's gay. He told me that." Something isn't right.

"*Stop*!" Doris's voice barrels down the hallway.

Nick and I race down the hall and see a woman, about my height—maybe a little taller—with long brown hair, running out of a room and away from us.

"It's the killer!" I shout as I take off after my impersonator.

Nick is hot on my heels, and I can only imagine from the thundering behind me, so is Doris, but I don't stop. Whoever it is has gotten pretty far ahead of me, but I still spot that long brown hair. The hair that's meant to implicate me. I'm not letting this bastard get away.

I turn a corner to find two gurneys barring my way. The killer turns right. I shove the beds aside and keep going. I'm not letting him out of my sight. He has my mother. I want her and my life back.

Nick catches up and actually passes me. He turns the corner before I do. When I get there, Nick has stopped. He's looking furiously around.

"Where did he go?" I'm out of breath.

"Or she." Nick is in better shape than I am.

Doris catches up with us. She looks like she's going to have a heart attack. I kind of love her for trying to keep up.

"What happened?" I ask.

"His wife…" she says between breaths, "she was holding a pillow over his face when I got there."

I gasp. "Is he okay?" Please, please don't let Dan die!

She nods and swallows hard. "I think I got there just in time. If you two hadn't come in…"

She doesn't finish the sentence, and I don't want her to. I don't want to hear what I know would be true if we hadn't showed up.

"I'll call the police and tell them to be on the lookout for Mrs. Presley," she says.

I shake my head. "Pastor Dan isn't married. And if he was, it wouldn't be a woman."

Doris looks at me curiously. "Really? She wasn't related?"

"Are you sure it's a woman?" Nick asks.

The nurse shrugs. "I thought so. But I didn't look too carefully. She came in when two victims from a car accident arrived. There was a lot going on. I can't be sure."

We follow her back to Dan's room to find two nurses in there taking the man's vitals. He looks so weak. So fragile. But he's alive. That's the good thing.

"Dan?" I take his hand in mine. "It's me, Nani."

Dan's eyes flutter open, and he smiles weakly. "I thought that was you."

"What do you mean?" I ask.

"The woman who tried to kill me. She looked like you. But it wasn't you. She didn't seem right."

At least I have an alibi for this one. "Did you recognize her? Was she the same person who hurt you last night?"

Dan nods in the affirmative and then grimaces in pain.

"You need to go," one of the nurses says. "He isn't in any shape to talk to anyone now."

I nod. "We're going, Dan. But I'll be back, I promise."

Dan smiles and then closes his eyes.

By the time we get to the front desk, Detective Ray is talking to Doris, and one of the uniforms from earlier heads down to Dan's room. We stand there until they are done speaking.

Doris says, "She looked like this woman. I think she might've been wearing a wig. The hair didn't look right."

I wanted to hug her. Maybe she should be a detective, because she's already better than Detective Ray.

"And where were you?" The detective turns his attention to us.

"I've been with her the whole time." Nick steps forward protectively. "We came straight here. Nani didn't do it."

Doris nods. "They came in and asked to see Mr. Presley. They were right here when I found the woman holding a pillow over that poor man's face."

There it is. The police would now have to know I didn't do it. And they'd have to know that this was the real killer coming back to finish off a witness who knew I didn't do it. And she was disguised as me, so it's obvious it's all a setup.

"Maybe." Detective Ray shrugs. "We don't have all the facts yet."

Say what?

"You must be blind if you don't believe us," Doris roars. It scares me a little. "That girl didn't do it. Someone dressed like her and tried to kill this poor man. You need to get your head straight!"

We watch as she storms off, looking very fierce. I really like her.

"I'm going to post an officer outside Pastor Dan's door," Detective Ray says before walking down the hall toward Dan's room.

"How does he not see it?" I rage. "Even Doris sees it!"

Nick nods. "I know this is going to sound terrible, but I'm glad the killer came back. She tipped her hand and destroyed her attempt to frame you."

I agree. "You're right. That does sound terrible."

Nick winks. I throw myself into his arms and press my face into his shoulder. He's not a bad guy—just eager. It's great to have him at my side right now.

Detective Ray comes back to the counter. He starts to walk away, changes his mind, and joins us.

"You must understand that I have to investigate every lead," he says expressionlessly.

This is probably the closest I'm going to get to an apology.

"You're just doing your job," Nick says after a moment of hesitation.

The detective nods. "I didn't want to believe it was you. You seemed sincere at Kua's and Leilani's funerals."

Finally!

"Did you see the lady in black at both funerals?"

Detective Ray nods slowly. "Yes. I don't know who

she is. She vanished before I could find out. But I don't think it's anything important. Just someone who mourns a little differently."

"I guess you found Leilani's remains," I say.

He cocks his head to one side but says nothing.

"Because of the huge orange coffin," I explain. "There wouldn't be a coffin if you didn't have a body."

"We never found the body," the detective says. "Just several quarts of blood. She couldn't have survived that fall."

"You declared her dead without a body?" I'm kind of shocked, but I guess the alternative would be to fight the shark that found it.

"Blood counts as remains," Detective Ray says. "It's connective tissue. It's proof that if she hadn't been washed into the ocean, we'd have a body."

I shiver as the detective leaves. "That's gruesome. Too gruesome."

Nick nods. "They've done that before. When remains can't be retrieved, people still buy a coffin so they have something to bury."

My cell buzzes. It's Mom.

"Mom! Where are you? Are you okay?" I put the phone on speaker so Nick can hear it.

"Nani?" Mom sounds shaky. "They have me here. They want you to turn yourself in and confess to the murder, or they say they're going to kill me."

Nick and I look at each other. *They*?

I think I stopped breathing. I just got out of being a suspect, and now I had to confess to something I didn't do?

"Let me talk to them," I say as calmly as possible.

"No, they don't want to talk to you," Mom says. I hear a strange rustling, like the sound of people walking through a cornfield. Growing up in Kansas, I heard that sound all the time.

Nick turns pale. He grabs a piece of paper and pen from the front desk and starts writing.

"Okay, Mom. I'll do it now. Tell them I'm on my way to the station right now."

"I'm supposed to tell you that once they know you're arrested, they'll let me go."

I look at Nick. The note he wrote says I should agree to the terms.

"It's going to be all right, Mom. I'll do what they say." The call ends.

"What was that all about?" I ask.

Nick grimaces. "I know where they are."

"You do? How could you know that?"

"Because," he says, "I recognized the sounds of the foliage. They're in my hedge maze."

TWENTY-ONE

THE CORNFIELD SOUND. "Are you sure?"

He nods. "The acoustics and the sound of rustling shrubbery. It doesn't sound the same as a jungle."

"You're certain?" But I know he's right. We used to go to corn mazes back home, and it sounded just like this.

"I *am* a botanist."

"So what do we do? Call the police?" I don't really want to do that. What if the killers hear the sirens and just kill Mom?

"We're going to go there. And then we're going to spring your mother."

Detective Ray studies my cell phone as if it's a purple centipede. "You want me to wait for them to call and tell them you are in custody?" He repeats the plan we've given him one more time.

"That's right," Nick says. "Meanwhile, I'll go to the hedge maze and rescue Nani's mother."

The detective frowns. "I should send a squad car."

I shake my head. "No. They'd hear it coming. Nick grew up running around that maze. He knows every part of it."

"If I'm right," Nick adds, "they have her in the center. It's a tight squeeze for three people, but it's the biggest area in the maze."

"And I'm going with him," I say.

"No," Nick says. "I should do this alone. I don't want anything happening to you."

I put my hands on my hips. "It's 'them,' which means it's more than one person. You can't handle that alone. So I'm going with you."

Detective Ray doesn't look convinced. "I think this sounds dangerous."

"It is. But they've got my mother in there. Which makes me dangerous," I insist.

Nick studies me. "Fine. But you'll have to stick close to me so you don't get lost inside."

Detective Ray insists on sending backup to the neighborhood. We are to call as soon as we find out if Mom is really in the maze.

Soon we're in Nick's car and on our way.

"So it's more than one person, and we know one of them is a woman," I say. "It has to be Gina and Elizabeth."

"I hope so." Nick is gripping the steering wheel so tightly his knuckles are white. "From what you've said, I get the impression that they aren't too bright."

"So they broke into Alohalani's office to get his notes on the murders. But why break into my house?"

Nick shakes his head. "Just to throw us off? Maybe the women are mentally unstable."

"That's a good point…" I think for a moment. "But Alohalani said things weren't as they seem. And he had that photo that said *deceiver*."

"It may mean nothing. We don't know that he knew anything."

"So why hide the photo in the uke?" I ask.

"For all we know, he was talking about the money they owed him. It could be anything, Nani."

I'm quiet for the rest of the drive. Pieces of the puzzle are swirling around in my head, trying to fit together. When we get a minute or so outside the mansion, Nick cuts his headlights and rolls slowly past the drive, parking behind some trees.

He opens the glove compartment and pulls out two flashlights.

"These are bright. They're LEDs. So don't use them unless you have to."

I nod. A full moon is going back and forth behind clouds. If it just stays clear, we won't need any flashlights.

I follow Nick toward his house. We keep to the jungle, hidden by the foliage. We have to move very slowly so as not to make any noise. Finally, after what feels like hours, we're opposite the hedge maze.

"I don't see anyone," I whisper. "How did the killers know about the maze anyway?"

Nick doesn't look at me. His eyes are trained on the hedges. "For a couple of years we had it open to the public at Halloween. Gina and Elizabeth could've been here."

That seems like a weak argument, but I say nothing. My hackles are rising. Something seems off. It's suspicious to me that the kidnappers chose Nick's hedge maze. Oh sure, it's brilliant, but there are tons of places on this island where they could hide my mom. They could just drop her anywhere in the middle of the island, and we'd never find her. So why this maze at Nick's house? But then again, whoever took Mom is probably crazy—maybe there isn't a reason.

The moon goes behind a cloud, and we make a run for the hedges. We don't go to the side facing the house, however. We move along the hedges to the other side. Is there a secret entrance?

I stare at Nick's back as we go. Binny's questions pop into my mind. *How well do you really know him? Don't you think he's moving a little fast?*

Nick wasn't with us when we spoke with the room-mates. The first time, at the restaurant, he was outside on a call. The second time he had to work. Does he know them? I think the thought I'd been avoiding. Is Nick somehow involved in this? After all—they are using his backyard.

"Come on," he whispers as he very carefully folds back what looks like a curtain of ivy.

It is a hidden entrance. I follow him inside. Wow. This really is scary. The dark walls are high, and the hall is narrow. He takes off on the right, and I stay with him. We try not to step on any twigs or leaves. The moon comes out from behind the curtain of clouds, and we can now see more easily.

What am I doing here? Nick didn't want police involvement. He wanted only me and him to attempt this. But doesn't that seem dangerous? We have no idea how many are here. We only assume it's Elizabeth and Gina. But what if it isn't? And what if Nick knows that?

Nick stumbles over a root, and before he steadies himself, I see that his cell has fallen out of his pocket. I snag the phone and stuff it into my back pocket. A little insurance, in case my suspicions are correct. He doesn't seem to notice.

We move left and right at strange intervals. It doesn't take long before I'm hopelessly lost. Nick clearly knows the way. And to think I'd wanted to try this out. Now it's too creepy. Now I never want to see it again.

Muffled voices come from our right. Nick puts his finger to his lips. We move much slower now. As we get closer, we hear a man and woman arguing. A *man* and woman? I'm still not able to make out the voices.

Something pulls at my arm, and I stifle a gasp. It's just branches. The maze seems haunted now. Like evil hedges pulling at our clothes.

I'm mad. I want to murder these people. For what they've done to Kua, Leilani, and mostly for Alohalani. I think of his office. All those treasures. What will happen to them now? I remember the night Nick and I broke in. Where we found the photo and…

A small idea pops into my head. It seems ridiculous. Absurd! There's no way what I'm thinking can be true. And yet, the idea won't go away. It sticks like taffy in my brain. I can't believe I didn't think of it before! All those puzzle pieces that didn't fit before, now fall easily into place.

If I'm right, then I know who the killer is. The idea is crazy. And yet, it feels right. In fact, I feel a little stupid that I didn't realize it earlier.

Alohalani gave it to us. The clues we recovered in his office. And I didn't even realize it at the time. If he'd just flat-out told me, he might still be alive today. I remember the things I saw in Leilani's house, and one thing stands out now. Something that I didn't give a second thought to before. And the picture of me playing the uke. It wasn't about me. It was about what was in the photo with me! Everything makes sense now. The break-ins. The funerals. All of it. And if we weren't maintaining total silence—I'd tell Nick.

The voices are a little closer now. I can hear them clearly. I'm right about who the murderer is. And the absurd becomes reality. The last few puzzle pieces pop into place with a satisfying snap. My theory is confirmed, and I want to laugh…inappropriately, of course. I know who's framed me. I know who the murderer is. It's too bizarre and too easy.

Nick stops. He nods his head to the left, and I see a glimmer of light. We've arrived. He looks me directly in my eyes, and I know now he had nothing to do with this. I trust him completely. As a matter of fact, I'm embarrassed that I didn't trust him from the start. It wasn't all my fault. He did act a little strangely. We'll have to discuss that when this madness is all over.

Then I realize that we've just put ourselves in danger. The people who have my mom could be armed. Nick and I aren't armed. I hear the man talking now.

"And you're sure she turned herself in?" The man is attempting to disguise his voice, but he doesn't fool me. I hear a *bleep* that sounds like a call ending on a cell.

"It's done. Nani turned herself in and confessed," the man says. "So we can let her go."

"No," speaks a woman's voice, harsh and mean. "We kill her and dump her in the ocean. One more way to frame that stupid Nani."

"That was not the deal," the man growls.

"I don't care," the woman says. "Kill her. Do it now."

Armed or unarmed, I need to stop them. I shove past Nick, turn the corner, and burst into the small open area. Mom is trussed up on the ground. She looks at me. And standing next to her, holding a piece of rope like a garrote, is Todd Chay.

And next to him is the murderer.

"Leave her alone, Leilani!" I shout as I launch myself at her, tackling the redheaded musician and knocking her to the ground.

"I hate you!" Leilani screams as she writhes beneath me. "I'm going to kill your mother, and I'm going to kill you!"

It sounds like a struggle is happening next to me, but I don't dare take my eyes off of this treacherous snake... this deceiver...the person I couldn't possibly think it was...the woman who had climbing gear in her closet... who also had a picture of me with my kauwila uke. We wrestle, and I discover that Leilani is extremely strong. She throws me off of her and climbs on top, pinning my arms to the ground.

"I should've just killed you when I had the chance!" Leilani's face is twisted into an animal sneer.

"Oh yeah?" I answer. "Well, you didn't. And now I'm going to take you in!"

I'm not totally sure how I'm going to do this. After all, the crazy lady has me pinned to the ground. Now I look over and see that Nick and Todd are punching each other. I hope Nick wins.

"You thought I was dead," the woman cackles. "Everyone thought I was dead. And they're going to keep thinking that until I show up on the beach, waterlogged and starving. Then I'll tell them how you attacked me. Then I'll have everything, and you'll have nothing!"

I bring my feet up and put them on her thighs and throw her through the air. As she lands, I flip her over, face down in the dirt, and pull her arm back so hard that she cries out in pain.

"Good luck with that," I say as I twist her arm a little more.

Leilani cries out, and I turn to see Todd's head swivel toward her. Just before Nick lands an uppercut that knocks him to the ground, unconscious.

"The rope." I wheeze a little. I'm not really cut out for hand-to-hand combat.

Nick brings me the rope that was meant to strangle my mother, and we hog-tie Leilani (something I learned in Kansas). I untie Mom and help her up as Nick uses her ropes on Todd.

"Why do I think you figured this out?" Nick grins.

I shrug. "I didn't until a few minutes ago."

"You figured out that Leilani was still alive. How?" he asks. He starts patting his pockets for his phone.

I hand it to him. "You dropped this."

Nick calls the police, and they arrive as we drag Todd Chay and Leilani O'Flanagan out of the hedge maze and dump them on the grass.

Detective Ray stares at Leilani for a few moments. "So she didn't die."

I shake my head. "Nope. I'd guess she saved up some of her blood for a while to make it look like she had.

Todd came down and stayed at the resort. It was him wearing the wig to look like me. She rappelled down the cliff in a harness and poured the blood onto the rocks."

"What gave her away?" he asks.

Two uniforms grab Todd and Leilani and clap handcuffs on them.

"A photo Leilani had of me with my kauwila ukulele. Rappelling gear in her closet." Ooops—I don't want the police to know we were in her house. "The reverend at the wedding where she allegedly died said she looked heavier and was wearing a large black dress. It seemed very odd to him. That's how she hid the gear. Leilani wore the same dress when she was the Lady in Black at the funerals," I say.

"Alohalani had told me that things weren't how they appeared. He'd said it wasn't a stranger. He had a photo of the Overlook, which gave me the idea she'd planned the whole thing. And then there was Leilani's birth certificate."

Detective Ray looks at us for a moment. "I'll need you to come down to the station and give a full report."

Nick and I watch as he turns around and starts ordering the other officers around.

"The birth certificate!" Nick slaps his forehead in an adorable eureka moment. "Lori Finnegan! Born in Canada to Irish parents!"

I nod. "She wasn't half Hawaiian. Alohalani knew that and was probably going to expose her. That might've been the last straw for her."

"Did you know Todd was in on it?" Nick asks.

I shake my head. "Not until I saw him in the maze.

He'd done a good job of appearing innocent. I knew someone was helping her, but not who."

"That's all you needed to figure this out?" Nick stares at me.

"It took me a while. Like right before we confronted them."

Nick takes me into his arms. "How? What gave him away?"

I grin. "Two things. First, the reverend described his build perfectly when, disguised as me, he pushed Leilani off the cliff. Secondly, Todd and Pauli drove away from the bar after Leilani's funeral in a white sedan."

"The car that followed you." Nick nods. "What about the break-in at Leilani's?"

"It was her. She couldn't let anyone know she was still alive, so she searched her house in the dark."

Nick frowns. "Was she looking for the surveillance photos?"

I shake my head. "The harness and rope. They were in her closet. I completely overlooked it."

Nick pulls me into his arms. "You really are Nancy Drew."

I kiss him. "I guess I am."

TWENTY-TWO

IT IS VERY early dawn before Nick and I leave the police station. I didn't have to provide much proof that Leilani killed Kua and Alohalani, because like an idiot, she ranted to the police all the way to the station that she should've finished me off at the Blue Hawaii Wedding Chapel. I have to admit, I was a little disappointed that I couldn't show off.

Oh, and the fact that she's still alive didn't help any. Turns out I was right about the blood. She'd been extracting it herself, a pint at a time, for a while—which is really gross and very disturbing.

Todd didn't say much. My guess is he's just a man in love. Which is sad. When it was all over, Leilani admitted she'd killed Kua and Alohalani and bludgeoned Pastor Dan. She'd put Todd up at the resort the night before the Parker wedding—with instructions written on hotel stationery. But Todd had only helped stage her death and kidnap my mother. Still, he's an accessory to murder, and he will be going away for a long time.

Nick and I walk out of the station, blinking at the light.

"I still don't know how you figured it out," Nick says as he pulls me against his chest.

"It was several things, really. The photo of the kauwila uke was key. So was Alohalani's photo of the Overlook. And then there was the lady in black," I tell him as I rest against him. "No one knew who she was. She'd appeared at both funerals. Something was seriously wrong about her being there. And I knew it wasn't Gina or Elizabeth, because they were in the front pew and seemed confused when I'd mentioned her."

"Why didn't you realize she was the key sooner?"

I shrug. "I had no idea who she was. I guess I always knew something was wrong with her. It was Alohalani's clue that cinched it. Things weren't as they seemed. Leilani appeared to be dead—only she wasn't. And her ego wouldn't let her miss her own funeral."

We get into Nick's beater, and for the first time I feel like a huge weight is taken off of my shoulders.

"I can't believe we didn't realize it when there was no body." Nick starts the car and tucks a strand of hair behind my ear.

"Something about that bothered me. But the detective seemed so convinced that she'd been eaten or something that I bought into that idea."

Nick shakes his head. "So she murdered Kua and Alohalani. Kua to frame you, and Alohalani because he was onto her."

"She thought it would be easy. And she did it for one other perk. By framing me for the murders, she'd be the only musician on the island," I add.

"Murder seems a little extreme to make that happen," Nick muses.

I nod. "But that's how Leilani operated. The woman

is held together by sheer hatred. Murder just seemed like the right means to get what she wanted.

The next day is the big resort luau. I wear a bright-orange muumuu with brown turtles on it and a kukui-nut lei as I play "Aloha O'e" for the largest audience I've ever had. Once I finish and the applause dies down, I step up to the microphone.

"I'd like to dedicate this performance to two great performers who, sadly, are not with us anymore. For Kahelemeakua Lui and Alohalani Kealoha. You and your music will be missed. Aloha."

"That was wonderful!" Mom kisses me on the cheek as I arrive back at our table. A troupe of drummers has taken the stage, and my gig is over.

"Very nice!" Perseverance Woodfield says.

Nick winks. It's all he needs to say.

"I got you a plate." Binny laughs, pointing to a huge platter of pork and ahi poke.

"Miss Johnson?" Julia Kekoa, the activities coordina-tor, steps up to the table. "That was lovely. I'm getting all kinds of compliments on your performance. Welcome aboard here at the resort!"

She nods once with a smile before visiting other ta-bles.

"So you're legitimate now," Nick says. "I could get used to you working here with me."

I elbow him gently in the ribs. No point in bruising my new boyfriend.

"Miss Johnson and Mr. Woodfield." Detective Ray stands next to us. "Thank you."

I wait for him to say something else, but he doesn't.

"You're welcome," I say with a smile.

He looks around. "We don't have many homicides here in this town. And if I was gruff over your involvement, I apologize. It's just…"

"Just what?" Nick asks.

"Well, you see, you weren't the only ones invading my turf to investigate here."

Nick and I exchange glances. "We weren't?"

The detective shakes his head. "We had a couple of undercover bounty hunters here from the mainland, chasing a surfer gang."

Suddenly, I know exactly who he's talking about. "Roberta and Robbie Lugosi!"

Detective Ray nods. "Yes. They're a brother-sister act from LA. They came here hoping to find someone who'd jumped bail."

"So the Sea Dogs really are dangerous?" I ask.

The detective laughs. "Not really. They had the wrong man. The guy they were chasing was from a gang called the Sea Bass. And they aren't from here. They're on Molokai."

Nick begins to laugh. "The Sea Bass? That doesn't sound very tough."

"Actually, they're much worse." Detective Ray nods. "Far more dangerous. But not my problem."

He gives us a chaka and walks away.

"The Sea Bass Gang." I shake my head. "I thought those two were acting weird." I start laughing.

"The name is pretty funny." Nick grins.

I shake my head. "No, it's not that." I'm laughing harder now, and tears are starting to roll down my cheeks.

"What is it?" He looks confused.

"Boy, are they going to be surprised." I wipe the tears away. "But that was a legal and binding marriage. Those two are stuck with each other now."

Binny grimaces. "Ugh. Brother and sister and now man and wife."

"They can probably get it annulled," Nick laughs.

"Probably," I reply. "But they're going to be horrified when they get the official license in the mail."

"Well, I'm just glad things have been cleared up and life can get back to normal on our island," Nick says.

Our island. Again, moving a bit fast, but I like the sound of that.

"I think I'm just beginning to figure you out, Nick Woodfield."

He looks at me. "I know I came on pretty strong pretty fast."

Binny starts to whistle and look around.

"Binny said something to you?" That seems a little out of place for my best friend.

Nick nods. "Yes. And I'm glad she did. Look"—he runs his hands through his dark, wavy hair—"I've been a loner for a long time. Avoiding any kind of relationship because my family is a bit famous here. When I met you, I felt at ease right away. I guess I just came off overly familiar."

I kiss him on the forehead. "It's totally okay. But you have to understand one thing."

Nick looks surprised. "What's that?"

"That life is too short, especially here in Aloha Lagoon. So I expect to make the most of the time we have together."

Nick reaches out and pulls my face toward him, pressing his lips to mine. I give in completely.

I'm still not considered a local, but Aloha Lagoon is definitely my home.

* * * * *

ABOUT THE AUTHOR

LESLIE LANGTRY IS the *USA TODAY* bestselling author of the *Greatest Hits Mysteries* series, *Sex, Lies, & Family Vacations*, *The Hanging Tree Tales* as Max Deimos, the *Merry Wrath Mysteries,* and several books she hasn't finished yet, because she's very lazy.

Leslie loves puppies and cake (but she will not share her cake with puppies) and thinks praying mantids make everything better. She lives with her family and assorted animals in the Midwest, where she is currently working on her next book and trying to learn to play the ukulele.

To learn more about Leslie, visit her online at: http://www.leslielangtry.com